About the author

Tom Lanoye (Belgium) is an award-winning, highly-acclaimed novelist, poet and playwright. He is a best-selling author and makes regular appearances at major European festivals. His novel *Fortunate Slaves* (2013) sold over 60,000 copies and was shortlisted for both the Libris Literature Prize and the AKO Literature Prize 2014. He lives in Antwerp and Cape Town.

About the translator

Michele Hutchison (UK) studied at UEA, Cambridge and Lyon universities, after which she started working as an editor. In 2004, she moved to Amsterdam where she continued to work in the publishing industry and began translating. Amongst the works she has translated are *Craving* by Esther Gerritsen, *Rupert* by Ilja Leonard Pfeijffer, *Hello Everybody! One Journalist's Search for Truth in the Middle East* by Joris Luyendijk and multiple thrillers by Simone van der Vlugt.

D1352161

Fortunate Slaves

Tom Lanoye

Fortunate Slaves

Translated from the Dutch by
Michele Hutchison

World Editions

Published in Great Britain in 2015 by World Editions Ltd., London

www.worldeditions.org

Copyright © Tom Lanoye, 2013
English translation copyright © Michele Hutchison, 2015
Cover design Multitude
Image credit © Corbis/HH

First published as *Gelukkige slaven* in the Netherlands in 2013 by
Prometheus, Amsterdam

British Library Cataloguing-in-Publication Data
A catalogue record for this book is available on request from
the British Library

ISBN 978-94-6238-035-6

Typeset in Minion Pro

The translation of this book was funded by the Flemish Literature Fund
(Vlaams Fonds voor de Letteren—www.flemishliterature.be)

Distribution Europe (except the Netherlands and Belgium):
Turnaround Publishers Services, London
Distribution the Netherlands and Belgium: Centraal Boekhuis,
Culemborg, the Netherlands

For R—my light, my life—who who turned
a country bumpkin into a traveller

'He loved his torments like loyal enemies.'
(From *Rebellion* by Joseph Roth)

'When I saw him for the first time, I thought:
the way this man is, that's how I should have been.'
(From *Damocles' Dark Room* by W.F. Hermans)

Contents

Prologue

WE DISCOVER TONY HANSSEN during the dog days of a virulent, suffocating, smouldering summer. Not on the crumbling continent where he first saw the light of day more than forty years ago. It is winter there now, raining filthy sleet on the streets and messages of doom in all the parliaments and stock exchanges. We come across him eleven thousand kilometres away, in the fertile gash beneath Brazil's tropically swollen belly, the open wound called Rio de la Plata, the Silver River. As wide as a sea, it smells of petrol and entrails, the purgatory of the Atlantic Ocean—a heaving, royal-blue universe full of hidden gas fields, shipwrecks, and whale carcasses.

There is a capital city on each bank of the Rio de la Plata. To the north, Montevideo. To the south, Buenos Aires—a city as big as a country. Here, in San Telmo, one of the oldest neighbourhoods, founded by runaway Italians and escaped black slaves, later the birthplace of tango, arms smuggling, and football madness, we find Tony Hanssen. Puffing and panting away in a kitschy, renovated town house, *una casa de turistas*, where, on the second floor, at her insistence and against his inclination, he is pleasuring a Chinese matron. A rickety fan turns above their heads; the charmingly antiquated air conditioner creaks and rattles louder than the bed.

Nevertheless, Tony is sweating like a pig. And he's not the only one, as he can tell from the skin he is thrusting against. He is disgusted at himself and feels sorry for Mrs. Bo Xiang. But he doesn't stop pleasuring her. She might take it as a rejection. Beware the wrath of an older woman scorned. Tony owes her husband a fortune, so he carries on thrusting.

It's not yet two in the afternoon. The lampposts outside barely cast a shadow.

TONY HANSSEN'S EXACT NAMESAKE is sweating, too—eight thousand kilometres away—though without moving a muscle. He is standing alone on a hilltop, in a remote corner of the private game reserve he infiltrated in a vehicle with false number plates. The park is called Krokodilspruit and has long considered itself the pearl of Mpumalanga, a province in eastern South Africa. Here, night is already approaching. The heat is subsiding, the greenery is losing its lustre, chirping swallows are swooping. Soon, darkness will fall, total and irrevocable, like a machete on a springbok's neck.

Tony Hanssen didn't choose this game reserve for its striking name but for the diversity of its wildlife, and its location. The modest airport at Phalaborwa and the border with Mozambique are nearby, the larger Polokwane airport is just two hundred kilometres away, and there are other escape routes, too. He managed to get hold of the fastest four-by-four pickup you could buy for cash on the black market in Johannesburg. There were disappointingly few on offer. The selection of stolen BMWs was larger. Alongside their invitingly chic leather upholstery and tinted windows, most of them had soft-tops. Doubly dangerous—carjackers in Johannesburg, bold lions on the reserve. The carjackers would blast out your brains without so much as a word; the lions would take a nap on your canvas roof before tearing it open with their claws. Before you know it, you're lunch. You didn't need to be neurotic, Tony told himself daily, to fear a worst-case scenario. These days, paranoia was another word for common sense.

During his previous stay, barely two years ago—still with his family—he and his wife had been horrified by a newspaper article about a solitary male elephant on the Kruger Game Reserve, not far away. The animal, by way of a feint, had charged at a sports car, trumpeting and flapping its ears. The panicked driver had got himself into the wrong gear. Forward instead of reverse. The elephant interpreted it as a counter-attack. It tore off the canvas roof with its trunk, tipped the vehicle over with its tusks, and stamped on it like a biscuit tin until the screaming under its feet stopped. The newspaper listed other recent fatal attacks in a sidebar. Mother hippos were the worst of the serial killers. It was best not to get between a hippo and her offspring, the item warned. She'd attack you at up to thirty kilometres an hour, as agile as a filly despite her two-and-a-half thousand kilos. She'd stamp you to a pulp, starting with your head, and waddle sedately back to her baby.

Tony has been here for an hour, already. The view continues to intimidate him. A reddish-orange globe, low-hanging and freakishly large, makes the landscape shimmer like a Bible illustration. In front of him, there's a gateway to nowhere, formed by two rock faces. They rise up hundreds of metres and recede many kilometres into the distance. A majestic scar, a ravine that lives up to its name: God's Window. The Porch of the Supreme Being.

Closer by, at the foot of his lookout hill, a watering hole beckons, surrounded by rushes and a few clumps of miserable, dusty bush. At the waterline, wading birds peck at bugs. The rising breeze causes the surface to ripple. Or invisible, toothed jaws just under the water do. You can't be sure of anything in this country—Africa is still Africa, especially for Europeans. Tony has one last look around and gets out the gun he has yet to use. His four-by-four is parked behind him like a tank.

It'll be the first shot he's fired since his military service. He's worried about the report next to his ear, but even more worried about the echo. How many minutes does he have after the last reverberations die away in God's Porch? How quickly can he reach the hole he cut in the fence this morning and hastily covered up? He's a long way from the wildlife paparazzi's usual routes. He'll have to use his iPhone as a compass.

He polishes the lenses of the telescopic sight with a corner of his damp handkerchief. Mosquitoes buzz around his temples. The skies grow even redder, as though someone has slashed their wrists into a bowl of warm water.

THE TONY IN KROKODILSPRUIT is a little younger than the Tony in San Telmo. Less broad in the shoulders and narrower at the waist. His hair is lighter and shows a greater tendency to curl, his lips are slightly fuller, and his face has a permanently injured expression, verging on the pained. But they are of similar height; their eyes are the same indeterminate brown. There are brothers who look less alike.

Perhaps there are even third and fourth namesakes of a similar age somewhere in the world. Hanssen is a common surname in their country of origin; a lot of men of their generation are called Tony. Maybe the third and the fourth share certain physical characteristics, too. But there will never be a bond between them as there is between these two. One despairs, the other takes aim and grits his teeth, and neither of them knows the other exists. Even less do they suspect their paths will cross on a different continent in just a few days' time. The crucible of the future.

But we're not there, yet. For the moment, African ants are making their way across Tony's dusty safari shoes. And, for the moment, the springs in Tony's South American mattress are squeaking as quietly and persistently as tortured rats.

PART ONE

Decline

1. Buenos Aires

WHAT WOULD MR. BO XIANG THINK OF THIS? Tony wonders anxiously in San Telmo, as he presses the soles of his feet against the bedpost, bracing to give his labour of love more traction and depth. With good results. The hitherto polite, restrained panting of the matron beneath him turns into moaning. Something low and bestial. Unreserved.

In social intercourse, Mrs. Bo Xiang is the picture of reserve. The eternal smile that people ascribe to Orientals has been bestowed upon her. The grainy layer of pale make-up she smears on her face each morning, over her shaven eyebrows, shows more and more cracks as the day progresses, as fine as the veins in an antique tile. They follow a double pattern: her age lines and the craquelure of her smile. A double map, a palimpsest of an eventful life.

God knows what that poor thing has had to go through in that outsized country of hers, thought Tony, a little less than a week earlier, in the plane on the way over, as he observed his benefactress from close up. She lay next to him in her reclined seat, hanging crookedly in her seat belt, an insect caught in a web, her eyes closed, her small mouth obscenely open. From time to time, she snored or smacked her lips. The Boeing thundered through the freezing, anoxic atmosphere in a composed, almost noble manner.

It was Tony's first opportunity to inspect Mrs. Bo Xiang undisturbed from this close up. There were several holes in her earlobes. Just before falling asleep, she'd removed her latest purchase—a pair of silver butterflies with a diamond on each wing—

and put them away in her Louis Vuitton handbag, along with her rings, her bracelets, and her Breitling watch. What was she afraid of? Pickpockets in first class? Her breath smelled of peppermints and her teeth looked like ivory jacks that had seen too much use. Tony had to stop himself from putting his hand over the obscene, wrinkled mouth until the breathing stopped.

A hell of a life, he thought at the same time, not without compassion—to be born in China, shortly after the war, a woman. He inhaled through his mouth to escape the odour of peppermints. Starvation, refugees, propaganda. Days and days of banging on pots and pans until the sparrows fell out of the sky in exhaustion. Now and again, a purge, or a week of euphoria. How many bullet-riddled bodies had she seen, how many show trials and rapes? And still she carried on smiling from early in the morning until late at night. Perhaps she was already growing senile. And that's the person giving me orders, that's the person responsible for my fate. His hand itched again.

But he turned his gaze away from her and asked the stewardess for a gin and tonic. Bombay Sapphire, please. A double.

In daylight, observed from a distance, Mrs. Bo Xiang resembled a flawless porcelain doll, as white as gristle. She drew on new eyebrows, blacker than engine oil. She painted her lips with a red that shone like the bodywork of an Italian sports car. She had everything her heart desired. She bought her clothes in Paris, her shoes and handbags in Singapore, her smartphones and cameras in Tokyo. Plastic surgery was the only thing she didn't subscribe to. The one time her smile vanished was when Tony cautiously enquired about it.

Four days ago, as they strolled along the widest boulevard on earth, the Avenida 9 de Julio, her countenance had already cracked by mid-morning. She had burst into peals of laughter.

Just like that. All Chinese people had that affliction, Tony knew by now, and the women most of all. A high-pitched, hiccupping laugh with a vengeance. He wondered whether there was a reason for it. Usually, there wasn't.

That same morning, during their very first breakfast on Argentinian soil, Mrs. Bo Xiang had explained her plans. This short trip would be no beach holiday, she'd warned. Idleness was the privilege of the young. She had no time to lose. She wanted to tick off as many sights as possible, with Tony as her guide. She was giving him a free hand. Wherever he went, she would go. It was all the same to her. Even so, she handed him a brochure with the top attractions circled in red pen. And, oh yes! Dear Tony! She laid her small, ringed hand on his. The claw was heavier than expected and felt cold and clammy—a bunch of wilted asparaguses just out of the fridge, pale against the Prussian-blue breakfast linen, the little vase containing a rose, the bowl of fresh strawberries. At the time, they were still staying in the Hilton on the Puerto Madero, the spectacularly modernized harbour district. Don't worry, dear Tony! The claw gave a couple of soothing pats and then remained on his hand. She'd pay for everything! As though she didn't always pick up the bill. There were more credit cards than banknotes in her purse, but there were a lot of banknotes, all the same. A whole range of currencies. She showed them off like a pimply boy with a handful of football stickers. Her complete collection—at home in Guangzhou—included a banknote in the largest denomination from every country she'd ever shopped in.

They don't have the same sense of pride as we do, Tony thought, nodding amicably as he carefully extracted his hand from under the claw. They imitate us. They imitate everything. They are delighted to forsake who and what they are, and they don't feel threatened for a second, because they are convinced they'll win in the long run. We think in centuries, they think in millennia.

23

We swear by the loner, they know better. They believe in hordes. In billions. No one is closer to the cockroach. He startled himself with his vitriol, but didn't tone down his thoughts. He quickly stuffed two strawberries into his mouth and stood up, shoving his chair away with the backs of his knees.

When she started to laugh on the Avenida 9 de Julio, Mrs. Bo Xiang was hanging on his arm. Her chubby flank was pressed against him as she pointed, gasping like an overgrown adolescent, at the Obelisco—a tall, chubby memorial column which rose up pontifically in the middle of the boulevard, as misplaced as a strap-on penis on a child's belly. Patriotic borders and lawns had been laid around the foot of the obelisk, full of flowers and dog shit. This was it, then, the famous Plaza de la República. The obelisk was not rounded off at the top, but crowned with a small, comical pyramid. If you felt compelled to worship a penis as a totem of your fatherland, Tony groaned—sullen and pale from the jet lag—at least do it right. Chop off that pyramid and put a proper bell end on top. He had woken up with a headache and a nauseated feeling, neither of which had subsided after the much-too-saccharine breakfast coffee, the strawberries, and the croissants that had been cloyingly sweet, too.

On either side of the Obelisco, hundreds of cars came and went along a full twenty lanes of traffic, most of them honking angrily. It wouldn't take much more to turn his headache into a migraine. He had lived in Jakarta for a few years during his peregrinations, and in Cairo, and Bangkok, so he was used to infernal traffic, but this was different. This exuded menace. He didn't belong here. He knew it, and this city knew it. It was already about to turn on him.

None of the hundreds of passers-by gave the unusual couple a second glance. Businessmen, young mothers, begging Falklands War vets, skateboarders, cops in short-sleeved shirts with sweat rings under their armpits and truncheons in their belts... No one gave anyone a funny look here, Tony chuckled to himself. Harried indifference is an asset. Or not. This was it, of course: the famous Argentinian cool. The gaucho's unflappability, the baccy-spitting cowboy who still believed he was descended from the conquistadores. The Indian-killer with his bow legs and his unshaven chin, his leather hat, his metal yerba maté cup, his incomprehensible Spanish. Perhaps they'd learned from their cattle to wear that indifferent expression. Socializing or flirting was for later, for after work, after the heat, in the new heat of the wood fires in the grill rooms where they would devour half a bull each, just for starters.

After that, they'd withdraw, as pissed as newts, to their shady *milonga*s, with their cheap wine, their sweaty accordion music, and their spastic dance steps, until daylight dawned. Ridiculous. What were tango dancers but a pair of tangled-up flamingos with epilepsy? Tony felt a surge of deep animosity, bordering on disgust. He'd already felt it the week before, when he'd opened his first tourist guide. 'City of roasted sweetbreads with Malbec!' 'Mysticism and romance immortalized in timeless music!' Each article came down to the same thing: glorified folk dancing and glorified barbecuing. Nobody mentioned the dictators and their coups, though they drooled all the more over their wives.

The only one on the Avenida who seemed bothered by this odd couple—a young gringo in designer jeans accompanied by a Chinese pygmy woman, hung with jewels and laughing like a lunatic—was a barking poodle. Clearly a creature with a pedigree. That's just perfect, Tony groaned. As he'd predicted, this place was 'Europe squared'. Even a dog was a status symbol. Yelpers like that didn't go down well with Muslims or Asians. Let alone blacks. They knew what a dog was for: to ignore or kick. The beginning of all civilization.

The poodle tugged, barking peevishly, at its incredibly long lead. The lead kept being pulled taut between the collar around its neck and the belt around the midriff of its escort: a sturdy, bespectacled girl barely twenty years old in a lemon-yellow top, lime-green hot pants, and dirty gym shoes. A princess from the upper middle classes, Tony guessed. Today a prissy student, tomorrow the petulant wife of an oil baron or a meat millionaire. She was wearing a pair of showy white headphones, the jewellery of contemporary youth, and her unbound breasts bobbed around boldly. There were four more leashed show dogs attached to her belt: the biggest was a pure-bred German shepherd, the smallest, a kind of chihuahua. It might also have been a rat. She was already the third of this type of dog walker they had encountered. Most of them were walking. This bespectacled girl was jogging, surrounded by her pack like a heavenly body with insane satellites. Only the poodle remained behind, barking angrily at Tony, bracing against the tugging lead each time: a mutineer, an Argentinian rebel, a four-legged gaucho.

It didn't stand a chance and was dragged along, tug by tug, once almost choking, to the renewed merriment of Mrs. Bo Xiang, who, after the Obelisco, now pointed annoyingly at the animal. Chinese people point at absolutely everything, Tony sighed. Except other Chinese people.

The girl with the dogs bobbed off into the crowd and disappeared. Mrs. Bo Xiang shook her ornamental porcelain head and snickered something in Chinese. Tony nodded without asking what she meant. He was just glad she was still enjoying herself. The first attraction he'd wanted to take her to—a guided tour of the Teatro Colón, one of the largest opera buildings in the world—turned out to be closed due to a union protest. In front of the entrance, a delegation of enraged comrades was making a racket with cowbells, panpipes, Inca drums, and firecrackers. What was it with this city and its cacophony? He apologized to Mrs. Bo Xiang, but she seemed to find the carry-on quite normal, even enjoyable, as though Tony had planned it all. She radiated happiness. Perhaps, Tony shuddered, she sees it as an homage to her communist origins. He quickly coaxed her away, before she got it into her head to go and shake the hands of the entire delegation of strikers, or hand out money to them. That woman was capable of anything.

She willingly let herself be guided away on his arm, smiling gratefully. He was almost convinced he could hear the layer of foundation cracking.

Her good humour stayed afloat even in the graveyard, a few hours later, when it turned out that Tony had made a mistake. Evita Perón was buried somewhere else.

He should have known. It had taken them half an hour to get there. Taxis were so cheap and so abundant here that the chauffeurs were all too eager to misunderstand you so that they could rack up a few extra kilometres. Or was it a genuine misunderstanding? Tony had asked for 'the cemetery with the famous dead people' because he'd forgotten the name of the neighbourhood. Perhaps the driver had liked music more than politics when it came to cadaverous heroes.

There was no lack of heroes in this sweeping boneyard: a genuine park with broad lanes, each one cobbled, each one bordered with graves that looked like miniature houses. They even had windows and ornamental doors—mausoleums custom-made to the dimensions of an extinct bourgeoisie. All of them built in the most flashy of materials, from marble to granite, topped off with a frieze of angelic hosts or a bust of the departed. The richest had had themselves anchored full length to the world they should have left behind. Fossils of bygone glory and self-importance. There were soldiers, eternally saluting in their dress uniforms of *bronzo bombarda*, and there were musicians, seated on chairs with bandoneons on their knees, frozen in everlasting ambiance. Nostalgia on a pedestal.

The undisputed high point was the grave of Carlos Gardel, Tango King, singer-songwriter of *'Mi Noche Triste'* and *'Volver'*, not to mention skirt-chaser, chain-smoker, and patron of Café Tortoni. He went down in a plane at the age of 45. His massively attended funeral disrupted traffic for an entire day. And that was in 1935. Tony remembered it all from his Michelin guide. He had still managed to hit a goddamn tourist jackpot!

And indeed, Mrs. Bo Xiang stood happily admiring the statue. Behold the eternally youthful, perpetually singing dandy, flaunting a bow tie and the smile of a Latin lover. He stared haughtily over their heads at the graves on the other side of the path, shining as though he had just been polished. There were fresh bouquets at his feet, and the wall behind him was adorned with copper plaques and enamel tiles covered in sayings, expressions of gratitude, and love poems written by admirers, most of whom had been born long after their idol's plane had crashed. Someone had threaded a white carnation through his bronze buttonhole. A real cigarette butt smouldered between the brownish-green fingers of his right hand.

Mrs. Bo Xiang got her compact red titanium Sigma camera out of her Louis Vuitton, peered through the lens, and gestured frantically with her free hand for Tony to stand closer and closer to the statue. She wouldn't calm down until he had climbed up onto the knee-high tomb and posed next to Gardel, mirroring his stance, right down to the cigarette in his left hand. Her gadget chirped like crazy—she had chosen an electronic bird sound for each snap. She had already taken shots of Tony at the gate of the Casa Rosada on the Plaza de Mayo, and next to the colourful houses on the Caminito in La Boca.

'You look exactly like him,' she crowed now.

Without breaking his pose, Tony shouted back that all Westerners were as alike as peas in a pod. To his irritation, Mrs. Bo Xiang didn't contradict him. No, she sank laboriously to her knees, so that she could take a picture of him and his doppelgänger from below.

Tony surveyed the boneyard as though it were a battleground. His headache finally seemed to be abating. He liked this peace and quiet. It made him long again for the sea, with its unbounded horizon. Three hundred and sixty degrees of nothing, as far as the eye could see. He missed the calm of the lengthy journeys on the cargo ships and cruise boats on which he'd been able to pass more than twenty years of his life unnoticed, sometimes with hard labour, sometimes with paid services of another kind, but always with total independence and a consoling insignificance. He had learned to live like a nomad, a compulsive tramp, a stowaway without a destination, and that life had suited him well.

He had left behind his home country with a bitter kind of pleasure. He went back sporadically just to keep the mass of paperwork at bay. What good are roots anyway, except as a way of wangling a valid passport? He had burned all his other bridges, starting with the frayed rope ladders that could have taken him back to his once-promising youth. He had nothing more to do with the scum and the provincial backwater that had spat him out. The spitting out was mutual. No one asked after him anymore; no one had anything to do with him. It felt like a kind of recognition. Tony had once been brought up to be successful, loved, an exemplary human being. He had become none of the three, and he flaunted it the way a fisherman shows off his catch.

His father's legal practice, sold to a complete stranger? Good riddance. He may have been cheated out of his inheritance, but that was just one less thing to worry about. His only motto was one he'd hated as a child because his family had professed it so sanctimoniously, though he'd given it a different turn. 'Live in the shadow, you'll live happily there' had become 'Live in the shadow, less shit will rain down on you there.' He didn't need any other principles or tenets than that. He had learned to love emptiness, the overwhelmingly infinite world which surrounded his home soil like a desert around a sewage cover.

A man has to feel at home somewhere, even if it's in the void.

'Please concentrate!' Mrs. Bo Xiang cried, her free eye shut. 'And look at me!' She kneeled down on the cobblestones before her idol, and it wasn't Gardel. 'Smile!'

Tony looked at the family standing behind her, waiting for her to finish taking pictures. He saw himself through their eyes. A hooligan with his feet on a beloved tomb, a barbarian posing next to a titan as an equal. The father of the waiting family coughed for the third time. He tightened his fists around the handles of a wheelchair in which an old man with a razor-sharp mouth and two cataract-filled eyes sat muttering away. The mother exhorted her two plump daughters, each of them blushing and holding bunches of flowers in her hand, to be patient. She didn't raise her voice but her face spoke volumes. The encyclopaedia of scorn.

Mrs. Bo Xiang didn't notice. She carried on taking pictures. No angle was too bizarre for her. She didn't quite go so far as to lie down on her side. Tony felt more and more ridiculous, and not only because of the designer jeans she'd bought for him during the stopover in Doha, which stretched grotesquely over his crotch and around his waist. What was she going to do with all these photos, he wondered. A slideshow with Ástor Piazzolla's *'Libertango'* as accompaniment? Entertainment for her husband? They called each other every day, Mr. and Mrs. Bo Xiang. Intercontinentally, sometimes for half an hour at a time. They laughed together. What were they saying in that filthy Chinese of theirs? Were they talking about him? What were they plotting?

Mrs. Bo Xiang noticed Tony's awkwardness. She let her Sigma drop and looked him in the eyes, tenderly, it seemed. It wouldn't have taken much for her to climb up on the gravestone, too, pinch his cheek between her thumb and forefinger and softly shake it back and forth.

One of these days, Tony thought, I'll wipe that smile off her porcelain face.

* * *

THINGS TURNED OUT DIFFERENTLY. By the end of the week, Mrs. Bo Xiang had even persuaded him to fuck her. No pain, no gain.

Tony had stopped resisting and given in. It had been on the cards for long enough. At a certain point, refusing became more dangerous than consenting. That was another thing he'd learned on the cruise ships he'd served on. Protecting your job security, and in some cases your hide, could take all kinds of forms. Love was the least objectionable. Love is always good, even though it's rotten to the core.

During their walk, he and Mrs. Bo Xiang had discovered San Telmo and taken it into their hearts. The antiques shops and the charming covered vegetable market in crumbling art-deco style certainly had something to do with that. Fading glory lends itself more to romance than new buildings.

Mrs. Bo Xiang, in particular, radiated joie de vivre once again. For anyone living in the lap of luxury, being confronted with deprivation is an unbeatable aphrodisiac. They instantly swapped the Hilton for a bed and breakfast in a ramshackle town house, cheerfully renovated on a tight budget in daring colours, and just by the Plaza Dorrego, the navel of San Telmo. This was the plaza where beggars and musicians held court from early in the morning, where every afternoon a flea market uncoiled, and where every evening an amateur dance display took place among the terrace tables of the many cafes and restaurants. Tango, tango—*el amor!*

Their own mating dance, on the second floor of the mansion, began staidly. In the tepid, heavy afternoon air, barely circulated by the ceiling fan, there was a wistfulness. Their journey home was approaching. Tomorrow they'd be checking out. Any kind of parting is sweet sorrow. The timid respect which with Tony had originally treated Mrs. Bo Xiang inhibited the intensity of their relationship.

But not for long. Intimacy breeds trust, and that trust increases as shame is reciprocally cast aside. Once Tony had braced his feet against the bedstead and slowly increased his tempo, a languid, noisy euphoria overcame Mrs. Bo Xiang and her worn-out bones.

Tony was embarrassed for her. The poor woman was lying prostrate and defenceless, her legs spread, one side of her face pressed into the pillow. Her whole body rocked backward and forward, assisted by her mild corpulence. Her face rocked along each time, as though she were trying to spread out the stiff pillow, using her head as a rolling pin. Just now she'd pulled the other pillow under her midriff to keep her hips raised without getting a cramp. When love comes knocking, you have to open your door to it. Mrs. Bo Xiang didn't take any persuading.

Just how old is she? Tony wondered. She smelled of violets and green tea. I really don't get it, he groaned inwardly, without sacrificing momentum. What do all these old bags see in me? Some objects attract flies, or iron filings. I'm a magnet for the motherly type. Or even the grandmotherly type, of late. What does Mrs. Bo

Xiang think I'm going to help her achieve, or recover? Or does she enjoy humiliating me? Is that the role I'm playing? Despite the heat, he systematically increased his pace.

The euphoria beneath him swelled just as systematically. 'More,' Mrs. Bo Xiang whispered in English, for the second time now, a little louder than the first time. 'Yes. I want more.'

Why didn't she say it in her own language if she was really that euphoric? Why did she use the lingua franca of the American porn industry? Did elderly women watch sex on the Internet nowadays, too? At each of Tony's thrusts, Mrs. Bo Xiang's shiny red lips poked out sideways between her squashed face and the stiff pillow. Her lipstick was coming off, her foundation, too. What she liked, she'd confided to him on one of the previous days, was being bitten in the scruff of her neck 'during the act'.

Tony didn't do it. On top of everything else, he was supposed to bite her? There were limits. 'I want more,' Mrs. Bo Xiang whispered, even louder this time. Tony was having more and more trouble empathizing. And the hardest part was still to come, he realized. The seduction and the foreplay were bearable; the action itself was a matter of not thinking too much and doggedly keeping at it. The aftercare, that was a terrible prospect. What could they possibly say after the deed? Two beings who were so different?

'More, Tony. More.'

Outside, the metropolis was taking its siesta. Spray trucks were driving around to mist up the pavements and beat down the dust. The heat managed to penetrate everywhere all the same, air conditioning or no air conditioning. It clamped around you like a truss. A shortness of breath was stealing up on him. Tony pounded away, anyway. What was the problem? It was years since he'd taken so long. It wasn't just the smell of violets and the creaking of the bed. It was also Mrs. Bo Xiang's husband and the fortune that

Tony owed him, of course. How could he have been so stupid? Roulette wasn't his thing. He should have never allowed himself to be seduced. Not then, not now. Not ever.

'More! More!'

Don't you worry, my dear Tony, Mrs. Bo Xiang had said to him a week earlier, shortly before falling asleep next to him in the Boeing with her mouth obscenely open. She was drunk; she'd had one gin and tonic after the other. You'll figure it out, you and my husband. He can be very generous and forgiving. If I ask him. And if you help me. Can you help me, Mister Tony? To avoid answering, he'd kissed her hand. She had pulled her hand away, giggling, and then kissed the back of it herself. Her own hand. With closed eyes, ardently, protractedly, not quite licking the place he'd kissed. It wasn't the first trip she'd taken him along on. She'd dragged him to Monaco, and even to Dubai. He'd always managed to ward off her advances. But not anymore. He knew what was coming. Buenos Aires would be his Waterloo.

'More!'

Just before falling asleep on the airplane, she'd stroked his cheek. She'd never done that before. It felt like he was being branded. 'My Tony is a little damaged, that's all' she'd jabbered. It sounded like a verdict. 'Damaged,' as in damaged goods. As in ruined. What was she then? A perfect peach? An immaculate saint?

'More!'

Stop whining, Tony thought, keep up the tempo and everything will come good. This is the fate of everyone who gets into debt; plenty of people are worse off than me. While thinking this, he looked at himself in the full-length mirror next to the bed. It was a shocking sight, the way he was mounting that hillock of flesh. Pale, veal-coloured, quivering flesh.

'More!'

I should learn to keep my eyes shut, Tony thought. But he carried on watching, focussing on his own pumping hips. Where his belly had once been taut, all muscle, now, in shock, he counted three rolls. I should learn to close my eyes to everything, he thought, and I have to stop complaining about my life. I'm not important enough to complain. I'm a louse in other people's bedsheets, nothing more. The traces I leave behind won't survive the first wash. So what? What have lice got to complain about, except that they exist? Where there's blood, there's hope. No self-pity! Everyone has to pay. Everyone looks for a scapegoat and everyone longs for a saviour, there isn't anything else to be said about life. Give up grousing and ejaculate.

But he didn't ejaculate. His breathing grew frantic, his floundering took on a desperate note. Liberation was a long time coming.

Mrs. Bo Xiang, whose head was still pressed solidly into the pillow, didn't take it personally. She began to help. She grubbed back up at him, harder and harder. The sounds she was making no longer resembled anything like words. The bed squeaked as though it were about to collapse. It was a long time since anyone had enjoyed themselves so much in Tony's company, and thanks to him, too.

He tried to pay back her efforts by trying even harder, but alongside desperation, melancholia began to delay his climax. What was he doing here?

And what else could he do but give in to that melancholy? Perhaps, moving forward on autopilot, he'd be able to achieve what he couldn't if he thought about it too much. Disassociation, the mind breaking free from the body, didn't have to be all bad.

My God, he thought to himself—eyes closed, his body making love unabated—how wrong I was about this city! Buenos Aires is fantastic! The past week seemed like a month, he and Mrs. Bo Xiang had seen and done so much.

They had visited a theatre converted into a bookshop, with the flocked wallpaper and the gilded the ceiling intact. They'd attended an equestrian show in a distant suburb, and after that, a procession in a square clamped between an ominous-looking barracks and a stinking abattoir. The difference between the two buildings had been minimal, the fiesta after the procession ecstatic.

They had explored the collection of the practically empty Museo de Bellas Artes. Rembrandt, Renoir, and Jackson Pollock all hung within arm's reach. You could stand with your nose pressed right up to them, no guards to tell you off. They had enjoyed the fantastic wines in the working-class cafés, with their stirring music and elderly waiters. Tony had seen an old conviction of his confirmed, there. If you wanted to know if a city was worth anything, you needed to look at the age of its waiters. The young studs and teenyboppers in Los Angeles and Sydney were after big tips and a different job, the sooner the better. An elderly waiter lived only for his profession. He knew people and their impatience. He had been serving drinks and the same dishes for thirty years; he'd been listening to the same sorrows and the same gossip for thirty years without scoffing or butting in. That took wisdom, and self-knowledge, and class.

This beautiful city had class in spades. After his initial crabby resistance, Tony had completely changed his mind about tango. They'd taken an actual lesson together, he and Mrs. Bo Xiang. Mad, carefree fun that he would have simulated in the past, but which he now actually experienced. All of the foreign students were bumbling around, laughing; only he and Mrs. Bo Xiang were complemented on their efforts by the teacher—a fat queen with a pointy beard and werewolf eyebrows, shrouded in baggy black drapes that resembled net curtains, but with steel-tipped cowboy boots sticking out under them.

After that, and indeed, all the way into the early hours, they, too, washed into the dance halls—the Porteños, as the inhabitants of the largest meat market in the world called themselves. Young and old, rich and poor, all of them together. They didn't need lessons. Dignified and frenetic, they lost themselves in the music that Tony had whole-heartedly hated a week before, but which could now touch him to the bottom of the soul he thought he had lost long ago. What had happened? What had Buenos Aires done to him? Why had he succumbed here rather than in Monaco?

Monaco had proven to be a façade. Disneyland for billionaires, a cardboard cut-out skyline, an expensive cordon sanitaire for upstart proles, sanctimoniously clean and laughably chic, an architectonic neurosis for operetta walk-ons. This city, Buenos Aires, was a city. Unabashedly dirty, sincerely impure, stubbornly recalcitrant. She didn't beg for compliments but swept you up into her orbit. Tony realized this as, in the middle of the night, rooted to the spot and increasingly drunk, he was watching a performance by El Afronte, an *orquestra típica* with one singer and ten musicians. Four bandoneons, three violins, a cello, a double bass, and a piano.

They played with the refinement of a symphony orchestra and the rhythmic passion of a heavy-metal band. Tony couldn't explain why, but when the bespectacled singer—an anomalous cross between an angular existentialist from the Paris of May '68 and a charming rocker from '59, and yet every inch an Argentinian—when this anomaly began to sing, tears poured from Tony's eyes, even though he didn't understand most of the lyrics.

Mrs. Bo Xiang, who was no less drunk than he was, cleaned up his waterworks with paper tissues. Tony let her. He capitulated, there and then. He no longer begrudged the woman what she was looking for. She was quite sweet, really. He had obliged more repulsive women than her, obnoxious battle-axes who had looked down on him because they desired him. Mrs. Bo Xiang didn't look down on him. She must have been a fresh-faced beauty once. He had been wrong about her, too. She seemed more patient and generous than he'd thought. Had she always been like that, or had she been chastened by adversity along the way, by some kind of trauma, or a series of disasters?

It didn't matter. She was who she was, here and now, and Tony felt neither judged nor mocked by her. To his surprise, he felt grateful, even moved. He kissed her two claws in the semi-darkness of the clammy, sweaty *milonga*. He stroked her neck and her pierced earlobes. Casanova for beginners. She giggled like a schoolgirl—no, like a drunken cocotte in an ancient opium den, her head cocked, her narrow eyes squinting even more.

No one gave them a second glance. Tony wasn't the only man in the buoyant company of an elderly woman. No one asked any questions, no one gave them judgemental looks, no one hissed. People took the night as it came. Tony saw a bony man dancing with an overgrown teenager—his daughter, judging by her features. A long-legged beauty with a skirt that was too short and a tragic look in her eyes. They focussed only on each other as they danced. It was more like elegant wrestling, an intense duel. If they hadn't been clothed, you might have suspected them of public incest. They only stopped to smoke, still gazing into each other's eyes. Finally, they walked out into the early morning, entwined, and just short of kissing.

The following day, the Calle Defensa, San Telmo's main artery, was transformed into an elongated flea market, just as every Sunday. And there was El Afronte again, this time in the open air, performing on the steps of a church the colour of a desert, with a silly little amp for the singer. Tony's inexplicable tears returned and, again, no one took any notice. An elderly charmer of around eighty, dressed as a gaucho, was inviting passing women to dance on the tiny balata-wood floor of about a metre square in size. Mrs. Bo Xiang refused. She didn't let go of Tony's arm, except to buy him a CD that El Afronte had brought out themselves. She put ten times too much money into the collection basket, acting like she couldn't hear the singer calling after her and trying to offer her change, and pulled Tony into a neighbouring *parrilla*. It was the only thing she'd chosen herself for the week's sightseeing.

Tony had even grown to love this type of folkloric grill room, part Austrian *Weinstube*, part Wild-West saloon. Chequered tablecloths, broad-beamed ceilings, battered wainscoting, smoky plaster. On every free spot on the wall hung the preserved head of some kind of animal, with beady eyes and two horns or a set of antlers. There was a whole stuffed cow on the pavement by the entrance.

Anyone going inside had to pass not just the stuffed cow but also the circular grilling area. It was around two or three metres in diameter. The floor and the raised edge were covered in enamel tiles; a knee-high log fire smouldered in the centre. Various animals were arranged around the languid, intense glow, as though around a nocturnal campfire in olden times. Stripped of their skins, hooves, head, and innards, and attached to iron crosses. A coven of decapitated messiahs, confessing the sins of mankind in general, and this metropolis in particular, as they slowly cooked. Hissing and scorching, they took on all the unresolved pasts, and all of history's sorrows, before being devoured by their faithful followers, the worshippers of the flesh.

Exhausted and pouring with sweat, Tony was finally able to let himself fall forward onto the bed, next to Mrs. Bo Xiang. It was done. He felt more drained than ever before.

Mrs. Bo Xiang seemed to have calmed down, too. Tony had pulled out just in time. He had caught the proof of his climax in his right hand. He wiped it off on the side of the mattress and rolled onto his back, still panting. The synthetic scent of violets had made way for more authentic body odours. The silence was deafening without the squeaking of the bed, even though the fan and the air conditioning were still whirring away frantically.

As always after the deed, Tony was hit by contrarian sadness. Why were they leaving this place tomorrow, already? He wouldn't have minded staying a little longer. Mrs. Bo Xiang was enjoying herself, too, wasn't she? A bizarre vision revealed itself, an image of a possible future. The most bizarre thing was that he didn't feel humiliated by it.

He and Mrs. Bo Xiang should come here more often. A few weeks, a few months, the whole summer. Maybe they could buy a pied-à-terre. Mrs. Bo Xiang had enough money, and he no longer had any objections. Why shouldn't he pursue the only thing he seemed to do well without too much difficulty? All right, he and Mrs. Bo Xiang would never be a perfect match. They hadn't had a real conversation yet; he didn't know what her interests were; this lack of understanding was clearly mutual, and the sex bordered on the problematic. But the same went for even the most straightforward marriages. If the frequency isn't too high, anything is bearable.

Why shouldn't he do it—become her permanent male companion? A male geisha offering her a lot of fun, and all kinds of titbits of information, plus the occasional furtive gratification. What was wrong with that? There were worse professions and crueller pacts with the devil. At his age and with his prospects, it wouldn't be that hard to adapt to profound servitude. And it would amaze him if Mrs. Bo Xiang vetoed the plan. He knew her well enough, by now. He turned towards her.

She lay with her head turned away from him. The poor woman must be recovering, Tony thought. Not that crazy, is it? She had seemed like a mustang trying to throw off its rider. It would take a while to catch your breath after that. At the same time, a terrible presentiment was creeping up on Tony.

He could no longer hear her breathing.

He quickly rolled her onto her back, facing him. She felt clammy but already cold, brushed from top to toe by the cool breath of the fan, which continued to rotate its wings of death above them.

Tony called her name and shook her thoroughly. She didn't respond at all. The layer of foundation had indeed disappeared. Her face, paler than ever, had a bluish sheen. The lipstick and the mascara had left red and black streaks around her mouth and her eyes. It hadn't made her ugly or macabre. Her face seemed frozen in deep, delirious ecstasy. Never before had Tony seen anyone radiate such intense happiness. It felt like a betrayal.

He shook the happy corpse once again. He refused to believe what was happening to both of them, and the irrepressible smile on her lips made him angrier and angrier. It was as though she were laughing at him, yet again, once more. As though she'd planned this all from the start. Not just the trip to Buenos Aires, not just the dinners, the tango lessons, the Renoirs, the Jackson Pollocks, El Afronte—but this, too. Especially this. She had used him, tricked him.

He had to refrain from punching her in the face with his balled fists. Again he shook her, as furious as he was impotent.

But all of a sudden, the happy corpse moved. It belched out a cough that was more of a rattle. For a moment, Mrs. Bo Xiang opened her eyes—two strips of shining white were all that was visible, then they closed again. What she did do, without losing her disconcertingly blissful expression, was raise one hand. The trembling claw moved slowly towards Tony, but fell halfway onto the clammy sheet.

Quick, Tony thought, fumbling for his smartphone in panic. To hospital with her! Maybe it wasn't too late. Maybe he wouldn't have to call his creditor, the most famous entrepreneur from Macau to Guangzhou, and tell him his wife had just died.

2. Mpumalanga

TONY HANSSEN COULDN'T BRING HIMSELF to press the trigger. He didn't know what was holding him back the most: his fear of failure, his fear of being caught, or his realization that he—yes, he!—was about to kill another living being.

Three times, already, he'd had the rhinoceros' right eye in the exact centre of his cross hairs while the creature was barely moving. It stood there chewing lazily, staring into space with the slow, short-sighted gaze common to all herbivores. 'The rhino is an armoured bovine' a blogger had written on one of the sites Tony had consulted—a site that, ironically, warned against the scourge of poaching—"an armoured bovine with two unfortunate weak spots: its eyes."

It was these virtually blind, unprotected peepers, deeply embedded in a vortex of skin folds, that unsettled Tony and caused his finger to freeze around the trigger. He saw innocence in that gaze, and a heart-rending plea for mercy. Horses looked like that when they had just been wounded or beaten, as Tony had once been forced to witness in Provence, not far from his former holiday home. Two men were flogging a worn-out draught horse that stoically put up with the rain of blows. All of a sudden, they'd had enough, and raced off, arguing.

Tony had been so aghast that he hadn't tried to stop the brutes, something he would feel guilty about for years. At crucial moments, he was clearly less decisive than he would have expected himself to be. He'd walked guiltily up to the horse, which had remained rooted to the spot, only its flanks quivering. He spoke soothingly to the animal without touching it, so as not to frighten it even more.

The horse neither started nor moved. It gave Tony a sad, human look. He felt doubly conscience-stricken. Would anyone—would he?—be capable of braving such torment without collapsing in pain, or going crazy with anger? This broken, tortured nag embodied something so noble, it was almost offensive. A sober heroism that Tony doubted he would ever be capable of.

Now, in Krokodilspruit, placing his finger back on the trigger, he tried to convince himself that such considerations were just mere projections, based on a deep longing for kinship. Show a man a stray cat, a cumulus cloud, or a weeping willow, and he will find something of himself in each of them. And each time it will be baloney.

And a rhinoceros was especially far from being human. A sea lion's brain was a hundred times more sophisticated than the grey matter of this stinking colossus, which should have become extinct thousands of years ago, along with the dinosaurs and the mammoth. It was an oversight of nature that it was still wandering around, serving the tourist industry. In the Middle Ages, knights had scoured the Old World looking for unicorns—elegant white stallions that could charm virgins with the twisted horn on their foreheads. In the modern Middle Ages, the era of globalization, Joe Sixpack could lay his eyes on the unicorn's cumbersome grey kinsman in any zoo in the world. Few people, virgins or otherwise, fainted at the sight of its squat double horns. If the rhinoceros possessed any charms, they were hidden beneath its robust hideousness, its surprising girth, its threatening, primordial strength. A primitive tank on four legs; it was hard to believe it would let itself be taken out by a single person with the right gun and a steely set of nerves.

Before the arrival of men with guns, rhinos hadn't even had any natural enemies. Wherever they weren't hunted, they thrived and flourished. They were the only species of tropical animal not to suffer from the Arctic winters and eternal nights of the menageries in the Far North, as long as they had creature comforts and a decent roof above their heads.

In that respect, they were only too human. All the rest was sentimental fantasy.

Tony had no time for sentiment. There was a knife at his throat. He had to bring off this appalling job or go under, himself, dragging everything he loved down with him. He wanted his family back, his reputation, and his old life. That creature, there, was the key. Backing out was no longer possible, anyway. He was already guilty of fencing, breaking and entering, and attempted poaching, plus illegal arms possession and forgery. And that was just the South African stuff.

It wasn't fair, though. This animal was simply unlucky enough to be the first rhinoceros to turn up at the watering hole. 'But hey, that's life! Things are tough for everyone!' The head of the trading floor had shouted that at the first furious clients who had telephoned to complain about Tony, and the inexplicably falling prices of the stocks recommended to them on the basis of his prognoses.

'When the prices inexplicably rise, you lot never call. Drop dead, you bunch of losers!' For a whole week, he'd had to maintain his defensive line of scorn and threat.

Then he'd begun to telephone Tony himself to complain about his own shrinking portfolio. He, too, called Tony a conman and a leech. Another week later, something happened that no investment fund, ministry, or rating agency had wanted to consider. The bank went bankrupt and pulled all its foreign affiliates down into the black hole with it. A fortune larger than the budget of some European industrial powers disappeared into the void, leaving behind as much of a footprint as a fart in outer space.

The night before, Tony had gone into hiding. Disappeared off the radar, along with his laptop and his twelve memory sticks. They contained encoded company secrets from throughout the years. Activities that had been kept off the balance sheets. Toxic investment products, cut with clean ones and then oversold as reliable derivatives. A list of demanding clients and their exotic bank-account numbers. A demanding client—and this could be a person, a fund, a country, or another bank—didn't like to share where the money came from or where it was going next, but demanded the highest interest rates and, if they didn't get them, put their eggs in the competition's basket.

The memory sticks were supposed to be a private database, nothing more—a way of keeping track in the growing rat's nest of data. Tony only consulted them when his laptop was offline, that was how worried he was about hackers and extortionists. He had installed all the firewalls possible, but didn't trust any of them completely. He had never wanted to use the sticks for criminal purposes. The thought hadn't even occurred to him. His loyalty and sense of duty were too great for that. Now, in retrospect, he could no longer imagine it, but as long as he'd worked for the bank, gratitude for his job had won out over doubts about his role. He had shown respect because he thought he was respected. Extremely proud was how he had felt about his career, his salary, and his domestic happiness, even though he seldom got home before eleven at night and usually left again by seven in the morning. His weekends were one day long—unless there was a crisis, then they lasted an afternoon. His holidays in Provence were never longer than seven days, one of which was spent travelling there and another getting back. For ten years, he'd begged his wife to be patient. Just before she turned forty, he'd granted her a pregnancy. After the birth of their daughter, he'd had himself sterilized.

The more blood he shed on the altar of his profession, the more fanatically he took up its defence. He even protected his employer from slander on Internet forums, albeit under a false name. He didn't want be known as a toady. Toadies didn't survive in investment banks. Indispensability depended on hard figures, not on soft-soaping.

On the Net, he had used ten pseudonyms in rotation to attack each new critic. He had the nine other usernames give his first alias the thumbs up, accompanied with little commentaries that attacked the details in the post but backed up the general gist. Sometimes the discussions between his aliases were longer than their collective brawls with the slanderers. This was how he conducted his chorus of swelling counter-voices to a climax: the detractors would grow tired of the unexpectedly large blowback and go and mouth off elsewhere, about some other financial mastodon.

Their departure filled him with more disappointment than triumph. He didn't have any other hobbies.

Now he, too, had departed. He was in exile. He took his incriminating memory sticks and his laptop with him in a sports bag bearing the bank's logo. He wasn't intending to do any harm with them. He wasn't a rancorous person; he found revenge barbaric. But he didn't feel like paying for what was on his sticks. They would be his life insurance, nothing more.

His real life insurance would be shut down a few days after his disappearance, he was certain of that. Not everyone found revenge repulsive. He had many superiors, and the urge to retaliate increased the further up the food chain you went. His good name would be dragged through the mud, his bank accounts and his credit cards blocked, his shares, warrants, and options would be confiscated or forfeited. Whatever value they still had.

He stamped his BlackBerry to smithereens in the main station in Brussels, right after he'd used the phone one last time to say goodbye to Martine, his shocked wife. He hadn't had Klara, their six-year-old daughter, on the line. She was still with the mother from the babysitting co-op, Martine sobbed. Tony didn't know whether to believe his wife or whether she wanted to spare Klara the trauma of two tearful parents. Klara was a hypersensitive child.

But Tony was the person who would have been able to calm her down. He and Klara often talked on the phone. They mainly talked on the phone. But there wasn't time to convince Martine. He wouldn't be surprised if his BlackBerry were already being tapped. I'm sorry, darling! Keep thinking of me, and tell Klara that Daddy will be back as soon as he can! He left the broken pieces and the battery in a corridor where there were no security cameras. He might be acting overly cautiously, but prevention was better than being arrested. A little fear of being followed wasn't unhealthy for a man in hiding with a controversial record.

Next, he took the metro to the terminus of line 5, Herrmann-Debroux station. It was a twenty-minute walk from there to his hideout on the Tervurenlaan, which bisected one of the prettiest neighbourhoods in the European capital. He hadn't dared take a taxi. He might just stumble on the one ex-Yugoslavian driver who had inherited a photographic memory from his partisan family. Or what if the Belgian security services, or who knows, even the CIA, kept lists of anyone arriving by taxi at what was supposed to be his safe haven?

No, no taxis for him. In Brussels, Tony figured, you'd stand out least as a pedestrian with a sports bag in a sweater. A sweater whose hood you could pull right over your head. He'd purchased the item especially for this purpose from a grubby little shop near the Fontainasplein. A low-key disguise. And even then, after leaving the Herrmann-Debroux, he'd be better off taking the quiet minor roads that would take him past Castle Hertoginnedal's gardens. Pleasant footpaths, pastoral greenery on either side, almost deserted at dusk. The fewer people who noticed him, the better.

He would miss Klara and Martine like crazy. He felt no remorse about the rest. They should have checked his work more thoroughly. But they weren't even capable of it. That was the essence of the collapse. It was also the reason that all of his peers had long been fired and he hadn't. Nobody in the world, except for himself and a handful of confrères, understood the details, let alone the scope, of the newest generation of econometric computer models.

If Tony were honest, he had to admit that he had found it hard to keep a handle on them, himself. They had outgrown the human brain, so to speak. It wouldn't be long before they became independently operating cancerous growths, autonomous digital organisms, spurred on algorithmically to ever-greater speeds, until they achieved perpetual motion with unprecedented purchasing power and no inhibitory mechanism at all. In virtual reality, where there were no days or nights and the free markets stayed open forever, the most diverse products could be purchased fully automatically and then immediately resold, even if they had long ceased to exist in the tangible world. Sometimes they had never existed in the first place. The market for financial derivatives was already ten times larger than the real-life global economy. The end of the tumescence was still not yet in sight.

The concept that a product must exist in order to be traded has long been outmoded. Just as old-fashioned is the idea that money should exist before you can spend it. In a career barely spanning two decades, Tony, as key witness in the front row, had been able to observe this natural progress on his ever-thinner, ever-higher-resolution computer screens. Trading had definitively freed itself from its two fetters, merchandise and money. The earth's produce and the bargaining chips to obtain it with? They had quite simply become superfluous. Just as art for art's sake had come into existence, now there was trading for the sake of trading. After the poet and the conceptual sculptor, now the banker and the stockbroker had entered the era of pure lyricism, in which you didn't have to take anyone else into account, least of all the public. Lucre became hermetic poetry. Even property could be a soap bubble.

At some point a real bill would be presented, for real money. Material money, old-fashioned money. They all knew that only too well. Fearful of being the first to be cast out of the pecuniary pecking order, they had all just carried on speculating and cashing in. This schizophrenia didn't even prove to be that unpleasant. When repression takes hold of a closed group of insiders, an enjoyable collective intoxication ensues. Especially if the concrete salaries and bonuses continued to rise in tandem with the phantom rates.

Intoxication becomes addiction, and addiction is the new Order of the Garter's badge of honour—*honi soit qui mal y pense*. In no time, a newfangled nobility had risen up, a coterie of untouchables, dancing on the lid of a cesspool that gained the allure of a blocked volcano as more and more yeast and toxic gasses escaped from the underground river of global crap. Its eruption had been a surprise, nevertheless, and was felt across the globe.

On Tony's memory sticks there were constructions and trajectories that undeniably fingered him as the architect and route planner. But why should he put on the hair shirt? He had been an errand boy, nothing more. He had followed his masters' marching orders without insubordination. If they'd been hoping he'd be the get-out clause that would ensure their collective impunity, they had the wrong man. For the first time in his life, he was going to categorically follow their beloved principle: 'Help yourself, no one else will.'

They had tried to hammer in the unwritten rule—'the Law'—from his first workday onwards. Each employee, they had warned him, would be judged on his quarterly results, not on the vague feelings of satisfaction of some client or other. This was neither cheating nor negligence, they thought. In the long term, it was the client in particular, each client, who was better off with a stronger bank. That was how it worked, the Invisible Hand, the tentacle that governed the free market better and more rationally than God his Creation. Help yourself, and the whole world would be better for it.

Tony hadn't openly protested, even though the Law clashed with his ethics as a programmer, his principles as a dyed-in-the-wool democrat, and his sense of duty as a spouse, and later, a father. And, above all, he didn't like to be forced to do anything he didn't believe in one hundred percent.

This internal conflict was the only thing that irritated him about his job. Ostensibly, he had submitted meekly to the banking uniform—a tie and designer labels. Internally, and that was what counted, he had continued to see himself as some kind of rebel. A latent anarchist. However fiercely he defended his corporatist pride to the outside world, it didn't prevent him feeling on the inside that he was a missing link. An autonomous pivot between the normal tribe he came from and the master race of high finance to which he would never be admitted.

And which he'd never wanted to belong to, in the first place. He was neither one nor the other. He was himself. And that secret feeling of honour was something no one could take away from him.

His latent resistance had turned into overt revolt shortly after his department head had called him a leech and a conman down the phone. The heads of other departments had come to threaten him, too, all the way to his office, which they had never set foot in before. One of them, a red-faced brute in a double-breasted suit, foaming at the mouth, had unexpectedly taken a swing at him with a balled fist covered in rings. The fellow was probably still coked up, too. Once one party drug wears off, you need another.

Tony had been able to turn his face away in a bewildered reflex. The punch had grazed his jaw without doing any visible damage, but his cheek was still sore a week later. A humiliating phantom pain that only let up when Tony made up his mind what to do. You couldn't even call it rebellion. It was more about finding an antidote for the poison.

From now on, he swore—as he emptied his drawers and collected his memory sticks, packed his laptop in the sports bag, not forgetting his framed photo of Martine and Klara—from now on he would live life the way he'd been brought up. Help yourself? You could say that again. He didn't just know the programmes for embellishing bank balances and pimping up long-term government budgets.

He also knew the paths a person of flesh and blood could take to go up in smoke.

And even here, Tony thought—sweating on this hilltop in Mpumalaga at the foot of God's Porch—even here, the Law worked. Even here, I and I alone am the master of my own destiny. He wiped his sweaty palms on his cotton safari trousers and shouldered his gun again. He hadn't been a bad marksman during his military service. According to his training officer, he possessed all the qualities you needed to become a sniper in urban combat. Accuracy plus patience, patience, patience.

It wasn't the kind of thing you could forget. It was a gift. The only thing you had to do was pull the trigger at the right moment. What could go wrong? There was hardly any wind; there wasn't a single reason to believe that the bullet would miss its target. Its head had been notched with a cross so as to burst behind the eye socket on impact. The animal would die instantly with a minimum of suffering. It sounded cruel but it was humane.

For minutes on end, Tony stood there, trying to gird his loins, but again he didn't manage to pull the bloody trigger. He was forced to watch helplessly through his scope as the rhino cow turned her head away again. She revealed the contours of her magical, majestic double horn, the price of which, per kilo, exceeded that of gold. She sniffed around suspiciously, her head back, her nose in the air. Then she bent down toward her baby. He was standing next to her, panting away after frolicking in the mud of the watering hole. The place where his own horn would grow was marked only by a small bump. How old was this calf? A few weeks? Months?

Tony let his gun drop. He couldn't do this. His right leg was shaking, sweat was running into his eye again. His armpits stank. Thank God the light breeze was blowing in his direction, away from the watering hole; otherwise his presence would have been betrayed long before. He rested his back against the pickup and rolled his shoulders around to relax them, breathing deeply in and out. A zebra stallion brayed in the distance, a family of warthogs trotted toward the waterline at a respectable distance from the rhinos, the wading birds were still pecking away like crazy, and the colossal red sun sank ever deeper into the horizon. How much time was left until darkness fell? Which escape route should he choose?

And what would happen if he missed the eye, and the animal

was only wounded? That wasn't an option. He had to hit his target with the first shot.

He pulled himself together and aimed again.

His heart winced. The endearingly clumsy rhino calf was searching between its mother's back legs for a nipple. It wasn't easy, with all those skin folds and layers of fat. The calf just kept on feeling around, searching.

The rhino cow didn't interfere. She stood there with her legs wide apart, somewhat peevishly—or was that more silly anthropomorphism? A little bird with a red beak was sitting on the cow's hunched back, pecking away at parasites. The cow just let it all happen.

Again, Tony had her right eye in his sights; again, his finger failed him. Now he was paralyzed by the thought of the suckling calf. What would happen to a calf like that in the African night? He shuddered to think. Next to a corpse that would attract scavengers from kilometres and kilometres away? God, he wasn't about to sentence one living being to death, but two. He could picture it already. The baby would be snatched and dragged off by a crocodile because it had dared to venture too close to the water's edge. Or it would be attacked in the middle of the night by hyenas with slimy, already-bloodied maws. Or by a pack of Cape hunting dogs. In ten minutes they could tear an impala to bits. They might need slightly longer for such a thick-skinned baby.

He wiped the sweat off his top lip with his wrist. Should he shoot twice, then, so as to grant the baby a merciful death, too? That would be even harder for him. He was no brute. Two shots would result in lost time and a racket, with all the attendant risks. The fight against poaching had been drastically stepped up in recent years. You could read all about that online, too. The government and the game managers were co-operating more closely. As well as night vision goggles and reconnaissance planes, they now possessed the most modern forms of communication, and had even gone so far as to acquire munitions, recently—the poaching gangs were becoming so foolhardy. In the Umfolozi game reserve, the former hunting ground of King Shaka Zulu, there had been a bloody clash between a poaching gang and a surveillance patrol, with deaths on both sides and a fuss in the international press.

It could actually be considered a miracle, Tony realized, that he hadn't already been caught red-handed. The risks he was running were outrageous. That was why he'd cooked up the plan on his own, without any nosy parkers or potential snitches, leaving no loose ends, no helpers who could turn against you on the way back. A life wasn't worth much in this part of the world. You saw plenty of stories in the papers. A single horn sold for enough money on the Vietnamese black market to ensure a dozen families a generous standard of living for several years. It didn't do much for his spirits. The one chance I have, Tony thought, is to act fast. I shoot, I drive over, I get out the axe, I strike, and I hurry back to the hole in the fence. The night and the unlit access roads will hide my retreat. That's the way it has to happen. Forget that calf!

He beat off a few mosquitoes and took aim.

To his dismay, he saw the zebra stallion he'd just heard braying many times appear some way behind the hunched back of the rhinoceros cow. The stallion was the first to descend a low ridge; the herd followed in his footsteps, in dribs and drabs, in a messy line. A family of giraffes ran along with them at a slow gallop, thirsty, majestic. Tony had been so focussed on his prey, he hadn't seen them coming. He suppressed an expletive. What else was about to turn up? A herd of gnus? A watering hole like this could be incredibly busy at this time of day, and that made all of the animals nervous. They were venturing into treacherous terrain. Lions often lay in wait here. Tony needed to strike before the rhino cow cleared off. Rhinos liked their privacy; it wasn't in their nature to share a lair or a watering hole. There you go! The cow was getting restless. Her large pointed ears turned in all directions; she sniffed for hostile odours again. Stepping backward, she began to rock her massive head to and fro.

Tony cursed and followed her with his gun. He couldn't get the eye cleanly in the cross hairs anymore. I should have pulled the trigger just now, he muttered. At the same time, he was overwhelmed by the hefty grace of his prey. Her nervous stamping carried all the way over to him; he saw quivers run across her dusty flanks. In her neck, under her legs, and in her groins there were folds like an old leather armchair, her armoured skin stretched between them, pockmarked like magnified, concrete-coloured orange peel. He saw the shaking of her heavy, hanging belly, the curling of her short but powerful tail. What an awe-inspiring, beautiful creature she was! Millions of years of precarious evolution and an irrepressible survival instinct.

Tony's own Klara flashed through his mind; he'd only spoken to her a couple of times in the past year. Surreptitiously and briefly, via Skype and all kinds of false accounts and digital back doors. His wife and his daughter were the bait he would have chosen, himself. Not only the government would be looking for him. The bank had a different name by now—its relaunch had been generously subsidized by the government—and it had hired not only most of the old bank directors but most of the researchers, too. Those Judases were good at their jobs. They had given Tony hushed-up information about clients often enough, or insider knowledge that bordered on the illegal. He couldn't be too careful.

But it was also high time he took the step toward his potential deliverance, towards rehabilitation, however bloody and difficult that step had to be. His odyssey had lasted long enough. His life's course couldn't just end here. He'd already given up too much, invested too much for that. He had the right to a second chance. A future, just like everyone else.

He determinedly took aim again, gritting his teeth with determination. And at last a crisp shot rang out at the foot of God's Porch.

Tony was surprised. He wasn't the one who had fired it. He let his gun drop and looked at the rhino in disbelief. One of her temples had been blown away, eye and all. Blood gushed out. An expert shot.

For the moment, the cow remained on her feet, shuddering. She bellowed briefly but dolefully, stamping her back legs truculently as the wading birds rose up above her, the zebras and giraffes fled around her in disarray, and the echo of the shot rumbled behind her, ever deeper and higher into the ravine.

Then she fell with a dull thud. In the distance, a songbird made its presence known again.

* * *

IT WASN'T A LARGE GANG that had stolen a march on him, as Tony feared for a split second—his heart skipping a few beats at the thought that he had accidentally found himself face to face with half a dozen poachers. Imagine if he had been the first to shoot, and they'd fired at him after that! With their superior numbers and undoubtedly automatic weapons! He could have been dead by now. Helplessly riddled with bullets, left behind to disappear without a trace, twelve thousand kilometres from home, eaten by vultures and worms, a carcass of uncertain origin.

But soon his panic ebbed away. It was replaced by a cautious sense of relief. His opponent turned out to be a lone man, just like himself. And, judging by his bold act, he hadn't even noticed Tony.

Even before the shot had died away, a safari jeep raced to the watering hole with a shadow at the wheel. The canvas protecting the back seat instead of a door featured the same logo as the bonnet: a graphic representation of a springbok, with the words *Nasionale Krugerwildtuin* underneath it.

For a moment, Tony thought that his opponent was simply better prepared than he was. This fellow hadn't bought a stolen four-by-four in Jo'burg; he'd carjacked one in the vicinity. An entirely appropriate vehicle, which no one would frown at if it were spotted, parked on the forbidden byroads of a neighbouring safari park. Brilliantly planned.

But when the man got out, surrounded by the cloud of dust his abruptly braking jeep had thrown up, Tony's mild admiration turned into enmity. This wasn't fair. It was Tony's right to be standing there, he thought, down there in that dust cloud, down there by that water. *His* right—after all the trouble he'd gone to to get this far, a foreigner in a remote, unpredictable country, and a numbers person at that, which meant he rarely came into contact with animals, and certainly not in order to kill them. His opponent, on the other hand, was a professional park guide. That was much easier.

Tony watched the man through his telescopic sights with increasing dismay. A black giant of around 50 with a gammy leg and bloodshot eyes, creamy white teeth, grey stubble, and a grimace that looked as gloomy as it was grim, he was wearing the uniform that came with the job: sturdy shoes, knee-high green socks, a dark pair of shorts with pockets on the thighs, and a khaki-coloured shirt with breast pockets and green epaulettes on which the reserve's emblem was repeated in miniature.

Tony remembered that uniform only too well. He had admired

it, not two years ago, during his stay in Africa's largest wildlife park with Martine and Klara. They may even have met this man in his capacity as guard.

That possibility made Tony's blood boil.

For ten days, they had exchanged their converted barn in Belgium for a country as big as Western Europe. They hadn't nearly enough time—they'd realized that right away. They hadn't seen much more than the Kruger Wildlife Park, two vineyards in Franschhoek, and the view of Table Mountain from Cape Town.

But what a staggering panorama that had been! The bright-blue bay with its V&A Waterfront, the lattice of the busy streets in the City Bowl, wedged between Devil's Peak and Lion's Head, the elongated Parade with its palm trees, the smoggy patches on the northern horizon... After the immense, ever-changing landscape that he and Martine had admired from the hire car for hours on end, this lavish vista made them feel even more regretful. They resolved to return as soon as possible and do this magnificent country justice.

Nothing ever came of their resolution. They just didn't have time. The ten-day trip was one of the very few real trips Tony had ever allowed himself. Martine had pressed for it for so long, and the bank, back then, seemed to be heading toward double-digit profit growth. They could, briefly, do without him. For once, he even accepted the risk that, while he was gone, the newly recruited whiz-kids would steal his niche. These days they were snatched from university even before their finals and given a five-year contract straight off, in exchange for that period in their lives when they didn't yet have a time-consuming family, but did have the endurance of an athlete. Those pups could work for two nights in a row without losing any of their enthusiasm. Well, just let them try it, the suckers. Let them muddle along without him for once. Just to play it safe, he'd stowed away a few files behind double passwords. There were others he'd failed to mention during the briefing. They'd just have to get on with it. He'd had to do that, too, when he joined the bank.

Klara had just turned four back then, during their jaunt, but two years later she still remembered the herd of elephants and the one lion they'd seen close up, not to mention the family of amusing meerkats, and the warthog with eight piglets. And the hippos! Once Klara got going about them? Their wide-open mouths with birds in, pecking between their teeth? And her very own pink Hello Kitty binoculars, used to spot everything? After that, Tony could just sit back and listen for a few minutes. Klara would rattle on endlessly to oblige Daddy.

At least it had once been that way. At home and on the phone. And recently, again, though much more briefly, on Skype. There was hardly time to talk about anything else; Tony didn't dare to speak to her or his wife for longer than ten or twelve minutes at a time.

Maybe it was better that way—Klara talking about the trip again. He wouldn't have known what to say if she had pestered him with questions like she usually did. He was already feeling sick about the fact that, in the space of three minutes and with her prettiest pout, she'd twice asked him when he was coming home, at last.

One consequence of Klara's extended safari story was that Martine barely had the chance to break into the conversation. As a mother, she clearly considered it more important that their sensitive daughter got to talk to her father than that she unburdened her sorrows as a wife. When Tony had cautiously sounded her out on the progress of the investigation, Martine had reacted strangely. She had gone white as a sheet, stuttered, stumbled over her words, and been completely incomprehensible. Was this his

Martine? Where was her self-control, the sangfroid he'd always admired? From the dismal sob in her voice and the sidelong, fearful glances she'd cast at her daughter, only visible to him, Tony concluded that she and Klara were still under surveillance, and that they were trying to track him down through his family. They were being tapped, watched, downright spied upon.

He not only cut the connection immediately, he logged off completely and left the Internet café without paying, disappearing into the ambling crowds in Istanbul's Old City. Two hours later, he had checked in at Atatürk airport, completing his stopover of almost a full day. Two hours later, and he was taking off in a Turkish Airlines Airbus A330 to O.R. Tambo airport, Johannesburg.

The uniformed black giant had hardly looked around as he got out, maddeningly calm, as though any cause for concern were unimaginable. He threw back the canvas of his jeep, tossed his safari hat onto the back seat, and still with the same air of appalling unflappability, got out a chainsaw. The rhino cow lay convulsing on her side next to the jeep. Blubber welled out of the hole in her head while her fat legs continued to move, slowly struggling as though making their way sideways through a sea of clotting mucus. The bottom of the sun touched the horizon. A sickly smell reached Tony's nostrils, carried on the evening breeze. Birds hovered high in the sky; Tony wasn't sure if they'd already been circling before, or not.

The birds flapped away when the man set off his chainsaw with a tug of the starter cord. The hysterical roar of the machine not only cleaved the newly regained Arcadian silence with just a few bird and insect sounds, it also cut Tony's heart in two. He no longer knew what he felt, watching motionlessly from his hiding place. Outrage? Jealousy?

Or was he simply angry?

Even as a student, he'd had a predilection for black people. Their history was deeply tragic; it seemed to cry out for vengeance. The nice thing was—and this country was a wonderful example of that—that the black masses, despite all the injustice done to them over the centuries, were able to forgive. At least as long as they had a leader like Nelson Mandela.

Unfortunately, they had also proved, in other African countries, that they knew what genocide was. They thought nothing of large-scale acts of revenge. Nor did they shrink from other major atrocities. But if you had the stomach to look at things from a historical perspective, the Europeans could hardly boast. They hadn't managed much better, even in just the twentieth century, even amongst themselves. And you didn't need to have studied economics to be shocked by the lasting havoc Europe had caused beyond its borders, primarily in its former fiefdoms.

Improving the local schools and infrastructure did little to lessen the responsibility, no, the liability, of the Old World. It was going to take generations for the West to even slightly redeem itself. That couldn't be said often enough, flying in the face of all that Eurocentric cynicism. What's more, Tony, like Martine, considered the black man to be more handsome and noble by nature than, well, representatives of all the other races. Race was a word they didn't like to use, but there was no other way to describe it. If you disregarded the unfortunate high number of dictators—their existence frequently playing a part in Europe's continuing interference—blacks were simply more photogenic and more likeable than the other inhabitants of the planet. This was something he and Martine had been able to experience during their admittedly brief stay.

The wealthy tourist received a warm welcome in every holiday paradise in the world, but the genuine, good-humoured geniality to which Tony and his family were treated for ten whole days?

Even on the street? And by all the South Africans—not just the blacks, but also the coloureds, and even the whites? Their love of life was almost unsettling. Certainly when you returned to the self-proclaimed navel of the world, that country of your birth, where you were re-confronted with all those snarling voices and sour faces, for whom a friendly word seemed equal to an insult, which could only be answered with a real insult. Even Klara—who, with her blond curls and her freckles, had been the centre of attention for ten days, treated to cries of admiration and tickling games by adoring strangers—seemed to sense it. "When are we going back to all the smiley black people again?" she'd pouted one evening at bedtime. And to friends and family, to anyone who had wanted to listen, Martine and Tony had been full of praise for the overwhelming country of their dreams, where, sure, inequality hadn't quite been eliminated, sadly enough, which they'd travelled to with a sense of apprehension, yes, that, too—but where, from the first day onward, they'd been treated like royalty and friends, and where the motorways, hear this, were better than those in Belgium.

And it wasn't as dangerous as you thought. But now Tony was being forced to watch a black man take advantage of a uniform aimed at tourists to commit a crime against the resources and the progress of his own country. He knew that he was ill-placed to lecture others, but it made him seethe. Everything that went wrong in Africa, everything that made its future look so hopeless, came together in this spectacle, this tragedy in a nutshell.

What had got into the man's head? In a region and a time of towering unemployment, you finally get offered a decent job, expenses and housing included, clothes on your body and a car beneath your ass, in one of the most beautiful parts of the world, and in a sector where the visitors' tips alone equalled the basic income of three quarters of your less-fortunate compatriots—and what do you do? You take them for a ride. You start poaching, too, thus increasing the damage perpetrated by those international gangs. You saw off the branch you are sitting on. How stupid could you be? And this, too, was Africa, with its epidemic skulduggery, its short-sightedness, its corruption at every level that just couldn't be stamped out. The ease with which you could buy a stolen pickup here, a rifle, even ordnance. Just like that! On the street, no questions asked. Tony kept a roll of South African rands in the glovebox of his pickup, brand-new notes in the highest denomination, now featuring a picture of Nelson Mandela, if you please. Notes he'd use to bribe customs so that his luggage, horn and all, would be set on the conveyor belt unchecked. Prior contact wasn't necessary; guts and canniness about human nature at the crucial moment were enough. This was something else he'd found out during his ten-day stay. Traffic fines? Half the money as a backhander to Mr. Friendly Policeman, and he'd tear up your ticket. No authorities ever needed to know. A wink and a mutual nod sufficed. The rituals of corruption were pathetically simple and catastrophically efficient. And then they were shocked that their rainbow nation remained a sunless mess.

But Tony's anger cut deeper than that. It had to do with the man himself. The man was acting in total cold blood. It was surely not the first time he'd got up to something like this. Everything about him was arrogant, focussed, and offensively authentic. Tony's safari outfit was a parody; the guard's was the real thing. He was a professional; Tony was a hobbyist, a miserable impostor, even in deceit. Without realizing it, the man was holding up a shaming mirror to Tony. He saw that clearly, now, and it shocked him. This was what he had wanted to do. This was how far he'd sunk.

But, in spite of this, he still felt a primitive envy of this part-time poacher, and it made his blood boil.

The uniformed brute didn't wait until the rhino's legs had stopped thrashing. He hobbled over to the dying animal, stood with his legs wide apart, and placed the roaring chainsaw against the root of the largest horn. Tony had to stop himself from screaming. The bastard! At least put the creature out of its misery first!

The man braced himself. The chainsaw's roar changed into a bellow, softer and yet warlike, triumphant. It sliced through Tony like a knife. The chutzpah of it—the man daring to use a chainsaw rather than an axe! You could hear the racket for miles. And he sawed deeper than necessary, too, not wanting to miss a scrap of horn. Drops of blood and bits of bone flew into the air. Tony loathed the man from the bottom of his heart. A faint smell of burning hair and hot bone reached him. He felt his teeth grate; he gagged in disgust. The man got ready to remove the second, smaller horn.

And then it happened. Still clearly visible despite the looming darkness—half of the sun had disappeared now—the rhino calf charged.

Tony had lost sight of the animal. It had probably run off with the zebras and only just returned. In any case, it charged desperately, with its still-virgin nose low to the ground. This was how it reached the giant, sideways from behind, not head-on. But it was still enough to send the man with the bad leg pitching forward.

Deafened by the roar of his saw, the giant hadn't heard the calf approaching. In order not to fall, he had to make a clownish jump, chainsaw in his hands, over the mutilated head of the rhino cow. His swearing was audible above the singing of the saw.

He regained his balance and turned around angrily to face the calf, who began a second charge from close by. Then the giant did something he shouldn't have. He raised the chainsaw, ready to mow down the calf. And Tony shot him.

In a fraction of a second, he had aimed and pulled the trigger, all signs of paralysis gone, and just as accurate a shot as ever. It *was* a gift, and Tony possessed it, even though he was a programmer and number cruncher by trade. He could see the result through the gun's sights. His shot had hit the giant below the neck, not far above his heart. Interrupted in his counter-attack, the man let out a gurgling scream, head back, mouth and eyes wide open in pain and astonishment. The chainsaw slipped out of his hands and fell across his knee, separating his thigh from his lower leg. Blood spurted out, mixing with that of the rhino cow. The man himself toppled theatrically, away from his amputated limb. For the second time that evening, the crack of a shot echoed deeper and deeper through the rocky crevice.

The howling of the chainsaw had stopped. It stood upright in the loose sand, like a knife in a tabletop.

The remorse would come later, along with the shame and the permanent dent in his self-image. ('Am I really capable of something that monstrous?')

For the time being, Tony felt none of that—aside, perhaps, from the adrenaline coursing through his veins. The only thing he did think was: I should have done this much sooner.

3. Buenos Aires

THE HAPPY CORPSE hadn't made it, after all. It had died a second time. No one could really accuse Tony Hanssen of not trying hard enough to bring Mrs. Bo Xiang back, though. Cautious pats on her cheek, repeating her name ten times with his lips pressed to her pierced earlobe, shaking her, imploring, crying, and cajoling, he'd tried it all and nothing had worked. Mrs. Bo Xiang had entered the Kingdom of God and flatly refused to come back.

Tony had been advised in his resuscitation attempts by the pension owner—a towering, extravagantly-dressed fake blonde with a face of granite and permanently raised eyebrows, both the result of plastic surgery. Her full lips enjoyed the benefit of the doubt—her mouth was the only thing on her face that seemed able to move easily. And yet she was still attractive in a wilful kind of way, Tony judged, like most of the women in this city. It didn't matter where Eva Perón was buried, the actress and first lady's spiritual legacy had not gone to the grave with her. The Porteñas, young and old, still had fiery temperaments and rock-solid self-esteem. And they continued to have just as many problems with their men—men whose domineering nature they criticized while refusing to tolerate any sign of weakness in them.

Tony had called her, the pension owner, in panic because she was the only person in Buenos Aires whose number he had saved on his smartphone. She interrupted him after his first sentence, ordered him to stay where he was, snapped at someone in Spanish—probably the cleaner—to alert the emergency services, and rushed to the scene herself. All of this without hanging up. She lived two floors above them. There was a good chance, Tony thought, when she entered still clutching her mobile phone, that the sounds of he and Mrs. Bo Xiang going at it had reached her upstairs.

She kept a straight face, but that could have been the Botox. Her gaze, though, directed at the mortal remains of Mrs. Bo Xiang, betrayed contempt, if not ridicule—as though she considered it typical of a Chinese woman to kick the bucket at the *moment suprême*. While they waited for the ambulance, she stood at the foot of the bed and gave Tony more orders than advice. Her father, she had told him when he'd checked in, had been a general during *los Años Difíciles*. Tony hadn't dared ask more. He had read in the Rough Guide that Argentina had had many difficult years. The difficult years outnumbered the easy ones. Her name was Mercedes. Her father had not only been a general, he'd also had a lot of German friends.

'Slap her face again,' Mrs. Mercedes commanded, looking down her nose at Tony and his happy corpse as if they were two street fighters down for the count. Her English wasn't bad for a Spanish speaker. From her tone, she wasn't too pleased that death had paid a visit to her *casa de turistas*. She managed two small hotels and twenty guest rooms, spread out over rustic San Telmo and hip Palermo, but this house was her HQ and the jewel in her crown. A former architecture student, she had supervised the renovations herself, and lived on the only floor that was never rented out. 'Have you already put a finger down her throat?' She sounded more and more sincere and more and more concerned, looking down with her arms folded across her stiff bosom. 'Maybe she's swallowed her tongue.' After that, she didn't say anything else.

What a difference from the first time they'd met, at check-in. Then, Mrs. Mercedes had monopolized the conversation in record time, as though she were worried her two wealthy guests might escape to her competitors if she stopped talking. Tony was forced to think about this now, in her mute presence, as he tried to lure Mrs. Bo Xiang out of her new-found homeland of the smile. The poor woman was naked under the damp, thin sheets. Only her head stuck out, with its shocking grin, open and bared. Tony began to massage her heart through the sheets even though he knew it couldn't be coaxed to beat again. He didn't want to do it, but he did it all the same. Again, he bridged the gap through dissociation. By reflecting on a trivial event from two weeks earlier, he could avoid thinking about the cruelty of the present.

The three of them had stood waiting in the entrance hall, next to a desk on which Mrs. Mercedes's laptop rested.

Mrs. Bo Xiang was supposed to pay for their three-day stay in advance by Internet banking, using this laptop and not her own smartphone. This was a strict condition imposed on all guests, Mrs. Mercedes had apologized. It was just a precaution. She'd been ripped off too many times in the past. She'd added that her bank was in the Virgin Islands, so it would take a while for confirmation of their payment to come through.

This is the kind of thing you have to deal with these days, Mrs. Mercedes sighed—as they still stood there waiting—all these long distances and passwords and devices you'd never have dreamed of in the past. My God! She still had vivid recollections of the tube radio of her childhood. Her hard face now showed a grimace of happiness, which she further improved on by rolling her eyes and shrugging coquettishly. *Dios mío!* The tube radio of her childhood! She was so caught up in her story, she missed Mrs. Bo Xiang's confused expression.

Her family, Mrs. Mercedes had cooed, was the first in the village to acquire one of those hulking great things. It was nearly the size of a cabin trunk, and you had to wait two minutes for all the lamps to warm up. Only then did the scratchy music come out, or the news, or hours of background noise. You could pick up Montevideo when the weather was bad. The neighbours gathered once a week for the radio play. She had shrugged coquettishly again, her voice taking on a languorous tone. The weekly radio play! My goodness! Everyone had crammed into their old drawing room around that one appliance, the way you'd gather around a preacher, all thirty of them hypnotized, half of them bursting into tears during the final episode because of the injustice of the heroine's death. And that was just the tube radio! Again she'd rolled her eyes, elatedly shaking her granite head. After that, there was the freezer, the washing machine, the colour TV! Unbelievable, wasn't it? The colossal changes that could take place within a single person's lifetime. And just look at this! She'd shown Mrs. Bo Xiang and Tony an outdated mobile telephone. Now she could even receive text messages from the *Islas Vírgenes*. Thousands of kilometres away. Handy, wasn't it? *Dios mío*, where would we be without mobile phones? She'd reply to the bank manager right away, and then everything would be in order. Her sincere apologies for the delay. But she couldn't help it.

'I've helped fill this country's bottomless pits more than enough times already,' she complained, her thumbs working away over the mobile's keyboard. 'Those blundering politicians should be happy with the likes of me, the people who haven't completely upped sticks to the *Islas Vírgenes* yet.' She determinedly pressed the send button.

To Tony's astonishment, Mrs. Bo Xiang stood there, nodding energetically. Her head was almost coming off. But her expression was disparaging. Did she actually understand what Mrs. Mercedes was saying? Or was she simply impatient, and all the more prepared to nod at everything the pension owner said, as long as it got them closer to the love nest on the second floor?

Mrs. Mercedes still didn't notice a thing. 'It's just the same with the beggars on the street,' she continued, checking confirmation of payment once again, this time on her laptop. 'Those penniless bums can count their blessings that there are still rich buggers like me left.'

Again, Tony had the impression that Mrs. Bo Xiang was nodding too emphatically, prior to accepting the room key, smiling broadly, and even bowing—it was more a curtsey.

The overt mutual contempt felt by the two ladies had begun there and then, with the curtsey and then the look they exchanged. One of them felt deadly contempt, the other felt she'd been caught out. The pleasant atmosphere could be heard shattering.

Despite her predilection for grand gestures, Mrs. Mercedes wasn't blind to the subtleties of human interaction at the micro level. She watched the curtsey, read the expression, and knew she'd been trumped. Ridiculed by someone who must be immeasurably richer than she. Someone who had come here to experience picturesque poverty, not the self-proclaimed wealth of a woman who shared a name with a German car.

A unconceded defeat doesn't count as a defeat. Mrs. Mercedes didn't say another word. She proved the benefits of the national dance tradition. She let her well-restored body speak in pantomime. With just as deep a bow, a cramped smile, and a theatrical wave of the arms, she showed Mrs. Bo Xiang the winding staircase that would take her and her young companion to seventh heaven on the second floor.

'You've got one last chance,' Mrs. Mercedes said now, looking at Tony and his lifeless mistress with ever more concern. 'Mouth to mouth. If that doesn't get results within two minutes, she's brain-dead.'

There was sympathy in her voice but no inclination to give the life-saving kiss and spare Tony, who was still trembling from his recent efforts. He'd already given so much of himself today. It was still boiling hot in the room. His armpits were dripping. He felt the same bleak despair as—well, how long ago was it? Fifteen? Five minutes ago? Half an hour? He had lost all sense of time. He was almost suffocating. His migraine had returned, more aggressive than ever. A trepan was boring its way through his head, from temple to temple. Nevertheless, he bent down over Mrs. Bo Xiang's beatific face, opened her happy mouth as well as he could, took a deep breath, and then, breathing out heavily, pressed his lips to hers.

Her mouth felt so cold, it was like kissing a dead sea creature. After the third deep inhalation and exhalation, he began to feel dizzy. He still didn't dare ask Mrs. Mercedes to take over for a moment. He wondered why. A human life was at stake. And, regardless of her age, Mrs. Mercedes's physical condition was probably better than his. She'd told them about that, too, as they waited for permission from the Virgin Islands. Her real wealth was her stamina.

Tony tried to remember all the details, so that he didn't have to think about anything else during the kissing.

Every night, Mrs. Mercedes had recounted, not without pride, she went out dancing in one of the nearby *milongas*. Yes, that's right, every night. At dusk, she'd leave her top floor to grab a bite to eat in the Plaza Dorrego. After the meal, she'd wash her hands in the toilets, dab perfume behind each ear to suppress the smell of food and anything else, pick one of the dance halls at random, and stay there until the early hours. She drank enough to forget her age, but too little not to be able to find her way home. Otherwise, she'd be condemned to accompany her last dance partner to his *casa*.

She'd never minded that in the past, but since her last minor procedure—she didn't say what it was—she'd stopped bed-hopping. Just as long as she could dance. Every day. That was the only thing that stopped her from moving to the place where her fortune was already housed.

'You can stop, Mister Tony,' Mrs. Mercedes said now, more gently than he'd heard her speak up to now. 'That's enough.' She gripped him by the shoulder, not at all reprovingly, not at all unkindly. It was the hand of an understanding nurse. 'The ambulance is here.'

Tony looked at the hand on his shoulder so as not to look at the face belonging to it, or the face that he had just been kissing so intensely. The consoling hand had an unexpected quantity of age spots and wrinkles—it didn't match Mrs. Mercedes's face. The gems in her rings were so disproportionately large, they couldn't be real. 'Mister Tony! Can you hear me?' Tony kept on staring at the elderly hand. He didn't dare stand up, he felt so dizzy. He heard, as in a nightmare, the deafening zoom of the fan's blades above him. Mrs. Mercedes's voice seemed to be coming from under a bell jar. 'Mister Tony?' His own lips seemed frozen, too.

He let two men dressed in white help him to his feet. They were careful and considerate, and looked with more concern at him than at the happy corpse. As one of them checked for a pulse, the other placed an oxygen mask over Mrs. Bo Xiang's cold, ecstatic smile. Almost at once, the man gave Mrs. Mercedes a look that said no, and did with his free hand what Tony hadn't dared to do. He closed Mrs. Bo Xiang's eyes. The truth could no longer be denied. Tony almost toppled over. His legs could no longer carry him.

He let himself be supported, and brought to a chair, by the medic who was taking care of him. A lovely, slender boy with black curly hair, a sensual mouth, and a scar on his chin. His eyes were greyer than Belgian hardstone and still deeply melancholic. He asked Tony whether he wanted a glass of water. Tony nodded. The medic let go of him and went into the bathroom.

Out of the corner of his eye, Tony, swaying backward and forward in his chair in a seasick way, saw Mrs. Mercedes bend toward the other medic and begin a whispering conversation with him. She seemed to know the man; he seemed to have some respect for her. Tony noticed that he hadn't removed the useless oxygen mask from Mrs. Bo Xiang's face. He was a corpulent man in his 40s, with the features of a galley slave and the expression of a domestic skivvy. He let Mrs. Mercedes stuff something into his hand, at first trying to give it back and gesticulating wildly, but then later putting it into his pocket, sighing, shaking his head, and looking away in shame.

Despite his nausea and his overheated exhaustion, Tony could make out a couple of the sentences that Mrs. Mercedes was whispering: 'She didn't die here, right? Somewhere along the way, or on arrival. But not here.'

* * *

GODFORSAKEN AND DOG-TIRED, Tony found himself in a room in the darkest depths of the hospital to which the happy corpse had been taken, and where it had died for the third time, this time officially. He sat bolt upright in the only chair, a monstrosity made of aluminium tubing with a green leatherette seat. It peeped and creaked with every movement. He tried to move as little as possible as he waited for the undertaker who'd been recommended to him by the youngest medic, the handsome one with the curly hair and eyes of melancholic bluestone.

Next to him, on a simple iron hospital bed, lay Mrs. Bo Xiang. Under a sheet, thank God; he didn't have to look at her smile anymore. His head was still bursting, despite the painkiller and the sedative they'd given him. They left him there, stupefied, yet still unpleasantly aware of the situation. He didn't need any mirrors to be able to see himself sitting here. He could have chosen a dog, but his mind imposed a scene from a black-and-white Japanese film on him. The last samurai, next to his shogun's open grave, on guard, exhausted.

But you could hardly call Tony Zen. He was seething inside. To his astonishment, even rage, thoughts of his mother had been popping into his head since Mrs. Bo Xiang's death. For the first time in how long? Her? The woman who had ordered him to address her as mummy, even when he was 16 and she well into her 40s.

Mummy! Mamaa-tje! There wasn't a language in the world as polluted by the diminutive as the Flemish variant of Dutch. Every other word had a -*tje* or a -*ke* tacked onto it to make it sound smaller and more precious. Every time you went into a post office: 'How many *envelopkes* would sir like?' A bank employee to his adult customers: 'Have you got your *kaartje* or do you know the *nummerke* of your bank account off by heart?' Mutual degradation under the pretext of politeness. And always, always, with that persistent, asinine immaturity, even as they prattled away so fluently. This was how he remembered Mamaatje's imperium, the little *landke* in which he'd grown up.

But why was he longing for it from the bottom of his heart? Now, all of a sudden? A little steak with a little glass of wine. A little stroll around the garden. A little newspaper, a little cigarette, a little cup of coffee—all at a nice, easy, little pace. It all sounded so damned tempting, so painfully tempting. Fuck no. He didn't want this. He'd never wanted this. If he had to choose between homesickness and cancer, he'd choose cancer. But he didn't have a choice, he realized, shivering, reeling with seasickness in his chair.

They were things you just got. Both of them.

What would she look like today, his Mamaatje? Twenty-five years after he'd made his escape. How had the ravages of time abused her?

He tried to imagine it, but dismissed the image right away. He didn't want to think about the woman who had pooped him out into this world. To his disgust, he was actually longing to see her again, as she was now. It both tormented and pleased him that he couldn't remember what she'd looked like the last time they'd met, their unexpected farewell—well, unexpected for her. What was the colour of her eyes? The colour of her hair? Her haircut at the time? He didn't know.

He did remember the scene. Her: incensed, stamping her feet, again. Because he'd well and truly failed his exams, and he—once her childish chatterbox, her immature entertainer—now gazed up at her like a deaf mute, a victim, a Roman Christian whose tongue had been cut out, ready to be set on fire for the empress' amusement.

The empress had stood there, hissing at him for ages. That was after Papaatje had barked at the both of them for quarter of an hour. Papaatje had barked the same tune ten times over before going, at last, into the new-fitted kitchen, where he wormed his mother-of-pearl cufflinks into the cuff holes of his silk shirt, which was already displaying sweat rings, and not just at the armpits. His final insults, echoing thanks to the marble walls in the kitchen, were all addressed to her. Not to his offspring. She screamed something ghastly back. Without taking her even ghastlier gaze off Tony. Her betrayer, her favourite eunuch, ever since he'd been born.

My two bawling begetters, always stamping their feet, thought Tony, staggering with seasickness next to Mrs. Bo Xiang's death-bed. Mamaatje and Papaatje, the two links that preceded me in the pointless chain of hundreds, perhaps even thousands, of ancestors in evolution's trap.

Evolution? Two pyramids stuck to each other at the base. I'm hanging on underneath on my lonely, dead-end ownsome. Him stuck to the top, also on his lonely ownsome. A hermaphroditic baboon with bleeding haemorrhoids the size of pumpkins. He'd been shitting on everyone's heads for thousands of years. Trickle-down absurdity. I never had any other idea of God, and I had a holy family of my own. I was the silly dove, our Joseph adjusted his ludicrously white Frank Sinatra dinner jacket in the kitchen, and our snake Mary had on her most civilized sequined dress, like a ridiculous temple harlot. They were ready to go to the War-egem Races sponsors' party, or the Bal du Rat Mort in Ostend, or to the Middelkerke Kursaal for a talent contest in a country full of retards. As long as they had a party to go to, that one time per year they could bear each other's company because they believed they were standing in the spotlights, arm in arm, waving at their imaginary fans, smiling at the travesty of their existence.

Better than her face, Tony remembered her desperate décolleté and her sad little beauty spot, diagonally above the left corner of her mouth. On the back of each of her legs, her stockings featured an old-fashioned seam, descending her calves to her stiletto heels. They were burlesque stilettos, and her only son, her Judas, hoped she'd break at least one of them, twisting her ankle on the cobbles of the driveway. As far as he was concerned, she could break both of her ankles, right before stepping into the silver Mercedes that would carry her away from him for good.

Did she ever think of him? It was inevitable. That's how it goes, with a piece of your own body, a chunk of flesh you'd put on earth yourself, and which you'd single-handedly taught to walk and read. And his father? Did he ever think of Tony? It wasn't inevitable. How did it look, that ugly mug of his? After all these years, all that whisky, all those Cuban cigars? All those macho tales of protracted court cases and inflated fees for routine divorces and debt collection, plus the occasional attempted rape or murder. It was a career of sorts, if you liked that, growing older, and powerless to escape the shadow of the Great Baboon high above you, the Endless Defecator with his bleeding pumpkins, the source of everything. It didn't always have to be a Big Bang.

Tony stopped rocking in his bucket seat next to Mrs. Bo Xiang's bed. He had to sit still or he'd vomit up his soul. Past, present, shame, hatred—it was all mixed up, everything was out of sync, everything was a mosaic. Now and the past kept swapping places; he wasn't where he was. It had been like this for years. Wherever he found himself, he was always in the same hall of mirrors, full of nightmares and shards of real memory. From time to time, a mirror would fall and shatter. Others bulged out or sucked themselves frightfully hollow, showing laughably distorted images from his previous life. He still didn't know what sliced through his soul the most: the shards of memory or the cartoon-like deformation. Who was he now? Who had he been? And how, in God's name, had he ended up here? In this city, in this life, this pretty kettle of fish? He wasn't himself. He was a heap of street litter with a body around it.

Outside, through the dusty net curtains, the sun and the metropolis were on the rampage, merciless, tireless. In the half light of the death chamber there was a sterile, oppressive calm. Was this really still Buenos Aires? A hospital room in Beirut or a suburb of Moscow wouldn't have looked any different. Off-white walls, floor tiles in a vague grey colour, wide wooden doors last varnished two decades ago. Transit buildings looked the same every-where, Tony groaned to himself, whether they were train stations, bus stops, or hospital rooms. Form born out of routine and necessity. Form? Ugliness. Thoughtless, hopeless, universal ugliness.

But not everything was the same all over the world. Customs and laws could vary remarkably. He glanced at the bed. He felt, to his amazement, that his cheeks were wet, and not from sweat. He wiped them dry with the back of his hand and looked again at the sheet with the form of a human being underneath it. Mrs. Bo Xiang would have to be repatriated sooner or later. He had no idea what that might involve in this part of South America. Where had that undertaker got to, by the way? There must be set protocols and tried-and-tested scenarios that the mortician could just fish out of his laptop.

Tony remembered the labyrinthine twists, the Kafkaesque developments, that had ensued when there were deaths on board during his career as host and, later, cruise director on the world's most luxurious ocean liners.

Given the average age of the passengers, it was a miracle that they didn't kick the bucket in droves on every cruise. They ate and drank themselves under the table, they fancy-footed and fornicated the whole night long. The next day, they'd toss and turn their fat bodies next to the swimming pool on the top deck, as though they were bald seals, bloated and lazy after being fed. An entire lifetime of stress and neglect had to be made up for in three weeks of luxurious loafing, on an ark that could have survived two Great Floods. Money was no object. When booking, anyway. During the crossing, you had more chance of getting the clap than a tip from half of them. The other half didn't give you anything at all.

A sailor's burial was permitted only when an on-board epidemic threatened. Other deaths had to be handled by the book. There were several editions of the book, and even more idiosyncratic translations. Tony still felt outraged when he thought back to the worst cases. The sickliest battle-axe in a group of wealthy widows had the misfortune to pass away while the ship of her dreams was moored in Bombay. She was carried off the ship on a bier with great pomp and circumstance. All that was missing was a band playing the funeral march. The woman would eventually reach her Canberra destination by plane, albeit two weeks after her female companions, who sailed back. They'd spent two weeks of the journey calling every authority they could think of in panic all day. Wasted efforts. Aside from smuggled uranium, a body left behind was the most lucrative cargo for customs officers, who would hold every regulation up to the light three times until a backhander trickled down to them through the pyramid of corruption. The same scandal occurred in Odessa, with the body of an asthmatic child. And in the Philippines, with the body of a deceased Pekinese, the pride and joy of two gay millionaires from Fort Lauderdale.

Forget the rule of 'Women and children first' in an emergency. There was just one law aboard ship. The more ailments and strokes on board, the less discretion and tact. Sick women and children were actually worth double points. The poorer their state of health, the more lucrative they were. Maintenance personnel passed on confidential information from the sickbay to onshore inspectors as soon as the ship came within range of a mobile-phone mast. If necessary, they used the ship's radio. One time it was discovered that people were placing bets on the chances of a diabetes sufferer who had fallen unconscious. If you considered what the maintenance personnel were paid, you couldn't really blame them, but one of them secretly feeding honey to the diabetes patient was a step too far for his colleagues, who ratted him out. As a reward, they were offloaded at the next harbour, along with the miscreant. Without papers, and with only the half-empty pot of honey as remuneration.

After fifteen years of pleasure cruises, Tony's disgust had won out over his pragmatism. He disembarked in Aruba, supposedly for just one night. After that, he never set foot again on a vessel that promised pleasure as its only destination.

On the cargo ships he'd served on after that, people showed even fewer scruples. Paperwork was a waste of time, time-wasting an offence. Employees who died on the way were kept in the cold-storage rooms, where exotic fruits ripened more slowly. Officially, they didn't die until arrival. No one asked any questions about the overpowering smell of pineapple.

On the last cargo ship Tony had worked on, four unfortunate stowaways were discovered two days after they'd set sail. They must have misunderstood their smuggler's instructions, or the bastard had deliberately dumped them there; whatever it was, they were travelling amongst the hundreds of quarters of beef in the freezers at minus twenty degrees. They all sat on crates and faced one another, as though gathered around an imaginary card table. Surprised expressions, crossed arms, and lips and hair that grew whiter and whiter. The captain locked the door, cursing, put the only key in his pocket, ordered his crew to keep quiet about it, and changed neither the course nor the speed at which they sailed over the fathomless deep. When the ship moored three weeks later, the freezer room turned out to contain only quarters of beef.

That was the day Tony quit. There were limits, even in places where there weren't any. He asked for his back pay in exchange for keeping schtum, and went ashore.

Not in Aruba this time, but Macau.

On that peninsula, a former Portuguese colony, the largest buildings turned out to be either casinos, or racetracks for horses and greyhounds. Gaudy oriental palaces full of fake brass and neon, interspersed with neoclassical temples in marble and gold leaf. Monstrosities somewhere between the Taj Mahal and the Roman Forum.

Modern flats lured visitors with revolving restaurants on the top floor and water features on the ground floor, in which—the whole night long and with ever-changing music—computerized fountains put on a multicoloured ballet of water and light. The biggest gambling hall in the world, The Venetian, was a city within a city. Thanks to the plentiful shopping precincts, restaurants, event venues, bridal suites, meeting rooms, massage parlours, dental practices, corrective-surgery clinics, sports clubs, and mini-golf courses, you didn't have to go anywhere else before or after the gambling. Even the entrance hall overshadowed the largest palazzo in the real Venice. There was only one commercial building in the world with a larger surface area—the flower auction hall in Aalsmeer in the Netherlands.

The most remarkable gambling hall in Macau was built in the form of a volcano. Plastic trees and polyester sheep made to scale were stuck onto its flanks. Every hour, the crater discharged a real cloud of black smoke, accompanied by threatening rumblings from hidden speakers. Under the crater there were hundreds of fruit machines, twenty-five blackjack tables, twelve roulette wheels, four entertainment rooms, various themed bars, and a world-class hotel, as the promotional billboards proclaimed in five different languages. Without forgetting the two tropical swimming pools, one of which had "tropical waves."

As the crater above him belched out an artificial column of smoke, Tony climbed the volcano and made his way, not to the floor with the blackjack tables that were his usual habit, but to the escalator up to the roulette. A chaotic crowd streamed around him in glass elevators and on other escalators, to halls with high arched ceilings and auditoriums in luscious red, past packed cocktail bars and exotic eateries, through noisy corridors and past restrooms with a lot of marble and few mirrors—you were encouraged to relieve yourself, not look yourself in the face. The crowd hurrying back and forth looked flustered, hysterical, intent. The omnipresent elevator music blended with a torrent of chatter and forced peals of laughter, screams of joy, and cries of horror. Rows and rows of fruit machines in neat lines rattled at hundreds of players, or advised them in metallic voices to double their stakes now. The women had eyes that could just as easily express lunacy as chemical intoxication; the men smoked like chimneys and hawked like fishwives. They all clutched popcorn cups full of coins.

Tony was the only European amongst hundreds of Chinese, Malaysians, and Filipinos. No one paid any attention to him, and he didn't try to make contact with anyone. It wasn't necessary. He was already one of them, without any distinction of rank, race, language, or origin. They'd all joined the Congregation of the Lucky Strike, the Brotherhood of the Windfall. All of them on a pilgrimage without penance, a hajj without a monolith. Tony elbowed his way through the heaving mass around the largest, central roulette table. A crystal chandelier, which outdid a merry-go-round in size and brilliance, hung from the rafters above. He paid no attention to it, elbowing himself forward.

Now there was just one man between him and the table. A Filipino who was clutching onto its edge like to the railing of a boat in a storm. In front of him, there was a wad of banknotes held together with a paper clip. Just before the croupier cried 'Rien ne va plus', he cast the wad onto a single number. All the people around the table looked on in consternation—or was it disgust?

The man had probably been standing there for quite some time. Did he have children? A business? Recently deceased parents? He only had eyes for his cash. It lay there forlornly amongst the many brightly-coloured chips, most of which were stacked up in neat towers. The ball's rattle slowed and then it dropped.

Raucous, multiple cries of horror swept through the group of bystanders. The croupier scraped up everything except for a couple of towers and loose chips on the green felt with his *rateau*, creating a wave of plastic coins that propelled the wad forward like a runaway raft. The croupier raked the wave toward a funnel-shaped drain hole in the table, a copper mouth into which chips clattered and disappeared. The croupier stripped the notes of their paper clip, laid them over a slot in the table, and smoothly pressed them in with a wooden spatula. The Filipino was still clutching the table's edge, motionless in his battle with the invisible hurricane. Suddenly he spun around and hurried away, as white as chalk.

Tony quickly took his place and bet on the same number. All in one go. His blood money, his pieces of silver. His reward. *'Faites vos jeux!'* He wanted to be rid of it. *'Rien ne va plus, messieurs, dames! Rien ne va plus!'* The ball dropped.

All hell broke loose.

In the death chamber in Buenos Aires, Samurai Tony got up from his chair. He went over to the window and slid the net curtain aside a little—a smell of dust and exhaust fumes asserted itself. There was nothing to see outside apart from a lawn, impossibly green and surrounded by blind, peeling walls, shimmering in the excessive sunlight. The pills were working. His headache was finally under control. Now, only the fear to deal with.

He felt his tongue stick to the roof of his mouth. Mrs. Bo Xiang's repatriation wasn't the greatest of his worries. It was time he called Mr. Bo Xiang and his interpreter. Were they staying in Guangzhou or Macau? What time was it there, now? How on earth was he going to explain this calamity to the man? What role should he invent for himself?

He'd rather not make the call at all.

He had ridden along with the ambulance. Dazed and confused from the shock, spurred on by loyalty and remorse. Halfway through the drive—they'd raced through the old centre of Buenos Aires, lights flaring, sirens blaring, lurching wildly and braking abruptly, screeching around every bend: a misleading externalization of a battle between life and death that had been long settled inside the ambulance—Tony had regretted getting in. Shouldn't he have scarpered while he still had a chance? The world was enormous. Who would ever find him if he covered his tracks properly?

Mr. Bo Xiang. If anyone could track him down, he was the man. His employees had plenty of experience with fugitive gambling addicts. Their tenacity wouldn't relent at the prospect of a debtor who was the only witness to their boss' wife's death. If that witness went into hiding, he would be covering himself in complicity, even guilt. Tony had no choice. If he didn't want to pass as the cause of Mrs. Bo Xiang's death, he would have to be its messenger. Waiting was foolish.

He got out his smartphone and sat down at Mrs. Bo Xiang's side, one buttock on the bed. He keyed in the interpreter's number. Sweat dripped down his back. He hadn't been able to wash since the lovemaking and the mouth-to-mouth. He smelled of stale love, despair and, faintly, of violets.

After a whole minute of intercontinental white noise, a mobile rang, somewhere far away in the Chinese night.

From Beijing to Guangzhou, the former Canton, Mr. Bo Xiang was known as the most powerful building contractor with the smallest pursed lips. His estimated fortune was deeper than a borehole and his ruthlessness was legendary. There were people who didn't dare to pay off their debts in one go, even though they were capable of it, out of fear of his reaction to an unforeseen loss of interest payments and the loss of power over another human being. The latter gave him particular pleasure, it was whispered. Above all, he was a bad loser. This was probably the reason he'd got into casinos in the first place.

Besides his cruel whims, Mr. Bo Xiang was known for his benign appearance, that eternally crumpled suit of his, his endlessly sorrowful laugh, his shortness of breath, and the bags under his tired, almost green, slanted eyes. He could have been a brother of the old Mao Zedong. He still had a membership card for the Communist party and a garden where he grew ginger and kept dwarf rabbits. He'd even shown them to Tony. The garden and the party membership card. In the residential suburb of Guangzhou, where he'd set up his imperium's home base in a modernist fortress full of oriental antiques and automatic doors. He and Tony looked at the garden while Mrs. Bo Xiang made preparations for a Japanese-style tea ceremony inside. She'd taken a quick course in it after shopping in Tokyo. She'd taken a lot of courses, Mr. Bo Xiang revealed via his interpreter.

A little while later, they moved to the salon to wait for her. It was a high and spacious room full of Ming vases, Persian carpets, and cubist paintings. Tony thought he spotted a Georges Braque on the wall. It might also have been a Picasso. Mr. Bo Xiang saw him looking around and announced, again via his interpreter, that he was proud not only of his ginger and his dwarf rabbits, but also of his wife. He burst out laughing.

The interpreter didn't laugh along. Tony did, although in moderation and rather uneasily. He still didn't know whether it was appropriate to laugh along when a high-ranking Chinese guffawed. Usually—as now—they'd stop abruptly and become even more serious than before. Yes, for sure, Mr. Bo Xiang told him, as sincere as could be, his wife was his pride and joy. Like his own, her parents were illiterate farmers. Now she was a master of all trades. Even Western opera held no secrets for her. She'd also put together this interior. Those kinds of paintings were too modern for him, but he'd made his peace with them. His wife meant everything to him. And he to her.

The interpreter converted all these communications into the international lingua franca—mangled English. Sentence by sentence, and tonelessly, despite the host's spiralling enthusiasm. Apart from his wife, his Ming vases, and his casinos, he didn't seem to have much enthusiasm for anything else, however, and spoke only of his dwarf rabbits with any tenderness. They reminded him of his youth, he'd just confided to Tony, as he held one of the animals upside down by its back legs in his garden, just for the fun of it. The animal's body had jerked, fearful of the rabbit punch, convulsing prematurely. But Mr. Bo Xiang changed his grip, clutching the rabbit to his chest like a newborn. He bared his smoker's teeth in a smile, kissed one of the floppy ears, and announced that dwarf rabbits were the best and the loveliest thing that America had ever produced. Even though they came from Canada, historically speaking, of course. He said this with a conspiratorial wink. The interpreter left out the wink, too.

At last Mrs. Bo Xiang entered the salon, carrying her authentic Japanese teapot and wearing a silk kimono. Her pouring ritual took several minutes. The silk rustled with every movement. Afterward they drank the tea, the Bo Xiangs, Tony, and the interpreter. The silence was eerie, apart from the slurping. They sat very still. Four terracotta warriors on the Great Wall, Tony couldn't help thinking, looking out for Mongolian soldiers and their barbaric leader, Timur the Lame, Tamerlane, with his towers of human skulls instead of stone angels.

In reality, they looked out of two high windows over a rockery and a kidney-shaped pond with two little fountains, dozens of koi carp, and horribly perfect water lilies. Two Porsche Cayennes stood next to the pond, more displayed than parked. One in metallic jet-green, the other in sand yellow, both with leather upholstery in simple Luxor beige. The chauffeurs stood between the cars, smoking. Their uniforms were a shade of blue that Tony recalled from his childhood.

That was what the farmer's smocks had looked like when potatoes were being harvested in the fields that still surrounded his parents' brand-new detached house on three sides, back then. The other side of the country road was just fields, too. Well-ploughed barriers against further land development, corn fields as a buffer against encroaching concrete. All in vain. By the time Tony had started his law degree, only one field bordered their garden. The rest had been developed and built up and surrounded by a high, green wire fence, crowned with barbs. It wouldn't have surprised Tony if that last plot of ground were now endowed with a brick house resembling a cuckoo clock.

Mamaatje and Papaatje. Did they ever even drink tea, let alone according to a ritual? Had they ever set foot outside Europe, let alone in China? Tony didn't care. They didn't pollute his thoughts for longer than a second. He slammed back his tea and, surrounded by slurping, looked again at the Ming vases and the Georges Braque. Or was it a Picasso?

He didn't dare to ask. Maybe it was neither, and that would only embarrass Mrs. Bo Xiang.

During that first visit to the Bo Xiang's home base, Tony had still simply been a family friend, not a debtor. Sometimes things moved quickly when you made friends with a tycoon in a country that housed a fifth of the world's population.

After your resounding victory on the roulette table, they courted you, all of them. It was no coincidence they'd invented the fortune cookie. If there was anything Chinese people respected, it was a man who seemed to have good luck on his side. They vied for your friendship; they touched you as if you were a holy icon, hoping your good luck would rub off on them. They didn't just let you slip away after your spectacular winnings on the green felt of the roulette table. They broadcast your name over the loudspeakers. It echoed through the interior of the smoke-spewing volcano. The raging mob, the waiters, the croupiers, the fruit-machine players, everyone looked up and sighed at the thought that they, too, might have amassed such a fortune. People clapped, they showered you with flowers, they took photos of you and the croupier, of you and your fellow players, of you and the hostess who brought the free champagne and caviar. You had to meet the big boss in his office, his penthouse, just under the crater. You had to accompany him in his private jet. First to his home base in Guangzhou, to meet his wife and fertilize her with your lavish prosperity. After that, back to Macau, where everyone treated you like royalty, as if you were now the impromptu adopted son of the boss and his wife, who didn't have a son of their own. You became their mascot, their human amulet, their walking talisman. Everybody's favourite fortune cookie.

You allowed yourself to enjoy it. You could use this consolation, this inordinate attention, this unexpected celebration. It pleased you beyond measure that, for the first time in years, you didn't have to put up with a superior: no commander, no captain, no entertainments manager. It caressed your ego; it clouded your common sense. Somewhere deep inside, you'd always known that, one day, something like this would happen. Caviar, champagne, private jets—why not? You'd wasted two decades flattering and pampering the super-rich. Now it was your turn to be pampered. That was called justice. You were worth it.

You were given the largest luxury suite, free food and wine, unlimited credit at all the gaming tables. You accepted this, too, by now solidly convinced that you were indeed a lucky devil, a child of fortune. Five days later, you were looking at debt that you never in your life would be able to pay off. At the same table where the Filipino had bankrupted himself, you lost more money than only recently you'd believed you'd won. Much more.

This time nobody turned up to take your photo. Your name wasn't called out. But you were summoned again by the big boss in his penthouse just under the crater.

This time he had you wait an hour before receiving you.

Far away in the Chinese night, the interpreter didn't pick up the phone. In Buenos Aires, Tony pressed his smartphone to his ear. He wished he knew how to pray. His heart thudded; his mouth felt dry and fibrous, like the inside of a worn-out wallet. What should he say if the interpreter did answer? Where to start? The ringtone stopped, more abruptly than Tony had expected.

It wasn't the interpreter. A cheerful woman's voice said something in Chinese, and after that there was a beep. Tony said his name as calmly as he could and left a neutral message—'Call me please, it's urgent'—before hanging up.

At that same moment, a total stranger thrust open the door to the hospital room.

He couldn't have been older than 30, and was dressed in a neat but worn suit. His appearance took Tony's breath away. Curly hair and a well-defined chin, steely blue yet endearing eyes, small Greek ears and a mouth with full, violet lips, almost negroid. The ancestors of all that beauty must have assembled from all corners of the globe to beget this heir, this silent golden boy. He gave Tony a questioning look that was also sorrowful, his hand still on the door handle.

'You must be the undertaker,' Tony managed to say, barely containing a stutter.

The young man nodded without letting his sorrowful earnestness drop. 'My condolences for your loss,' he said, entering with a discreet glance at the bed and the sheet with a human form. He closed the door gently behind him, as though not to wake up Mrs. Bo Xiang. 'You have the deepest sympathy of our entire firm, mister, sir.'

'Call me Tony,' Tony said, 'Tony Hanssen.'

The golden boy nodded understandingly. 'I am Pedro. And how can I be of assistance to you, Mister Tony?' He got out a notepad and a ballpoint pen. 'The head nurse was unable to provide me with many details.' He had the voice of a singer—a performer of *fados*, lamentations about endless wastelands and eternal decay—and he could use a good shave, unless you liked stubbly beards. He could use a splash of deodorant, too, unless you liked the crude, spicy odour that had driven Tony wild for so many years. The armpit odour of the Mediterranean *jeunesse dorée*, of the muscular Latino still filled with dreams and the desire for action, before the humiliation of ageing struck him, too.

'Just start at the beginning,' the golden boy suggested.

'I've been waiting for you for a very long time,' Tony began. Almost stuttering.

He had renounced homosexual love years ago, along with love in general. After a certain age, people were better off not entertaining any illusions about physical relations. On television, you saw controversial directors defending their pornographic neuroses with the term 'functional nudity'. Tony defined his amorous life that way, too. It was all about the contacts it could deliver, or quite simply, dosh. Apart from that, love was like playing football or letting your hair down in a disco. After a certain age, it just became pathetic and bad for your health, to boot.

Tony had acquired this wisdom the hard way, in what must be the mecca of sexual fantasies—the beach at Copacabana, also known as Princesinha do Mar, the Princess of the Sea. Maybe because half of the men were parading around with the sole intent of royally fucking the other half. With or without a limp wrist, with or without the loose hips. Backward and forward, up and down, wiggle wiggle, tirelessly looking to get laid. 'Cruising', it was called in the gay handbook.

Rarely was a term more appropriate. At the time, Tony was serving on the largest cruise ship in his career, the *Liberty Oasis*. Three thousand seafaring souls, not even counting the crew.

First disembark, then clamber aboard somebody. That had been Tony's plan, when, looking out from the top deck, he'd seen the bay of Rio looming up, dotted with rocky islands. Shortly after that, the city's hilly skyline had appeared, with its domed Sugarloaf Mountain and the statue of Christ on his own woody sugarloaf. The Saviour with his outstretched arms seemed to rise up, slowly spinning, between the colourful sunlit skyscrapers. The *Liberty Oasis*'s ship's horn asserted itself deafeningly as the mastodontic vessel began a slow, elegant turn to reverse into its mooring at the terminal festively hung with flags. Fragments of samba music were blown back and forth, and the wharf was packed with waving tradespeople and hustlers.

Not yet familiar with the customs in Rio, Tony sunbathed and cruised until dusk, as if to increase the approaching pleasure by putting it off for half a day. Temptation is like good wine: you mustn't drink the whole bottle at once.

For the time being, he enjoyed himself in snatches—the winks, the compliments, the outright advances. There was no end to it. Men, women, and transvestites, they all looked at him with one thing in mind. Tony Hanssen, first in the white uniform of the *Liberty Oasis*, later in a pair of shiny black Speedos. Both times strutting like a cat in heat. Cruise ships had plenty of unused exercise machines; for weeks on end he'd spent all his free time in the gym. He wanted to look fitter than ever during his first stay in the samba city. He turned down the advances made in the first few hours for a reason. Too easy wasn't worth much. He had trained for this like a marathon runner. Now he was demanding his laurel wreath.

He still wanted to be conquered. Back then.

He was still worth it. Back then.

The beach at Copacabana was already dusky and abandoned when Tony unrolled his towel for the tenth time, this time in a far corner near the crashing waves. Far enough from the front— the famous boulevard with its beautiful marble mosaic and arty lanterns. If he was visible to the naked eye, it would only be as a shadowy figure. A disciple of the night, whose contours contrasted with the foam of the surf from time to time. Making love wouldn't look any different from fooling around.

He had just lain down on his side, resting on one elbow, when a guy came running toward him along the waterline, right at him. He doesn't waste any time, Tony thought, just before the guy started screaming from afar. He seemed furious.

'Have you lost your mind?' He came to a stop, panting—barefoot, well built, and attractively dark, even though he was sporting silly yellow sports trousers and a sleeveless light-blue T-shirt.

He had a boyish rucksack on his back in fluorescent green. His hair was close-cropped, his skull perfect, his teeth shining white.

'Why don't you just stab yourself in the belly with a knife?' His English was adequate, his accent awful. He pulled Tony up by his arm. 'Quick! Or do you think they wait until it's completely dark?' He grabbed Tony's shoes and trousers and walked off, stumbling over the loose sand, heading toward the beach boulevard with its pleasant lighting and its sauntering crowds.

Tony had no choice but to run after the guy, stumbling in turn, with the rest of his hastily gathered belongings in his hands. It was only now, as he ran, that he saw a handful of shadows appear on his right and on his left, scarcely thirty or forty metres from him. They shouted and cursed at both Tony and his rescuer. They'd been creeping up on him. How long had they been following him? One ran after Tony hesitantly, the others began to throw stones, or were they shells? Two projectiles landed feebly in the sand a few metres away from Tony. The rest of their clamour died down behind his back, increasingly absorbed by the sound of the waves, and soon completely drowned out by the surging hubbub on the boulevard.

His rescuer stood there waiting, panting with both hands at his waist, grinning from ear to ear. He held out a hand: 'I'm Rafael. And you're crazy.' Tony guessed he was about 25. Rafael continued to laugh and shake his head as Tony got dressed, his knees still knocking. After that, he good-humouredly led Tony through the crowds. 'I've got a nicer surprise for you. Come!'

Even at this time of day, half of the women walking along the boulevard were still wearing bikinis that left them practically butt-naked, despite their high heels and their opulent hairstyles. The men were all bare-chested. All of them going from party to party, from terrace to terrace, from dalliance to dalliance. Dancing and dancing, drinking and drinking. Expensive sunglasses, expensive jewellery, the barely-disguised assurance that came from cocaine and party pills. Rafael gave a running commentary on everything they passed on their stroll. Despite all the wealth, he warned, the favelas were close by. Morro dos Cabritos was literally around the corner. The gangs didn't shy away from anything, certainly when drugs were involved. They'd shot a police helicopter out of the sky with a bazooka in Ladeira dos Tabajaras. What was to stop them from nailing a naïve tourist on the beach?

'That's why, even here'—he pulled Tony through the staff entrance into the expensive hotel where he worked—'you can't invite anyone into your room without signing them in at reception, name and surname, passport included.' Once they were in the service lift, he began to kiss Tony without warning even before the doors had slid shut.

By the twentieth floor, he was already groping Tony's crotch. Tony let it happen, horny and grateful, and still shaking from the adrenaline. He returned the kisses with virility. It was as if they were biting each other in a small cage. On the sixtieth floor, the top floor, they pretty much fell out of the lift. Clawing and grunting, caught in each other's clutches. If it were up to Tony, they would have got down to it there in that empty, long corridor with dozens of doors, just on the fitted carpet. But Rafael broke free, held his finger to his lips, opened the door to a suite with his master key, and pulled Tony into the room, a teasing grin on his face. 'Look!' he said with a smile, soon afterward, tugging open the curtains with both hands.

Tony's mouth fell open. He'd been lucky enough to behold many panoramas before, but this view belonged to the top ten. The windows reached from ceiling to floor, showing the dark ocean on the right and the shimmering city on the left, riveted together by a gully filled with sparkling lava—the boulevard they'd just walked along. Copacabana by night. In the distance, sticking up between the crests of the hills and the buildings, you could even see the funnels and the top decks of the *Liberty Oasis*, quivering in the orange glow of the harbour lights.

Tony laid both hands on the cool glass and wanted to say something. About the garlands of motorways in the distance and the crescent moon above them, the winding boulevards and the slope of the illuminated mountains of the city, and how even they seemed to exude eroticism, like the whole of Rio. Nothing came of it. He was hit on the back of his head by the truncheon Rafael had brought along in his green rucksack.

When Tony came around, he was tied to a chair, with a pounding headache and a crusted ear. There were a handful of people present—laughing, guzzling, snorting. Each of them bellicose and strident. Rafael did most of the talking and knew no mercy, whatever Tony asked or said. For two days and two nights, he was beaten, raped, and drugged by the gang. Until he'd confessed all of the codes for his bank cards and all his accounts had been emptied. They even paid for the room service with his money.

As a parting gift, Rafael gave him the master key—stolen or bought off somebody, who was to say?—and a final kick in the face. A day later he was discovered by maintenance personnel. Naked, torn, dehydrated, beaten black and blue, and in shock. He recovered remarkably well from the ordeal, without too many permanent injuries, if you didn't count the six porcelain crowns and the scars on places that seldom saw the light of day.

After that, you didn't run into him in the fitness centre anymore. And he'd given up love.

'I think I've got enough here to be going on with the golden boy,' undertaker Pedro, nodded. He looked satisfied. After listening to Tony's account, he'd first noted Mrs. Bo Xiang's name and the cause of death—heart attack during siesta'. Beneath that, he'd written down Tony's telephone number and that of Mrs. Mercedes, followed by her address and the address of the Hilton where Tony and Mrs. Bo Xiang had originally been staying. Finally, he'd also noted the details of their arrival and their planned departure, as well as the name of the airline company. Not for one moment during the note-taking had he let his sad smile slip. His writing hand was like a pianist's, slender and agile with tidy fingernails.

Tony hadn't given him the phone number of Mr. Bo Xiang's interpreter. He didn't want to run the risk that Pedro, for whatever reason, would contact China before he did. Although he *had* instructed the young undertaker to get in touch with the Chinese embassy that same day to start the repatriation process in conjunction with the local authorities.

It would be no mean feat, Pedro had warned, putting away his notepad. Nevertheless, he foresaw a good outcome. Their firm had plenty of experience. If it had been Angola or Albania, the picture would have been a little less rosy. They hadn't had any problems with China for years. No, really, Mister Tony could get a good night's sleep, Pedro placated him—in a voice that seemed made to sing *lamentos*, with a mouth that seemed shaped for kisses, rather than listing the costs of various different kinds of coffin. He would ask his boss, he soothed, to give this case top priority. For just a trifling supplemental fee. That wouldn't be a problem, would it?

He gave Tony a questioning look.

His proposal barely registered with Tony. He had said yes and nodded his consent to everything that was asked. What was happening? He was falling more and more under the young man's spell. He had to do his best not to ask him for a hug. The urge was sudden and irrepressible. Even if it was just for two seconds.

Why not, in fact? For a professional undertaker, it wouldn't be that absurd a part of the service. Obviously you could charge an extra fee for it. It might even turn out to be a successful part of the enterprise. Everyone could do with a good hug. Especially a man, alone in life, yet confronted with death at close quarters. People in that situation needed professionals who could offer the physical equivalent to all their pretty words of hope and support. Without a palpable complement, those words would risk remaining hollow and inadequate. It was common sense, wasn't it? Tony was becoming more and more convinced. Proper funeral services began with cuddling the survivors.

And yet he stopped short of asking Pedro for a hug. Not because he was afraid of being rejected. He had long got beyond that kind of embarrassment. It was more the opposite. He couldn't be held accountable for his actions if Pedro really did wrap his arms around him. It wouldn't stop after two seconds, and it wouldn't stop at a hug.

He wondered, in despair, where this intense urgency was coming from. Was it a side effect of the pills and the exhaustion? Was he suffering from a kind of decompression after the humiliating sex with Mrs. Bo Xiang, followed by her shocking demise? Or was it this goddamn heat, and the general feeling that his chest was caught in a wolf trap he just couldn't get out of? Whatever the case, he had to force himself not to jump Pedro's bones and make love to him without preliminaries. Whimpering, foaming at the mouth like stray dogs, blinded by carnal desire, hungry for gratification. Here on the floor, if necessary. Right next to the bed with the happy corpse. Or no, on the bed. On top of the body, separated from her only by a sheet, a sheet that might just tear during their violent lovemaking. Why not? Pedro was used to being around bodies; it was part of his job, and Tony didn't give a shit anymore.

It wasn't even lust that had taken hold of him. It was sexual homesickness. He saw the past few years of his life flash before his eyes. The vacuum, the missed opportunities. He realized, with a start, that the imperturbability he'd always been so proud of—his 'glorious indifference' as he'd always described it to his colleagues, when he still had colleagues—was nothing other than disguised pain, an efficiently bandaged wound. This realization doubled his pain now. The stabbing feeling was unbearable.

Begone with it! It was time for reparation. He had let himself be curbed and repressed long enough. Why don't we lead the lives we might? He was entitled to one more moment of splendour, one more blast. An instant of pure, raw emotion. Then the curtains could fall, as far as he was concerned. Definitively, if needs must.

But first he would take what was coming to him. Here and now. Willy-nilly. Just as he so often had been taken.

It was a matter of justice, nothing more.

'There are just two little problems,' the golden boy, Pedro, said. He bent forward to release the brakes on the small wheels under the iron bed frame. Four little wheels, four blocks. Each time Pedro bent over and his buttocks strained against the threadbare suit trousers, Tony had to swallow a lump in his throat.

'And which problems might those be?' he asked. It sounded more hostile than he'd meant it to be. His fists were balled, his nerves taut. He didn't manage to take his eyes off Pedro's lower back.

'I need a document confirming Mrs. Bo Xiang's identity,' Pedro said. He'd straightened up, sighing, edged between the wall and the head of the bed, and grabbed the shining bars of the bedstead as though he were getting ready to roll Mrs. Bo Xiang through the door and disappear off to his funeral parlour with her.

Tony went to stand at the foot end. 'What kind of document would be acceptable?' he asked, looking Pedro in the eye. His voice sounded hoarse.

'Doesn't matter,' Pedro shrugged. 'Bank card, driving licence, passport. Or all three, of course. Authorities like official papers.' His pianist's hands gripped the iron bars even more tightly, but his face remained sympathetic and sad.

'Pass me that handbag, would you,' Tony said. His voice still sounded hoarse.

'Which handbag?' Pedro asked, now with an amused twinkle in his eye.

'*That* handbag,' Tony snapped. He pointed at Mrs. Bo Xiang's Louis Vuitton. It was in the open storage space of the iron night-stand next to the bed. Pedro only had to squeeze his way between the wall and the head end to get it and hand it to Tony, over the happy corpse. The twinkle in his eye had turned into a touch of resentment.

Even that resentment turned Tony on. He knew what was in the handbag, but he began to rummage around in it at length, as though he were really searching for something.

Tony hadn't come out of his state of shock until the ambulance men at Mrs. Mercedes's house in San Telmo had actually carried the happy corpse out of the room on a stretcher. He'd stumbled down the stairs after the trio, taking his wallet and her handbag. It was just like the time he'd grabbed his belongings on the beach at Rio as he fled: hastily, and without thinking.

And it wasn't until he was in the swerving ambulance, sitting next to Mrs. Bo Xiang, to the background music of the blaring siren and the swearing of the two ambulance men in the cab, that he'd examined the contents of the Louis Vuitton. Not even out of curiosity, more to kill time on this endless-seeming journey. His amazement was none the less for it. Apart from a few pieces of jewellery, some make-up, her passport, and her Sigma camera, the Louis Vuitton also contained a small fortune. The real treasure wasn't her purse with its many credit cards and its range of notes in foreign currencies. It was a collection of thick rolls of euros in the highest denomination.

Now, at last, Tony understood why her handbag had seemed so much heavier over the past few days. Each roll easily contained thirty or forty notes. They were accompanied by a statement, printed by a small Argentinian bank in the centre of Buenos Aires. Other statements indicated transfers, payment orders, of dizzying sums. When had she managed it? Presumably during that one hour she'd been so keen to shop without him. She'd insisted that he stay in the Hilton on the Puerto Madero and treat himself to a foot massage and manicure in the wellness centre. He didn't have to accompany her on every shopping spree. No, no! She insisted! She'd only feel guilty. He hadn't needed much persuading. Even though he'd just hung around in his room, without a manicure or a massage, raiding the minibar and zapping from one TV channel to the next. There were more than a hundred of them.

The date and address on the statements confirmed his theory. She'd withdrawn the euros a few days previously in Buenos Aires. Why? He couldn't care less. But sliding around in the ambulance, he gasped for breath when he re-counted just one roll. There were fourteen of them. He had a fortune on his lap, hidden away in a camel-coloured tote.

Did Mrs. Bo Xiang have a secret hoard of money in this city? She'd always maintained she'd never before set foot in Buenos Aires. Had she been lying to him? He hadn't expected that of her. Had she kept other things from him? And Mr. Bo Xiang—did he know about it? What if he didn't? What if no one knew anything about this money? Tony's head spun. True, there wasn't nearly enough money in the bag to buy his freedom. But it could be a considerable contribution to his ultimate escape route. His secret exit. Thanks to his own hidden stash.

His lifeline, well hidden on the Bahamas. Not even that paltry a stash. He'd won a few times at the blackjack tables on the cruise boats. He'd spent a lot of time there since he'd stopped having to slog it out in the gym.

After his robbery and torture in Rio, he'd done what he'd always hated his parents doing, and the many social climbers they counted as their friends: legal colleagues and well-known surgeons, project developers and captains of industry, even a few sporting heroes of yesteryear. Tony had always looked down on their eternal search for back doors and enterprising constructions to keep them one step ahead of the tax authorities.

Every last one of them took part in a schmuckish ritual that was popular in all echelons of society. They asked restaurants to double the amount of their real bill on the VAT receipt. Tripling was all right, too. They asked insistently enough to make it clear to the restaurant owner that, without the inflated VAT slip, they'd be eating their fondues and *raclettes* elsewhere in the future. Some went in again the next day and asked at the counter for a new phony receipt. Without even ordering any food. Why not? There were plenty of other clients who hadn't taken their VAT slips, weren't there? They'd be happy enough with one of those unused slips. *Merci!* See you next week! Just until they'd amassed enough VAT receipts to pad their tax-deductible expenses up to the annual limit. It was something of a national sport. Some milked pigeons, others restaurant bosses.

His parents' friends were more ambitious. With the help of financial advisors, specialist tax technologists, and widely respected bankers, they put in place a close-knit carousel that mimicked the earth in its rotations. Backhanders, under-the-counter gratuities, and good old-fashioned bribes made a hop, skip, and jump from continent to continent. Sometimes, after a negligible penalty, they'd alight, whitewashed, in their country of origin. Usually they marked time, flourishing in the shade of a sunny tax haven, before making their final intercontinental leap.

Tony had one of those accounts now, too. Out of pure necessity. What had happened in Rio would never happen to him again. Betting it all away and having to start all over again, building a new nest egg for his, well, his "old age." That was another thing he'd once scoffed at, but no more. That vague, monstrous threat. That slowly building hurricane that would lead to physical helplessness and a dependence on other people. For now, it was still swelling beyond a far-off horizon. But each year, the infernal tornado grew a little closer, roaring ever louder, slowly but inevitably building up to its ultimate onslaught—a rampage that would leave nothing and nobody standing.

Tony didn't have any bank cards or statements; there wasn't anything that could lead back to his savings account, or even to a suspicion of its existence. All the information he needed—all the telephone numbers, the names of his contacts—was in his head. They could interrogate him and torture him as much as they liked, he'd never give it up. He'd rather die a real death right away.

That even Mr. Bo Xiang's employees, usually so skilled at tracking down their debtors' spoils of war, still hadn't discovered anything, reinforced Tony's conviction. His high-tech banking specialists in the Bahamas had done a top job.

And he, himself, wasn't a total write-off. There was still a remote possibility of a way out. At least, if he managed to escape the clutches of Mr. Bo Xiang and his hired guns.

Where there's blood, there's hope.

'Take a look at this,' Tony said to the golden boy, Pedro, still in that strange, hoarse voice. 'This should do you.' He handed the young undertaker Mrs. Bo Xiang's passport and one of her many credit cards. He was still standing at the foot of the bed, blocking Pedro's escape route.

'It's certainly a good start,' the latter agreed, again sad and serious. He respectfully stowed away the passport and the credit card in the inside pocket of his jacket. For a moment he seemed to stroke his heart. Or his nipple. Tony had to swallow another lump.

'But then there's still that second delicate point,' Pedro said.

He was standing at the head of the bed again, ready to flee, away from Tony, into the metropolis. Away from lust's momentum.

'I'm curious as to what kind of delicate point the two of us might be looking at,' Tony replied. The pitiful flicker of hope in his voice was noticeable even to him.

'Embalming,' Pedro said.

'Embalming?' Tony asked. He didn't know whether to laugh or to cry. He desperately tried not to picture this, but instead got a very clear image. Mrs. Bo Xiang being laid out on a cold stone table, first being emptied, and then filled up again. As though the poor woman were a jerrycan. The woman he'd almost ejaculated into just a short time ago.

'Embalming,' Pedro nodded, sadder and more earnest than ever, 'according to the rules of the art.'

'What's so bloody delicate about embalming?' Tony asked. 'You either do it or you don't.' He was aware that he was raising his voice, but he was no longer in control of himself. He was feeling more and more ridiculous by the minute, still standing there, holding the Louis Vuitton. What was he supposed to do with it? Hang the strap over one of his arms, up to the elbow? Or just throw it over his shoulder? Like an old woman dawdling in front of a window display? He didn't dare abandon his spot to stow the bag back away in the nightstand. He could see that Pedro might be capable of quickly rolling the bed out the door behind his back. He could already feel the footboard pressing against his legs.

'You are absolutely right, Mr. Tony,' Pedro said. Despite his submissive sadness, there was something impatient about him now. As if he wanted to leave the room as quickly as possible. 'We either do it or we don't. But if we do it, we need your permission. As soon as the medical examiner has seen her, we can make a start.'

'The medical examiner?' Tony asked. His heart missed a beat. He felt the foot of the bed starting to bump against his legs again. A few times.

'Are there medical examiners in Argentina?' In all the brouhaha, it hadn't crossed his mind. The happy corpse would be examined from top to toe. Would the examiners ask themselves why the unfortunate woman's expression was so blissful? Would they search for a deeper underlying cause? And would it still be detectable, hours after penetration? Thank God he hadn't come inside her. But how advanced was DNA research in this country? Hair, saliva, sweat, and flakes of skin. All from him; all of it on her.

Given the smile on his face, Pedro must have considered Tony's question a mildly cynical joke. 'Naturally we have police doctors here. With the many violent crimes here, they rank amongst the best in the world, sad to say. But what do you think?'

'They'll have to do what they have to do,' Tony said weakly, 'but I hope they don't make too much of a mess of her.'

Pedro looked at him. It was several seconds before he said, 'The embalming. Is it a yes or a no?'

'Go on, then,' Tony said. 'Embalming is fine. As fast as possible,

I'd say. Don't put off to tomorrow what you can do today.' He was feeling dizzy again. His concentration was weakening visibly. His desire for the young man was beginning to ebb away, too. What a killjoy, with his pianist's hands and his black man's mouth. With his silly, unctuous tone.

'Speed is no problem,' Pedro continued, with some hesitation. 'The delicate part is that the embalming fluid is so unbelievably expensive.'

'That doesn't surprise me,' Tony said. He only just managed not to laugh. It was all too sad for words. 'Imagine you lot doing anything for free.' A catastrophe had taken place, a tragic death—and what did it all come down to, once again? A game of questions and answers and readies in the pocket.

Pedro even adopted an injured expression. 'It's not an obligation, Mr. Tony. It's a question. We're a business. The choice is all yours. We could just give her a wash.'

'A wash would be great!' Tony was laughing unabashedly by now. 'She loved hygiene.' He had to stop himself from slapping his thigh. 'And how much does a wash cost? Soap and shampoo included?' He shoved the bag strap over his arm now, up to the elbow, and placed his free hand, fist clenched, in his side. He didn't care what he looked like anymore. But that poseur shouldn't think that he, Tony, was planning to step aside. He was going to stay where he was. If necessary, they'd have to run him down.

Pedro let go of the head of the bed and pressed his palms together, at chest height, as though in prayer. He moved his folded hands gently up and down, like a priest addressing his parish. His tone was in keeping—concerned, pained, and gentle.

'Mister Tony, I realize you must have had a serious shock, so I don't hold any of this against you. We deal with matters like this all the time. It isn't easy for anyone. I'll do my best to get all the paperwork arranged as quickly as possible, but if there are setbacks, it could take quite a few days, if not weeks, before Mrs. Bo Xiang is repatriated. Does she have any relatives? Children, grandchildren? Don't deprive them of the chance to say goodbye to her as she was. At her best. We do have cold-storage facilities, obviously. But the cold isn't flattering when it comes to good conservation. Do yourself a favour, Mister Tony, you and all the other people she cared about. With a small down payment, I can make a good start. We'll settle the rest later.'

His plea hit home. Tony's giggly anger subsided.

'You're right,' he said, after a few seconds. 'Forgive me.' He took a step to the side and opened the handbag. 'Here,' he said, not long after. He showed Pedro one of the rolls. Why not? The whole idea that he might be able to pocket the fortune was ridiculous. He could hardly take the risk that Mr. Bo Xiang and his heavies might know about it already. If one of the rolls got lost, Tony would have created a motive for murder, with himself as prime suspect. What had he been thinking? It was the same kind of bravado that had made him think he could seduce the young Pedro. He hadn't had a cat in hell's chance of either, right from the start.

'This should cover the current expenses,' he continued, still holding out the roll to the young man. 'And, once again, forgive me. I wasn't myself.'

Pedro took the roll with an understanding nod and respectfully stowed it in the other inside pocket of his jacket—stroking a nipple once again, Tony couldn't help thinking. And there was that lump in his throat again.

'You've made the right decision,' Pedro assured him, already manoeuvring the bed past Tony and toward the door. 'Mrs. Bo Xiang will be in the best of hands.' He stopped only to open the door, and returning, to give Tony a handshake.

Then he swiftly disappeared, bed and all, down the corridor. Without looking back. And without the hug that Tony had still been hoping for, against all odds.

Tony sank, exhausted and humiliated, into the leatherette armchair. He had to stop himself from throwing the handbag across the empty room. How could he have been so stupid? He had made an absolute fool of himself. That poor boy was just a sorry devil with a job he was trying to do as best he could. Of course financial gain was part and parcel of it. Everything costs money. Given the circumstances, the boy had coped wonderfully. Incredibly professional, incredibly polite. Tony was the one who had behaved badly, with his ridiculous randiness—in the presence of a dead body, at that.

But more than the injury to his pride, the consequences of the tragedy started to sink in now. Mrs. Bo Xiang was going to be examined by a police doctor. How long would it be before one of those bastards alerted the local paparazzi with the scoop, paid or unpaid, that the wife of a controversial Chinese magnate had died in San Telmo, of all places? Where she had been enjoying the company of a much younger man. God knows what grotesque stories they might make up. They were the same everywhere, those gnats that dared call themselves reporters.

Shouldn't I have gone to more trouble to avoid causing a commotion, Tony fretted away. Mr. Bo Xiang loved his wife and his dwarf rabbits, but he didn't like publicity. There were enough stories about him doing the rounds. He'd had one of his competitor's tongues cut out, it was said. He'd fed the tongue to the lapdog of the man's mistress, apparently, while the poor girl had been forced to look on. In another version, the lapdog was served up as glazed duck while the man and his mistress were lounging in the Jacuzzi in their penthouse in the tallest skyscraper in Shanghai.

And that was the crux of the problem. All the threads, all the gossip, came together in the El Dorados of the Far East. Each year, Shanghai gained a new record-breaking building, even taller than the last, and Mr. Bo Xiang owned at least five per cent of every one. It was said. People said the same about his home base, Guangzhou, and about Beijing, and about Hong Kong. His stake in the three largest casinos in Macau was supposed to be more than fifty per cent. He was said to have more shadow companies than employees, and more pawns in the Chinese Communist Party than there were croupiers in Las Vegas. They remained rumours, dished up by rivals, or by foreign xenophobes with wild fantasies about anything to do with the Far East. There were enough business partners, from Singapore to New York, from Moscow to Jakarta, who insisted that Mr. Bo Xiang was an honest colleague about whom they wouldn't hear an improper word.

Mr. Bo Xiang did little to debunk the myths, himself. He acted as though he were above everyone else. But people gossiped that there was one kind of person he secretly hated even more than his opponents and his debtors. Journalists. They put that down to his childhood. Mr. Bo Xiang had grown up without the concept of private property and without a free press. He still had trouble with the latter.

Tony's telephone rang. The name of the interpreter lit up on the screen. For a moment, Tony considered just letting his vibrating, wonderfully old-fashioned-sounding smartphone ring.

Finally, he decided to pick up.

He was given no time to gently broach the issue.

'There isn't anything wrong with Mrs. Bo Xiang, is there?' the interpreter barked, without civilities. Tony had never heard him speak so fast and loud. The man seemed almost hysterical. Or scared to death.

'Mister Bo Xiang can't get hold of her. Where is she? What happened? Speak up, man! Tell me!' There was an uncanny intercontinental rustling silence, more killing than a real silence.

And just as Tony was about to begin to tell the story that would inevitably culminate in a tragic revelation, another total stranger opened the door.

It was a tall, elderly man with sideburns. He was wearing a black suit with a white flower in the buttonhole. If he'd been wearing a top hat, you'd have thought he'd stepped out of a time machine. He was sweating like a horse.

'You must be Mister Tony Hanssen,' he began, practically bowing. He had the voice of a drunkard in the morning. His English sounded far from perfect.

'I cannot deny that,' Tony said, with some hesitation. He had stared at the man, agape. He'd let his smartphone drop to chest height. The interpreter was still raging away, but his voice now sounded puny and insignificant. ('What's going on there, man? Tell me! Hello?')

'And where is our dearly departed?' the man asked, gazing around the room in amazement, wiping his forehead with a handkerchief. Either he'd run here or he had a poor constitution, one that was culturally embedded. Red meat, Malbec, and cigarettes each day. An odour of sweat and garlic began to fill the room.

That's what an inferno might smell like, Tony thought, as a terrible foreboding began to take hold of him. He cut off the connection with China as a precaution. At least the interpreter's voice fell away, as weak it was.

'Mrs. Bo Xiang has gone to the undertaker's,' he declared. His voice was differently hoarse than it had been.

The man looked genuinely shocked. 'I am your undertaker.'

'You're lying,' Tony said. 'You're lying!' He felt a devastating rage come over him. But he wasn't able to get up out of the bucket seat and hit this sorry boozer, this conman, this bearer of lies and calamity in the face as he would have loved to. His legs seemed to have been amputated.

'Pedro came to pick up Mrs. Bo Xiang!' he shouted. 'I've agreed terms with Pedro. We have a firm arrangement. A good arrangement.' His smartphone started ringing again. It was the interpreter, the screen showed. Let it ring, Tony thought. What you don't know won't hurt you.

'I know no Pedro,' the undertaker said, deathly pale himself now.

'That's a shame for you,' Tony cried, still seated, his ringing phone pointed at the man. 'You're hopelessly late, you've been beaten to it.' Without waiting for an answer, Tony took the call from China. 'Leave me alone, man. I have to sort out something here first. I'll call you back in a moment.' He ended the call and looked up again. The old man was still standing there. It wasn't a nightmare. He was flesh and blood. And he was sweating even more.

'Please,' the man stammered. He, too, seemed to be staring a nightmare in the face. 'Please don't tell me that you gave money and identity papers to this Pedro. That's how they operate. They scour the hospitals. Nobody warned you?'

'You're lying!' It was the only thing Tony could think to shout. He felt tears welling, and vomit, and bile. His smartphone was vibrating and ringing again.

'Have you got an address for this Pedro?' the man asked. Given the circumstances, he remained calm and concerned. 'A telephone number? Have you got anything at all?'

Tony couldn't even summon the strength to shake his head. His smartphone slipped out of his hands and bounced, still ringing, across the floor. The truth hit him like a freight train. He'd been set up, once again. He hadn't just fucked his creditor's wife to death, he'd managed to lose her mortal remains. Along with her passport.

4. Mpumalanga

TONY HANSSEN IN KROKODILSPRUIT WAS LEFT WITH JUST one way to make it through his new ordeal. He had to keep thinking about his daughter Klara and his wife Martine. One day he would finally be reunited with them, and everything would go back to how it was. Salvation was close. He just had to round this cape.

Wielding a woodsman's axe, he stood in the semi-darkness between the moribund man he had just shot down and the rhino cow the man had shot down. Both were convulsing.

This was limited, in the cow's case, to infrequent shudders of the belly, and a single, colossal leg that pawed the air ever more slowly. From time to time, her mutilated, partially dehorned head made a weak snorting, almost gurgling, sound.

Tony didn't dare take a second look at the black giant. The sight of him had been unbearable, despite the merciful twilight. Apart from the amputated leg, the man's face had shocked Tony. It was contorted and carved with deep grooves of pain. An oriental warrior's mask with a purple, protruding tongue. The poor fellow was groaning continually. Splinters of bone were sticking out of a hole at collarbone height—a slowly issuing source of blood and cloudy bubbles. They were lit up obscenely in the half-light, along with the groaning giant's teeth and the whites of his eyes. He kept on rolling his eyes; they kept on rolling away, two ping-pong balls.

Tony stood there, retching yet mesmerized, paralyzed, not knowing what to do. The pupil-less whites of the man's eyes reminded him of the oily white of lilies. Martine's indestructible lilies, her pride and joy, on the windowsill of their converted barn in Wolvertem on a summer's evening. A veiny, leathery white.

The man coughed up a splash of blood. His teeth changed colour, from obscenely white to glutinous red. Tony finally managed to avert his gaze, his fascination giving way to shame and disgust.

He turned his back on the dying man and walked over to the rhino. But he couldn't possibly ignore what was going on behind him. No matter how hard he prayed for the poor wretch to be granted a swift death, the plaintive groaning wasn't getting any weaker. It started to mingle with the unsettling sound of pawing, kicking limbs. And even though the watering hole's soft sand absorbed sound, and even though the man only had one leg left to kick with, the drumming sounded to Tony like someone banging away on an accusatory tambourine, a reproachful kettledrum as big as the watering hole itself. And were all the sounds he could hear coming from the felled giant? Wasn't that something else crunching a short way off? And over there—what was that? Sweat ran down his back. His heart raced. Anything could turn up: scavengers, other poachers, game wardens accompanied by intervention teams, all of them armed to the teeth. He had to act without delay. Pronto.

Yet there he was, rooted to the spot again, this time not with a gun but with an axe in his hands. He was wired on all the adrenaline—he really had fired and hit home. At the same time, the shock was making him feel ill—he'd killed a man. Or almost, listening to the groaning. Stop thinking about it! What had happened, had happened. There wasn't anything more to do about it; plenty of time for regret later. Back to work!

He bent over the rhino's head. It sputtered again, weakly, plaintively. A sickly smell rose up, mixed with the stink Tony recalled from the touring circuses of his youth. The day after the show, the entire class had been allowed to see the tigers' cage, as well as the accommodation for the sad-looking elephants, each with one leg in shackles, standing in a neat row in the wings of the circus tent.

It had smelled exactly like this—straw, shit, piss, and misery. The rhino's wound bubbled again. Tony felt sicker by the minute. His knees began to buckle again.

And his lower lip burned with pain.

Immediately after the shot, excitement had had the upper hand. He had felt omnipotent. He had tossed his gun almost effortlessly onto the back seat, started the vehicle, and driven over to the watering hole, exactly as he'd watched the black giant do. Foot to the floor and straight ahead.

Tony, however, had to drive down a hill whose slope was littered with boulders and treacherous potholes. The four-by-four had hobbled and bumped like a sloop in a storm. It was a miracle that the creaking vehicle hadn't flipped over or fallen onto its side. Once, a downward plunge followed by an upward blow had been so hard that Tony had first hit his head on the roof and then his teeth on the steering wheel. He felt something crack in his neck; he felt something crack in his mouth. He suspected he'd hurt his bottom lip and blood was already dripping from his chin. A quick glance at his safari shirt confirmed the suspicion. A coral-red corsage on the light-brown cotton, a rapidly opening, blooming bouquet. But he didn't feel any pain yet and he didn't lose control over the wheel for a second. On the contrary. He'd never felt as focussed as he did now, so sharply present in the here and now, so scintillatingly alive.

It surprised him. Until now, he'd only experienced this feeling in moments of extreme tension at work. There was no arena as exciting and addictive as that of a business bank with its deadlines and dramas, with the daily suspense of the rampant equity markets all over the world.

'Try your luck somewhere else then, mate! Get a teaching job!' That had been the regular response that he and his colleagues had thrown at one another every time one of them threatened to collapse or burst into floods of tears. The one time they hadn't said it was at the crisis meeting when a colleague had jumped out of the window. The taciturn eccentric had opened a window to feed a sparrow, climbed up onto the sill with dignity, and taken a step forward as though stepping off the edge of an outdoor swimming pool. All that was missing was the splash.

No one had said anything, then. For hours on end. But most of them had thought the same thing: 'Should have got a teaching job, mate!' Why shouldn't they think it? They formed an elite corps, not a charitable institution. Selection was part and parcel of it. Up to a point, that is. It wasn't supposed to lead to burnouts, nervous breakdowns, divorces, fights, let alone deaths. But the fact that they happened? Burnouts and the rest of it? It strengthened the motivation and pride of those left behind. One man's sickness is another man's treasure.

The line of demarcation—the gaping chasm between fiasco and success—was merciless and unbridgeable, even though the washouts complained or threatened legal action. If you ever heard from them again. Silence was more common. They'd spent years at your side, they'd put up with more shit from you than from their closest family members, they'd cursed and praised your opinions more often than the mafia of analysts at Bloomberg and Sky News Business, they knew your favourite drink and the smell of your farts—and then, all of a sudden, they'd gone. The only thing they left behind, apart from fading memories, was an empty chair occupied two days later by the bank's latest recruit.

His initiation consisted of being told for an entire week how easily and quietly he could be fired, too. The old hands, grinning, didn't shy away from parallels with Stalin's purges. You'd be summoned by your supervisor without a clear reason, given a ninety-second dressing-down, while behind your back, security swept all of your personal belongings off your desk and into a cardboard box. Another security gorilla would immediately take you from the executive floor to the back entrance, where you'd be ceremoniously handed your box in exchange for your entrance badge, your company credit card, your car keys, and your work phone. That was that, then. A closing door and a cardboard box in your arms. Your laptop left behind, your email account closed, your photo erased, your name deleted from the organogram.

If former colleagues ever did turn up, they'd stand on the other side of the street, calling out your name, waving like they knew you. The watchword was: don't wave back. The reunion would be too uncomfortable. For both of you. The odd one didn't wave but raised his fist, an angry look in his eyes and foam on his lips, ready to infect you with his pathetic defeatism. Those were the ones who took legal action, all of it doomed to fail. Those sorts never blamed themselves. They'd signed the same contract as everyone else, they'd been amenable to the group and the regime for years, they'd made the same jokes as the rest of them about the naivety of their clients and the ignorance of their supervisors. Now they were turning against their old firm. Always using the same arguments. They'd been chewed up and spat out by 'the System', or the CEO, by which they meant the same thing.

The survivors knew better. They didn't need a CEO. They worked their asses off. Bring it on! The challenges, the torments, the exhaustion, and everything else. The generous payslip was a nice extra; the real reward was the honour. Despite everything, they were still standing. The bruises from the school of hard knocks had faded. They were talented; the others were simply unlucky. Tough break for them, but they couldn't count on much sympathy. An amateur footballer didn't sue FC Barcelona because he didn't get into the first team, did he?

The recruits took note of all the advice and boldly dug themselves in. They were excited the first time they spent Christmas in the office instead of at home. Half of them were already wearing a sorry face by the time they missed their second Christmas dinner. The third Christmas separated the sheep from the goats. One resigned, another took pills, the third reeled in an order that made up for his entire year. No better moment than Christmas to strike an unexpected blow, whether the markets were up or down. Across the globe, less than half of the usual investor riff-raff were at their computers. A shortage is always a good thing.

Except when it came to your results. In which case, a shortage was a scandal. Abundance, that's what it was about, and abundance lurked everywhere. The world had an abundance of herring shoals. All you had to do was hang your basket overboard at the right time and bring it back up, brimming. But you had to find out where the herring shoals were. You had to be the first— and ideally, the only—person to find out. That took continuous research, and round-the-clock vigilance, and knowledge of the latest updates for the most advanced computer programmes, and groundbreaking hardware, procured even before it hit the shops. You wheedled the prototypes from their manufacturers in exchange for rave reviews of their gear on a site for investment fanatics, or, if necessary, in exchange for insider information on their competitors. As long as you got hold of the new toys before your competitors did.

Everything was a race against the clock. Some offices moved, management and all, to a building that was just twenty kilometres away, but right next door to the skyscraper of one of the largest Internet providers. The reduced physical distance between their computers and the notebooks in the neighbouring office provided a digital gain in real time of a fraction of a second. Enough to buy and sell electronically just that fraction faster. Within less than a year, the costs of moving had been earned back and written off.

A year later, all the other offices had moved, too. All of them around that one skyscraper, like termites around their queen. Once again, the playing field was levelled; once again, the search was on for that extra fraction of a second. You had to give it your all. No effort was too great, no sacrifice too crazy. You had to suffer and genuinely enjoy your suffering. Otherwise, you wouldn't stay the course.

Tony raised his axe high above his head with both hands, calculating the angle at which he should let it fall to sever, preferably in a single blow, the smaller of the two horns from the rhino's head. The cow looked properly dead, now. The largest horn already lay beside her head. The black giant had done that job. In the place of the horn there was now a horrible open wound with jagged edges. There was no more bubbling, but blood and gunge were still slowly oozing out.

For a moment, Tony had considered using the chainsaw himself, but he'd abandoned that thought. He was worried about the alarming noise it made, and he didn't know how to work it. He contented himself with his axe. Somehow an axe was more fitting, more honest. Using his hands was an act of homage. Right before striking the blow, he had another quick look around. He couldn't see anything, nor did he hear any trampling footsteps approaching in the semi-darkness. Get on with it, then. He whacked with all his might.

The axe grazed the rhino's low forehead without doing much damage. The blade had missed the small horn by two handbreadths. Tony felt a twinge of embarrassment and humiliation.

He couldn't even do this. Drive down a simple slope without almost breaking his neck and half of his teeth? He'd barely managed that, either. What was he doing here, in God's name? He felt his lower lip throbbing, he felt his shirt sticky with blood in front and sticky with sweat at the back. He was risking his life for, at most, ten kilos of horn. It wasn't even horn. It was made of fused and hardened hair. A kind of petrified wig, that's what it was. A backcombed moustache, two false noses. Look at him now, about to hack off a hairy costume nose with a genuine woodsman's axe. Wasn't it laughable? Especially because he couldn't even manage it. He grew furious with himself. Do it, then! Prove you can do it! He raised it again, his axe, high above his head, both hands gripping the handle firmly, close to the end to take maximum advantage of the leverage effect, his body tensed like a bow, one foot resting on the rhino's shoulder for better balance, more precision. He struck down with all the strength he could muster.

Missed again. Badly, too. He'd hit the animal just above the one eye socket that had been spared, with a resounding crunch. The blade was buried deep in the greyish, rubbery hide. The remaining eye had been thrown half out of its socket on impact. Tony failed to repress a disgusted expletive. Why was he such a klutz, all of a sudden? He was lucky he hadn't chopped off his own foot. Could easily have happened. The axe wasn't the problem. Sharp as a chisel, as merciless as a scythe. He had to lever it backward and forward to prise it out of the rhino's skull; that was how deep the blade had gone. Next time, he wouldn't even be able to get it out. He'd be left standing there like an even bigger prick. It wouldn't be long before it was pitch-black. What would he do, then? Strike randomly and chop both of his feet off? He could hardly turn on his four-by-four's headlights. That would draw attention for miles around. He might as well just call the police himself. No, he had no choice. He had to chop off this bloody horn. Now! Quick!

The axe finally came free. Tony went to stand on the other side of the cadaver. The striking angle was better here. Wasn't it? His breath raced like a lunatic's; his heart pounded in his throat; his bottom lip throbbed. Never in his life had he felt this hunted and cornered. The websites hadn't informed him about any of this— the pure horror of an encroaching African night, with its whining insects, its zooming mosquitos, and all the rest of his its winged armies. The rushes around the drinking hole swished in a deceptively idyllic way; in the distance, there was roaring and screeching. All around him, tenacious life and mortal danger rustled. Barely a couple of metres away, the black giant's groaning continued, a nagging lament, accompanied by the muffled, sporadic drumming of his convulsions. Why was it taking so bloody long for that poor doomed sod to give up the ghost? Why was life so horrifically tenacious sometimes?

And what was he doing here in this wilderness, thousands of kilometres from the place where he belonged? Everything here was suffocating and dirty and incomprehensible and tragic. You were never in control in a region like this. He couldn't have felt more out of place in the deep sea. He'd been on the run for so long. For months, he'd been longing for his converted barn in Wolvertem, with its clear hard lines, its architectural class, perfectly integrated into its once-rural but now well-organized surroundings. Healthy and green, but never threatening. He could have been there right now, sitting on his terrace, the sliding windows open, a view of the south, in a chair designed by Maarten Van Severen, next to a matching dining table, with a glass of Gouden Carolus beer, a bowl of Laughing Cow cheese blocks, and some slices of dried sausage. Yeah right. Own fault. Why had he stayed at that bank for so long? Anyone with any brains had seen the worldwide crash coming, and they had all cheerfully looked the other way. Racing forward at breakneck speed without a seat belt, or an airbag, or a handbrake.

Why hadn't he taken early retirement a few years ago, at the frothy crest of the wave? He could have cashed in his options and started a modest investors' club. He could have written articles for the Internet and provocative opinion pieces for the newspapers. Newspapers, as such, didn't exist anymore; journalism had been traded in for a catwalk of provocative opinions, a comedy casino of serial abuse. To everyone's surprise, economists had evolved into indispensable media stars, the most sought-after Cassandras, the intellectual pin-ups of their day and age.

If you just looked at who was calling the shots there, and with what kind of minimal baggage, Tony himself could have been a star. He didn't have model looks, but he couldn't complain about the amount of surreptitious attention he'd had from the women, and even the few overt queers, at the bank. Him, the cute nerd. Still waters? Animal appetites. Those were the kind of daydreams he inspired in strangers.

The general public wouldn't have thought any differently. He'd been so stupid! He could have been welcomed with open arms at all the radio and TV studios. He could have had a fan club. A Twitter account with a hundred thousand acolytes. His own talk show. Why not? If you saw the kind of people who had talk shows. At least he would know what he was talking about when it came to economics. And everything came down to economics. From wheat bread to equity derivatives.

He even missed Brussels. Brussels the city. The reality around the office blocks. He hadn't taken enough pleasure in its overwhelming, multicoloured chaos, its cacophony of languages, its array of striking-looking people from all over the world. A year ago he couldn't care less about it; now he longed to go back. The bewildering maze of metropolitan Brussels. Its excess of civil servants and beggars, its irritating tunnels and sweet little metro network. Its potential greatness, which it screwed up again and again, with its endearing talent for ugliness and failure. Nevertheless, it had plenty of parks and neighbourhoods where you could have fun. The Marolles district, the square next to the Schaarbeek town hall, the market next to South station, the fish market, you name it. Even its museums were ideal, small but world-class, ambitious on a human scale. You came out satisfied instead of laden with guilt because you hadn't even seen half of the exhibits. One of the last things he'd done before leaving—walking to Fontainas Square to buy the hoody—had been a painful wake-up call to how blind he'd been for years. Brussels was unruly but fantastic. He'd felt more at home than he'd ever wanted to admit. When Klara turned 12 and started secondary school, they'd simply have to sell the converted barn in Wolvertem and move to a renovated building near Flagey Square, the three of them. Cost what it may.

He still had so much life left to live! A surplus! And he'd spend it in one of the world's smallest belly buttons—the glorious, mongrel metropolis that held Belgium and, in fact, all of Europe together. He would get up close and personal with the world's big shots but still have a working-class pub on the corner, a flea market, and four affordable, cosy restaurants. *Bruxelles, je viens!*

At last, Tony thought he had found a satisfactory angle. He planted his legs wide and laid the edge of his axe against the root of the smaller horn. This was where it must land. He looked intently from the horn to the blade of his axe and back. Here. He concentrated. His breath raced. Here! For a moment he felt like throwing in the towel. He repressed the thought at once. He hadn't gone to all this trouble for nothing. He had lied and broken into a place; he had destroyed a stranger's life. It was simply unthinkable that he'd go back empty-handed now, or with just one of the horns. He had to complete this challenge successfully.

Here. Here!

And yet he hesitated again, paralyzed and crushed by the importance of the moment. To give himself courage, he summoned them up in his mind's eye—his saviours, his beacons of hope. Klara and Martine, Martine and Klara. Would they take him back? He'd lied to them for so long, and to himself. They'd been putting on an act for years, a parody of the family they thought they were.

Tony had missed more family milestones than he'd witnessed. Klara's first words? Her first steps; her first school play, as Little Red Riding Hood? He only knew them from the home videos. Or thanks to action replays at the kitchen table when he got home.

Martine turning her sweetest smile on Klara-with-the-pouty-lip in her baby chair: 'Come on. Clap your hands again for Daddy. He's here now. Come on! Do it! Do it for Daddy! Now, Klara, dear. That's not nice. You'll make Mummy cry.'

And then the same, Martine, now with her most pitiful expression, would say to Tony-with-the-raised-eyebrow, 'She did it so well this morning. Completely on her own. About ten times. I just don't understand it.' At which she would push aside his reheated meal and throw herself at him for a kiss. No holds barred, voluptuously. Her eyes squeezed shut as she undid his shirt and flies. As if she wanted a newer, better child from him, there and then. Despite his vasectomy.

They left Klara in her playpen. (Tony: 'Aren't you worried she's going to cry?' Martine: 'It's good for her lungs.') They barely reached the bedroom. Man is a creature of habit, yet with an astonishing ability to adapt. Both of them had learned to make love fast and furiously, to make the most of every available minute. They fucked faster and more phlegmatically than rabbits, keenly conscious that Tony's ringing mobile could drag him away at any moment because all hell had broken loose on the trading floor in Frankfurt or Kuala Lumpur. They screwed among the share prices, they fucked between the Nasdaq and the Nikkei.

'Our bedroom antics are going from bearish to bullish too,' Tony had bragged, sniggering as he revealed details of his sex life to just one colleague, the most boring of the bores in the dealing room.

The bore had sniggered back. He and Tony: a conspiracy of two in a palace full of one-hit wonders.

'You do realize what you are?' he said behind his hand, glancing around archly. 'A pigeon-fancier.'

'A pigeon-fancier?' Tony could have thought of many different comparisons, but not this one.

The bore: 'You're racing straight widowhood, only cocks.'

'I'm not racing anything,' Tony said, all jocosity gone. 'Betting is for losers, and both my wife and I are as fit as fiddles.'

'When a competition is approaching,' the bore continued unperturbed, 'the hen pigeon is separated from her cock for a few days. That way he'll fly home more quickly to mate with her. You have to get him off after five minutes or he'll fuck her to death. Absence makes the cock grow fonder, Tony!' The prick almost split his sides laughing. 'And your hen must know that. Absence makes the cunt grow fonder, too!' A month later, he'd gone as well. Never heard from him again.

The only thing Tony would remember about him was that expression. 'Straight widowhood.' He often wrapped his tongue around the two words. 'Straight widowhood.' He had to admit there was a lot of truth in them. A truth that left him feeling both proud and slightly bitter. Sure, he and Martine, though alive and well, were often each other's widow and widower. But so what? There was an upside. He was the right man in the right place. That was how much he'd given up for his passion; that was how much time and energy his career had cost him, and he didn't resent it.

He felt all the more admiration for Martine because she'd done her bit, too. She didn't try to stand in his way like most narrow-minded bourgeois bitches would have done. She was, just like him, as hard as nails.

Enough of widowhood, Tony swore now, raising his axe for the decisive swing. Their Spartan discipline hadn't been a virtue, but miserable self-deception. Martine deserved so much better. It wasn't even about the sex. How pathetic, all those lustful gymnastics. In the best-case scenario, sex was a by-product of affection; generally, it was a childish waste of time. True love required much more commitment. Longing and trust. The camaraderie between man and wife, and their unbreakable bond. He and Martine hadn't seen each other now for more than a year—Tony could hardly believe it, that's how long he'd been on the run—but when he thought about her, her body wasn't the first thing to come to mind.

Although it was impossible not to think about her well-toned body. She still had the same taut, firm buttocks. Her small but full breasts had sagged unattractively for a year after Klara's birth—'two used teabags' she'd sobbed one evening, naked in front of the mirror of her dressing table—but she'd made them rise up out of their lethargy with fanatical fitness and relentless dieting. Martine! His Martine! His fellow traveller since their 20s, with her fiery eyes, her long straight hair, and a mouth that made him think of a French *chansonnière*. Her attractive calves, her still-girlish knees, her lovely ankles. Tony would have given all the gold in the world to lie between her legs, licking her until she sobbed, getting drunk on her taste and her smell. But what really moved him was the thought of her fidelity. The years of sacrifice for his obsession. He'd freeloaded off her dedication. He hadn't been a lover or a husband, he'd been her cannibal. He had only one excuse. She'd been happy enough for him to devour her.

Enough of that shameful abuse. Martine deserved a new start, too. No more part-time widow and widower. Forever at each other's side. With a happy Klara hanging on Daddy's arm. (She and her mother: already as alike as two peaches.) Love conquers all.

Tony relaxed his body and brought his axe down on the rhino's head full force.

Judging by the noise, at least it wasn't a complete cock-up this time. The handle still reverberated in his hands. He bent over to examine the results from close up. Darkness surrounded him entirely now. The night would have to do without a moon. He used his iPhone screen as a weak torch.

His heart leaped. The blade had landed where he'd hoped, penetrating deeply, slantwise. The small horn was hanging half off. Just one little tap from the other side, and the job would be done. Relief and a burning feeling of triumph came over Tony. At the same time, he became aware of the last thing he would have expected in this setting, and under these circumstances. He had a hard-on. And not one to be argued with.

It wasn't just due to the thought of his dearly-missed Martine, or her body. It was also, Tony realized, a pure sensory reflex. His feelings of fear and anger had turned into euphoria. And add to that the disturbing scent of sweat and fresh blood, of animal dung and sticky mud, the proximity of death and his hope to be the only one to escape her. All these impressions translated into something physical. His cock was straining against his underpants. People could think what they wanted: the mind is defenceless against the body.

The officer who had trained Tony during his military service, and even seen a future sniper in him, had gone into this in depth during their last summertime exercise together. At night, in a pine forest in the Ardennes, next to the inevitable campfire, when he and Tony were the last ones left, drinking whisky and staring into the smouldering ashes as if into a crystal ball.

The least discussed and most disturbing feeling on the battlefield, the officer had told him—it sounded like a warning—was not cowardice, not tears, not the blind hatred toward the strangers on the opposite side. It was the inexplicable horniness a battle could bring on. A controversial German poet had written a masterpiece about it after the First World War—about the feeling of intoxication as he and his fellows had stormed out of their trenches. Surrounded by incoming grenades, rains of bullets, clumps of mud, pieces of dead horse, human remains. An intoxication that bordered on orgasm.

When Cossacks invaded a foreign nation, the officer continued, they pulled out the border posts and trotted into terra incognita, their saddles becoming the new border. Inch by inch, they conquered their enemies' most cherished possession—the land they'd been born on. Their efforts were rewarded with massive erections. Penetration at a gallop. Mass wartime rapes, the officer continued to lecture, might seem like an orchestrated attempt to shock and demoralize an enemy civilian population. But, in fact, like monkeys entering the territory of other monkeys, very few soldiers actually needed orders to rape mothers, schoolgirls, infants. 'It can all be traced back,' the officer concluded, allowing himself another drop of whisky, 'to the caveman in each of us. You too? One for the road?'

Tony had nodded without speaking. Fascinated, amused, but also wondering whether he wasn't having his leg pulled. At least it was good whisky. 'Here's to your health!' They chinked. A mountain steam babbled away next to the encampment.

Now, as he rolled a fag, the officer told the story of a pal of his.

The pal had been a former professional, now a mercenary, recently employed by Belgian arms traffickers as a sniper in the former Yugoslavia. Excellent at his job, looking for a new source of cash after his second divorce and his third bankruptcy. 'The thing he hated the most, my friend,' the officer said, passing his cigarette to Tony, 'wasn't even shooting defenceless civilians. If you can't deal with that, you shouldn't be a mercenary. He barely heard them scream, he was shooting from so far away. Thanks.'

He took the cigarette back from Tony, who'd barely taken a puff.

'After each direct hit, my pal got a whopper of a hard-on. That erection of his was the only thing that brought the victims closer by. Not their weak cries, not the little bit of blood he'd seen through his telescopic sight. His hard-on. It made them tangible. He felt soiled by it. That was the word he used. Soiled.' He shook his head and threw his dog-end into the ashes.

'How did he solve his problem?' It was the only question Tony could think to ask.

The officer's eyes remained fixed on the ashes. 'He jerked off and reloaded his gun.'

Tony hadn't seen the officer again after he was discharged, but he'd never forgotten their night-time conversation. In hindsight, he was sometimes struck with the uncomfortable thought that his temporary mentor—through a strange ritual, a mixture of intimacy and machismo—had been trying to seduce him. All that talk of 'whoppers of erections', 'penetrations at a gallop' and 'a hard-on from here to Tokyo'? He'd never heard the man mention his wife, or children. He always just talked about his mates, his buddies. 'Our lads.'

But if it had been a bizarre attempt at seduction, why hadn't the man made any advances earlier? There'd been ample opportunity. Not just during the exercises. That was what had bothered

Tony so much about life in the barracks. An oppressive, all-male barracks, in which love and sensuality seemed so far away that even stupid, bestial sex—orgasm for orgasm's sake—had seemed like an attractive prospect. Even if it was just to chase away the boredom.

Tony had nothing against gays. He simply didn't understand what they found so attractive about one another, all those muscles and rolls of fat, all that body hair everywhere, not to mention the rest of the male body. But back then? As a fresh, young, inexperienced 22-year-old? When circumstances dictated, he might have let others give him a hand job, in the showers or so, even though he was going out with Martine at the time. Why not? When the mood was right? And you didn't want to disappoint a friendly superior? There are worse things in life. Spunk will out.

Why else had that guy told him all those weird stories?

Now, in Mpumalanga, wrestling with an axe that once again seemed to be wedged, with a hard-on that made every movement even more painful and pinched unpleasantly in his crotch, Tony knew the answer. The man had been right, that was all. A battle is exciting, in every sense of the word. It seemed that the officer had wanted to prepare him, all those years ago, for this exhausting night. Don't be afraid, Tony. Accept your fear and your brutality. You have to realize that you, numbers whizz, master of algorithms, are just a poor fellow of flesh and blood. Don't be alarmed, give in to it, go with the flow. The axe finally gave up its purchase.

Tony got ready for the final, decisive blow. All he could see now were the contours of the rhino's head, but that was enough. He knew, he *felt* how and where the blade needed to come down. He was about to complete his mission. He felt stronger, more potent than ever. His crotch pinched pleasantly. He raised the axe for the last time, tasting victory, his body nicely relaxed, one foot in the sand and one on the animal's head, just behind its fuzzy ear. It was a pity no one could take a photograph of this moment, he just had time to think, before the discharge. Then he got the shock of his life.

Something had clawed his ankle. He screamed. It took him a few seconds to realize what was happening. It was the black giant.

The man must have dragged himself over with courage born of despair. He clamped Tony's ankle in a vice-like grip with his last scrap of primal force. Tony yelled and cursed, wrenched and wrung, but didn't manage to kick the man away from him.

The giant was still groaning and gurgling but also talking now. In fits and splutters. Tony couldn't make out much of it, and was so panicked, he could hardly listen anyway. He was still trying to tug his foot free, kicking like you would after a shipwreck, standing on the edge of an overcrowded lifeboat. A matter of physical survival.

To no avail. The man didn't loosen his grip. It was astonishing how much strength he still had, in spite of the bullet wound, the partial amputation, and his recumbent position. He gave Tony a grim, determined look. His pupils were back. Accusingly, they picked up the very last rays of light. 'Please!' he groaned more than once, in English. He also said lots of other things in another language. Was it Afrikaans? Dutch's pretty sister language. It had made Martine laugh so much, and Klara, too, because it had sounded so infantile. '*Hospitaal.*' He said that more than once, too. 'Clinic. Please!' Tony carried on kicking, hounded by his attacker's piercing eyes.

Until the man said something that sobered him up. Had Tony misunderstood it? Was this Afrikaans or English? 'Daughter.' '*Dogtertjie.*' It could also be something completely different. 'Do it.' Or rather, 'don't do it'. But this was what he made of it: 'daughter'. He was sure of it. And the idea that this half-corpse, this recumbent zombie, might have met him and his family earlier as a park guard during their dream holiday, and that he even remembered Klara, and that he had the temerity to draw that innocent child into this, into this mess, this debacle, this unnecessary bloodbath—it made Tony white-hot with rage. Unthinkingly, he brandished his axe. With just one hand, yes! A perfect swing. He was learning fast. He always had. An elegant, masterly blow. Driven by anger, pity, and inexorability. The groaning stopped at once.

Both of them were freed. One of them for eternity.

5. Buenos Aires/ Mpumalanga

'WHAT'S THAT?' TONY ASKED, GROGGY WITH SLEEP. He was lying on an iron bed now, and he hated his weak voice. How long had he been unconscious? Was he still in the same hospital? Mrs. Mercedes had carefully shaken him awake and placed an oversized cocktail shaker on the nightstand, next to the vase of plastic flowers and the old-fashioned telephone—a bizarre still life in search of a painter. Her face was as motionless as ever, her gaze and her mobile mouth expressing all the more concern.

'Why have you brought me that?' Tony persisted. He sat up and gazed, awestruck, at the shining cylinder. An aluminium thermos flask with a belly, without spout or handle, without any kind of opening. He saw himself reflected in it, stretched at the top and the bottom, blown up in the middle, with crazily big eyes. A drugged owl flanked by a psychedelic telephone and mad flowers. He saw the way a deformed claw, his own hand, reached out towards the owl, as if to drive it away forever.

Mrs. Mercedes held Tony's hand. 'That's Mrs. Bo Xiang,' she said. Her voice brooked no doubt or contradiction.

TONY LOOKED TO THE LEFT AND THEN TO THE RIGHT. The dirt track that had taken him away from the hole in the fence had turned into a motorway, just like Google Maps had predicted on his iPhone. The highway was unlighted. Not one set of headlamps rushing toward him anywhere, no blue flashing lights, and no low-flying helicopters with spotlights. He'd made it. And he had the whole night to make his getaway. 'Don't forget to stay on the left,' he reminded himself.

The darkness would have mercy on him. Only the stars twinkled in the firmament, so much more numerous here than in the northern hemisphere. A poet might call them stationary fireworks. The valleys of Mpumalanga seemed solidified under a layer of opaline glass for as far as the eye could see. The ink-black highway swayed over it from horizon to horizon. Tony followed it with his eyes, from left to right and then back again. In the back of his ticking-over four-by-four were the two horns and the still-assembled gun, sloppily hidden under the mat in the trunk. He'd left the axe behind. He'd wrangled it free enough times for one night. He'd kicked off the smaller horn with his right heel. It had already been half off. Two kicks were enough.

Left or right? Limpopo or Mozambique? He hesitated once again. Nevertheless, his heart was still in overdrive and his head whirred from the tension. He really had done it. He tried to shut out thoughts of the human price paid. He was happy he hadn't had to see the result of his last blow. Another gift from the merciful darkness. But his mind was no less troubled for it. He clung to one certainty. There was no question of malice. He hadn't set out to kill the black giant. It could have just as easily been the other way around. What if Tony had been the first to shoot at the rhino? How would the giant have reacted? Maybe even more barbarically.

He knew only too well that this was no cancellation of debt. Despite his joy, he still felt them gnawing away at him—the horror and the remorse. You'll just have to learn to live with it, he thought, trying to man up. What happened was sordid but irreparable. You'll just have to give it a place. It was the same for a soldier, the conscript returning home from the front who had left behind the intoxicating fug of combat and would now have to offload the abomination. The abominations he'd seen and the abominations he'd committed. The two were inseparable, just as peace cannot exist without war, and just as an indiscretion was usually accompanied by remorse.

Tony felt remorse. Unutterable remorse. He'd always be indebted to a stranger; a debt that no one would ever know about. An anonymous death that would disappear into the folds of time without leaving a trace, just like hundreds of thousands of other nameless people on this continent alone—but for which he, Tony, would bear the burden for the rest of his days. He solemnly pledged this to himself. Then he indicated—an automatism, even here—turned his wheel in the same direction, changed gear, and accelerated, shooting along behind the two piercing headlight beams of the four-by-four.

He slid open his window, let the warm breeze blast his battered face, and turned on the radio. Deafening, pounding *kwaito*. A few seconds more, and the dashes along the middle of the road would start to look like a solid line.

'YOU SHOULD COUNT YOURSELF LUCKY,' Mrs. Mercedes said, 'that you called me.' She spoke as though she were clearing out a property in the presence of its former owner. Hurried and slightly embarrassed. She spread out the clothes he'd last been wearing at the foot of the bed. Shirt, socks, jeans, underwear, all washed and ironed. The smell the clothes gave off was the only thing in this room that seemed comforting and familiar to Tony. He lay naked under the sheets. His migraine threatened to return.

'I've become an expert,' Mrs. Mercedes said. 'Last year, a big shot from Chicago gets off the plane with a calf as big as a balloon. He's dead-set on checking in with me, so does that first before going to the hospital with his girlfriend. He dies there in her arms. Embolism. What does that silly goat do, in her distress? She gives his body to the first person who comes asking for it. Along with his passport and an astronomical fee. Just like you.'

She shook her granite head in disbelief.

Behind her, Tony noticed now, were both his and Mrs. Bo Xiang's suitcases, next to the wall with their trolleys. Had Mrs. Mercedes brought them herself or had she had help? From whom? The real undertaker, her housekeeper, the ambulance men? Who else knew about this?

'I managed to fix the mess, once again,' Mrs. Mercedes said. 'With a little help from the powers that be.' She held up Mrs. Bo Xiang's Louis Vuitton, clasping the strap with one hand and using the other to rummage around in its gaping maw. 'Passport, wallet, mobile phone. Earrings, watch, bracelet. Plus all the money, right down to the last cent. Go ahead and count it.' Without waiting for a reply, she clicked the bag shut.

'Mister Bo Xiang!' Tony sat up with difficulty. He felt dizzy. His throat hurt. 'I must call Mister Bo Xiang.'

'The embassy and I did that ages ago,' Mrs. Mercedes reassured him, pressing the handbag into his hands.

'He'll never forgive me,' Tony said. He tried to ignore it, but the handbag smelled of violets and green tea. He could also feel the lumps of the rolls of euros. He swallowed with difficulty.

'Mister Bo Xiang knows little of the true facts,' Mrs. Mercedes said, 'and you and I are going to keep it that way.' She had come to sit next to him on the bed, her face and her torso turned toward him, her legs crossed away from him. An aging Amazon, a *gaucha*. The mattress gave a little.

'Mister Bo Xiang,' Tony said, bracing himself so as not to roll toward her, 'will find out everything. He's known for it.' What was it now with this bloody handbag? Once again, Tony didn't know what to do with himself with the thing in his hands. He didn't dare let it slide onto the floor. That would seem disrespectful. He continued to hold it in his crossed arms. All the while avoiding looking at the urn again. Swallowing was tricky.

'Mister Bo Xiang knows what he needs to know,' Mrs. Mercedes said, 'and he is touched. He is grateful. He is expecting you. He will reward you.'

'I know about them,' Tony said, 'his rewards. Mister Bo Xiang is known for those, too.' Despite this, the sweetest of medicine, a smattering of hope, now welled up in him. Did Mrs. Mercedes mean what she said—that perhaps all was not lost? Perhaps, miraculously, there was a way out.

'I praised you to the skies,' Mrs. Mercedes said soothingly. 'Mister Bo Xiang was crying in the background when I told his interpreter over Skype that you single-handedly gave his wife CPR and mouth-to-mouth, in the ambulance, all the way to the hospital, up until her deathbed.'

Tony looked at her in astonishment. 'You told Mister Bo Xiang that I gave his wife mouth-to-mouth resuscitation?'

'And CPR with your bare hands,' Mrs. Mercedes nodded. 'I emphasized your efforts and your grief. I didn't need any imagination for that. You did try your best. The ambulance workers and the head surgeon confirmed my story to the ambassador most fervently. To prevent any further rumours, and, let's say, humiliating investigations, we came to the joint decision to cremate Mrs. Bo Xiang with expedited proceedings. We gave it a cultural twist. Muslims have to be buried within twenty-four hours; Chinese have to be cremated within forty-eight. Not one civil servant raised an eyebrow. We might just as easily have said that she had to be sent into orbit around the earth. When it comes to the Chinese, no one asks questions. Certainly not when the bill is paid that quickly and that generously.'

'How's she going to get to him?' Tony asked. He did glance at the urn now. The drugged owl stared back at him with huge eyes. 'International procedures are time-consuming,' he explained. How full was an urn like that, he wondered. How much is left of a person? And didn't the ashes in the oven get mixed up with the ashes of strangers, after a while? He shuddered, squeezing the handbag like an adolescent squeezes its secret teddy bear, an old toy, one he doesn't want to throw away. Tony had never thought about it before, but what about when his time came? He didn't want to end up in a garden of rest, or in a columbarium. A garden of rest made him think of fertilizer, a columbarium of a bowling alley. He wanted a burial at sea. Or no! A real grave. All the knobs and knockers. He felt a nasty stab in his chest when he realized. He wanted a traditional grave in the country where he'd been born. Hardstone and marble. Carved letters and numbers. In the country that he hated and had been fleeing all his life. It was a humiliating thought, but his bones belonged nowhere else but there. A man should die where he was born. Otherwise, what was the point of it all?

'We'll leave the international procedures be,' Mrs. Mercedes sniffed. 'Mister Bo Xiang doesn't want any fuss. So far, we've managed to keep the press out of it. That's why he isn't coming to Buenos Aires himself. It would only cause a stir. Anyway, his interpreter told me he hasn't set foot outside of China or Macau for years.' She grinned. The mattress sagged a little more. 'I'm sure that's not only to do with being afraid of the press,' she whispered. 'What do you think?'

Tony had to brace himself again. 'How is she going to get to him, then?' he asked.

Mrs. Mercedes looked at him as if he were a recalcitrant child. 'You're going to take her to him, Tony. In your luggage. Or in hers.'

She stopped just short of saying, 'You started it; you finish it.'

TONY RACED THROUGH THE AFRICAN NIGHT like a spear. The wind forced its way through the window; his hands gripped the steering wheel; the *kwaito* pounded compellingly; in his mind he ticked off his list. Blood-stained clothes: to be dumped, perhaps even burned, somewhere along the roadside. Afterward, he'd get something more conventional out of his luggage than this silly explorer's get-up. Gun: to be dismantled. But not to be discarded bit by bit, as was his first plan. You had to be able to earn a pretty penny from it in Mozambique. Black markets are everywhere, certainly in countries where the scars of a civil war are still tangible. Alter ego: a rough version before he reached the border would do. He could wash away the blood and the dust with the drinking water from the twelve-litre container that he'd bought, thank God. A comb through his hair, and hey, presto! He'd just have to accept the swollen lip. And for the rest of it—he'd have to count on his talent for improvisation. Every border had a cash-strapped customs officer or an unmonitored dirt track used for trafficking. It was all over the South African press—the state borders were apparently leaking like a sieve. Admittedly, in the opposite direction. The entire continent was trickling down into its southern tip. That was to Tony's advantage. Who would worry about a solitary foreigner who, going against the current of job-seekers, freeloaders, and adventurers, wanted to take a trip to the former Portuguese colony he'd heard such wonderful things about?

They'd welcome him with open arms. The brand-new rands in his glove compartment would clear away any remaining obstacles.

TONY FELT LIKE HE HAD BEEN REBORN—albeit still a little shaky on his legs and light-headed—once he'd put on clean clothes. Just before she left the room, Mrs. Mercedes had urged him to get ready quickly. The officials from the Chinese embassy could arrive at any minute to escort him to the airport. He didn't have to worry, they'd arranged everything. He could check in just like any other traveller, but his suitcase and Mrs. Bo Xiang's would have special labels. Just before saying their farewells, Mrs. Mercedes grabbed his wrist. She was still sitting next to him on the bed. 'You must promise me one thing,' she'd said.

'Don't worry,' Tony nodded, 'everything happened exactly as you described. That's what I'll say to everybody, I promise.' He didn't dare tear his wrist away. Her grip was anything but gentle.

Mrs. Mercedes shook her head. Even her hair seemed chiselled. 'Watch out for those people,' she said. Tony hadn't heard this beseeching tone before. 'I got to know the Americans when they helped me dig out that hotshot from Chicago. That was small beer compared with these Chinese people. They don't pull any punches. And that Mister Bo Xiang of yours? They'd go through fire and water for him. Out of fear or respect, or both.'

'May I ask you something?' Tony tried to politely worm free from her grasp. 'Do you still have much contact with your parents?' He didn't understand where the question came from, all of a sudden. It wasn't an impulse, he realized. It was a confession. He could have kicked himself.

'My parents?' At least Mrs. Mercedes relaxed her grip now.

'Your father was a general with a lot of German friends, wasn't he?' Tony asked. He'd gone down this path; now he'd have to persevere. 'You haven't mentioned your mother at all.'

'They're both dead,' Mrs. Mercedes said.

'I'm sorry,' Tony said, 'my condolences.' He rubbed his aching wrist as inconspicuously as he could.

'It's too long ago to be sorry about,' Mrs. Mercedes said. Her expression told him the opposite.

'Do you still think about them a lot?' He didn't want to be having this conversation. It should have come to an end already. The smell of the freshly-laundered clothes at the foot of his bed was enticing. He couldn't believe it. Soon he'd be stepping outside, unburdened. A hero, not a suspect or a criminal. He would be given an escort. A reward was waiting for him.

'My father,' Mrs. Mercedes said, looking away, 'disappeared without a trace during our Difficult Years. My mother died of grief. She also could have gone and demonstrated every week with all those other women. It wasn't her style.'

'And you?' Tony asked. The conversation would just have to be continued until they reached some stopping point. 'Did you cry a lot?'

Mrs. Mercedes looked at him as though he'd turned into a moron. 'I dance tango every night. Just like my mother did. Nothing else is necessary. There isn't anything else.'

After that, she'd bent towards Tony. The mattress had sunk a little more as she kissed his cheek with her surprisingly warm, mobile lips. 'Look after yourself in China. That's all I ask.'

She left the room without looking back.

TONY SEEMED, THANKS TO THE DASHBOARD LIGHTING, to be sitting on both sides of the windscreen at once. The other Tony also had a steering wheel in his hands, but was sitting with his back to the oncoming asphalt, facing Tony. And even though the reflected Tony was semi-transparent, and even though the black motorway with its white stripes cut right through him, Tony still looked at him with astonishment. He'd never seen himself look so rugged and self-confident. Something has shifted irreversibly in me, he thought. I've bitten down on life. It was bitter, hard, unpleasant, and it suited me perfectly. Him there? That's who I am, who I really am. Tony was beside himself with joy in his blacked-out Audi on the way to Buenos Aires airport. He was being treated as though he'd won big-time at a busy roulette table again. Respect from all sides. Even bodyguards. He raced through the crowded inner city, not only toward the tarmac but also toward his own liberation. He had to stop himself from waving at the Porteños along the broad *avenidas*. They couldn't see him behind the tinted windows, anyway. Mozambique was so much better than Limpopo, he congratulated himself. Extra-difficult to trace him, once the poaching was discovered. And thanks to the formerly Communist Frelimo government, there would be a big Chinese embassy in Maputo, like the one in Brussels on the Tervurenlaan. Still in hospital, waiting for his guards of honour, he'd counted the rolls of euros again. Not a single note was missing. He hoped to skip across to Madagascar from Maputo, or to Zanzibar. After that, eastward, following the trail of the old monsoon route, where fortunes had been amassed trading saffron and incense, muscular slaves and near-transparent porcelain, for centuries on end. His lip chafed. His head spun. He didn't care. As he felt the airplane's wheels breaking free from the Argentinian tarmac, he could only think of one thing—Mr. Bo Xiang's sorrowful, grateful face as he handed over the urn. As he stared in contentment at the rugged apparition he was driving out ahead of himself in the African night, he could only think of one thing, aside from Klara and Martine: the admiring and approving expression on Mr. Bo Xiang's face as he handed over the two rhino horns.

PART TWO

Union

1. Guangzhou (fiftieth floor)

WE RUN INTO TONY HANSSEN on another continent, in the middle of a winter that people in his country of origin might brand a promising spring, or a mild autumn. Not much rain, pleasantly sunny, a light breeze. There was nothing to suggest how remorseless the summers here could be, with their suffocating heat, their low, dense clouds, their stifling monsoon rains, and rapidly forming cyclones. Bursting dykes and floods had been claiming thousands of lives in these parts for centuries, as a toll for so much fertile, arable land, natural mooring places for fishermen and merchants from all four corners of the globe, and a culture that was hundreds of years ahead of the rest of the world. Misery sharpens the mind. Especially if it returns every year.

These days, it was mainly the smog that returned. Every day. It didn't bother Tony. He was on the fiftieth floor of a skyscraper in the heart of Guangzhou in the unvaryingly cool, air-conditioned climate of an international hotel chain. He looked out over the chaotic traffic and a many-forked flow, the Pearl River. It wound its way from here to its estuary in the South China Sea, which stretched from Taiwan to the Strait of Malacca. Once the busiest sailing route on the entire planet, now well on its way to regaining that status.

It did its name justice, the Pearl River. Despite being filtered by the smog, the sunlight was reflected in its water in thousands of ripples and eddies. Shattered glass in motion. And so it swept on tirelessly, under bridges and ships' bellies, around old islands and recently reclaimed land, and between the banks built up with high-rises, which continued to broaden and fork into a mighty delta. The funnel-shaped lap of an unparalleled megalopolis. Already over one hundred million inhabitants, and each day dozens more country folk left their remote farms to start a second life in this fresh new Babylon of the East, as beggars if need be.

Just before it plunged into its destination—the South China Sea, that vestibule of the Pacific Ocean, which was the largest one of all, and which contained the deepest place on earth—the Pearl River passed another double crown. On the left, Hong Kong, on the right, Macau. They were so far apart that the inhabitants of either city state could not discern the skyline of the other. Not even from their tower blocks, the basilicas of modernity.

The estuary was also too far away for Tony to be able to see it from his hotel. He had to make do with the panorama that presented itself through the full-length windows—a labyrinth of viaducts and boulevards full of western cars, thousands of pedestrians, cyclists, trams, and taxis, united in double streams of traffic, coming and going, riveted together by a zip made of crash barriers. They swerved only for enormous building sites and cranes. All this was surrounded by a forest of skyscrapers. Just visible between two reflective office fronts was a park with antique pagodas, weeping willows, and a pond full of swans. Billboards were scarce. Half of them featured the head of the Communist Party, standing in a dynastic pose and wearing a business suit. On the others, languishing models offered perfumes and watches. Their smiles were just as broad as those of the apparatchiks, but their logos were bigger.

Reflected over all of this, Tony saw a phantom of himself, lonely in his brightly lit room. A luxury suite with wall-to-wall carpeting, crystal chandeliers, and a noticeably low ceiling. The coffee table, upon which he'd respectfully placed the urn containing Mrs. Bo Xiang's ashes when unpacking his luggage, was now bare. Somewhere in the city before him, her funeral was taking place, perhaps at this very moment. Perhaps in that park over there, where he'd just seen a column of black limousines pass by, driving at walking pace, all the tinted windows closed, despite the lovely weather.

What did the Chinese do with their dead? The same as everyone else, most probably. Put them in a crypt, buried them, or scattered their ashes, and swore they'd never forget them.

The interpreter was the one who'd come to collect the urn. Discreet in his conduct—the knock on the door was barely audible—but arrogant, even forbidding in his facial expression. He was the same age as Mr. Bo Xiang, somewhat shorter and more corpulent, but with a similar perpetually crumpled suit and bags under his eyes just as large as his boss'. Judging by the colour of his teeth and the smell hovering around him, he was a chain-smoker. It's not just dogs that start to look like their owners. Loyalty as trauma.

He conveyed his boss' message with visible reluctance, although in the same formal language as always. He'd dropped the almost-abusive tone he'd used over the phone to Tony when enquiring about Mrs. Bo Xiang in Buenos Aires. Still standing in the doorway, and with even a slight bow, he had announced that Mr. Bo Xiang wanted to convey his eternal gratitude to Tony, but that Mr. Bo Xiang begged him to understand that they couldn't yet meet in person. Then he came into the room anyway. He closed the door cautiously and continued his account, as stiff as a rod. His voice didn't become any friendlier. The little hair he had left was stuck to his scalp; the skin on his cheeks and forehead was pockmarked.

Officially, he continued, Mrs. Bo Xiang had died unexpectedly in her own home. Mr. Bo Xiang didn't want to awaken the bloodhounds of the international press, nor the vultures of his own party, by inviting an unknown Westerner to his wife's funeral—a young foreigner into whose arms he might even fall, as overcome by sorrow as he was. That was how Mr. Bo Xiang was—overcome with grief. Just as Tony himself was, no doubt. The interpreter rolled his eyes at these last words, letting out a mocking sigh at the same time. Although he didn't pause in his communiqué. Mr. Bo Xiang, he continued, solemnly promised to invite Tony for a closed ceremony, as soon as possible. In an intimate setting, Mr. Bo Xiang wouldn't have to feel ashamed of showing his pain. On the contrary, he would offer Tony the thanks due to him, as well as an appropriate reward. At the latter, the interpreter sniffed like someone who was indignant but powerless. Mr. Bo Xiang, he continued, completely understood the feelings of awkwardness and neglect that Tony must be feeling now. That was why he was being put up in this hotel, the consortium's pride and joy, the most expensive place to stay in Guangzhou, which had a Cantonese top chef and a sommelier from Geneva. Tony had but to make his wishes and desires known to the reception desk, and they would be fulfilled immediately. After that, the interpreter fell silent. Without looking at Tony, he got out a pair of white gloves, put them on, went over to the coffee table, and respectfully took the urn in both hands before walking to the door with it.

'And what about the rest?' Tony asked, only daring to speak now, for the first time. It distressed him to see someone about to take to their heels with Mrs. Bo Xiang's mortal remains, again.

'The rest of what?' the interpreter snapped. Now that he was speaking for himself, he no longer had to keep up appearances. He had stopped short provocatively, holding the urn out in front of himself. An incriminating piece of evidence, a damaged relic. 'What could be of any importance, Mister Hanssen, aside from this?'

'Her clothes,' Tony said. He stood between the interpreter and the door. 'Her make-up. Her luggage.'

'It seems to me,' the interpreter said, 'that, thanks to you, Mrs. Bo Xiang no longer needs those.'

'Her bank cards, her papers, her passport,' Tony continued. 'Someone will have to deal with them, won't they?'

'I presume you are mainly referring to her money?' the interpreter grinned, baring his smoker's teeth. His voice sounded both muffled and triumphant. A walk-on, uttering his only successful one-liner.

'What money?' Tony asked.

'The money in her handbag,' the interpreter said, still grinning. The urn shook in his hands momentarily. 'The cash in there with her credit cards, her make-up, her passport.'

Tony could make no reply.

'That sum is for you in its entirety,' the interpreter said, this time without grinning. 'Mister Bo Xiang said he wouldn't even want to touch that unlucky money. That's your first gift. You don't need to worry about the other things. In due course, people with more scruples than you will take care of them.' After that, he snarled an order in Chinese.

The door was opened from the outside by a bodyguard in a black suit, with a skinny tie and sunglasses. A colossus, fully pumped, by looks of him. There were three more in the corridor behind him, all three of them looking around, one hand to their ear, playing roles in a Hollywood action film. The interpreter slowly walked past them, silent, his nose in the air, like a cardinal with a ciborium.

Just before the colossus pulled the door closed, he gave Tony a brief nod. A bashful, almost-embarrassed nod. The nod of a man with a golden heart but an iron fist. The solid door closed with a sigh, leaving Tony abandoned.

That had been days ago. Since then, he hadn't heard anything more from the interpreter. The only living beings he'd seen were the cleaner and the room-service waiters. Apart from three words of mangled English, they spoke Chinese. The receptionist's language skills weren't much better.

Tony didn't fancy the swimming pool on the top floor, and the gym in the basement was even less attractive. Television bored him, despite the one hundred and fifty channels on offer, two of which showed adult entertainment for an extra fee. He'd considered the possibility for a moment, but immediately decided against it. Renting a porn film? To stimulate some apathetic self-gratification? Mr. Bo Xiang might learn what he had ordered. A grief-stricken magnate, whose wife he'd been the last person to see or speak to. It would hardly be tactful, on what might even be the day of her funeral. Now wasn't the time to offend his creditor.

But what *could* Tony do to console or gladden a widower? And where had the mourner got to, with all his fine promises? The telephone didn't ring. Tony felt more suffocated and threatened by the hour in this golden cage, with its ugly carpet and oppressively low ceiling. He was sick to death of the traffic panorama; the walls were closing in on him. He didn't dare leave the hotel building, not even for a short walk. It hadn't been explicitly forbidden, but neither had it been explicitly permitted. It troubled him that he was pretty much trapped here, but he was wary of just walking out without notifying anyone beforehand. What was this about? Were they hoping he'd make a run for it?

My God, perhaps that was his so-called generous reward? To be able to disappear unhindered into the sunset with a bag full of money. It made him feel sad. To slip away like a thief in the night—was that all, then? On the other hand, perhaps it was more than enough. Maybe he should just make his getaway.

Or maybe not?

If only he had someone he could consult, Tony sighed, trimming his toenails. He'd taken a bath in the hope that the Jacuzzi would calm him down. Wasted effort. The sense of isolation couldn't be washed off. He'd seldom longed for company over the past twenty years, but now? Lonely, uprooted, abandoned, still ignorant of his future… He yearned for a travelling companion, an insider, a bosom buddy with whom he could broach the most personal of issues without embarrassment, in the hope of at least a listening ear. He was tempted, for lack of anything better, to call Mrs. Mercedes. But what could that woman do from Buenos Aires? Supposing she was even willing to speak to him. What was the time difference again? It seemed like an eternity ago that she'd urged him to watch out for those Chinese.

She hadn't been wrong, Tony thought, putting away his nail scissors. Just look at him now, sitting here in his aquarium, his oubliette, his Western reservation in the middle of a metropolis where he couldn't communicate with anyone. And what if the magnate's sorrow should suddenly turn into a crazy desire for revenge?

How much was the word of a power-mad maniac worth?

At least the food wasn't bad, thank God. He'd ordered another snack over the phone. He'd let the chef choose. 'Surprise me, please!' On the television, his favourite film, *Hable con ella*, was about to start. Perhaps it would bring solace; at least it was a way of passing the time. Certainly with a glass of top-quality wine and an exquisite bite to eat.

And guess what room service came to serve him? Duck breast. Not glazed in the Cantonese manner but roasted the French way, with caramelized chicory, like they had in Belgium. The chicory, in particular, had a strong effect on him. Just the smell of it. That delicious bitter-sweetness. All those memories.

Tony sat in front of the television with the untouched plate on his knees, the title song to *Hable con ella* playing. A cautious but infectious tune with melancholic violins and a Moorish plucked guitar, backed by rhythmic Andalusian handclaps. His mouth was already watering, and now his eyes grew damp. And the mournful flamenco singer hadn't even started yet above the violins. Tony fought against the easy comfort of nostalgia, the temptation of self-pity. In vain. He felt a ridiculous tear trickling down to his chin. Ridiculous but trenchant. You could say what you liked about Mamaatje, but she could cook with the best of them. Chicory in her famous ham rolls. Chicory in her renowned Ghent chicken casserole. Chicory with her partridge *à la Brabançonne*.

There was a knock at the door. Not a gentle one.

Tony placed his untouched plate on the coffee table and turned off the sound. Who could it be? The interpreter, again? If so, the violence with which he was knocking did not bode well. Mr. Bo Xiang himself? Then the prospect was even worse. Room service? A cleaner? Impossible. No one who worked in this kind of luxury hotel would dare to bang on the door of a luxury suite that hard. Unless there were an emergency.

But in an emergency they'd knock on the door a second time. It must be a mistake, Tony reassured himself. He reached for the remote control to put the sound back on. Again, a knock on the door. This time even harder and longer than the first time.

Tony switched off the television completely, stood up, hesitated, dried his cheek with his sleeve, made himself look more respectable—his flies were still open, his shirt, too—and opened the door.

He was standing face to face with a black man in his 50s in a scruffy suit and glasses that were much too big. You wouldn't call him slender. His hair was greying and short, his chin badly shaven, his eyes ringed in red. You'd swear he were suffering from frustration and a lack of sleep. Nevertheless, he smiled. He took in Tony from top to toe.

'You're Tony Hanssen?'

'That's right,' Tony said, uneasily.

The man looked left and right along the corridor, as though to ascertain that it was indeed empty. 'Belgian by birth?' He had a bass voice and spoke English with a comical accent that Tony couldn't quite place.

'Indeed,' Tony admitted.

'That's all I need to know,' the man said. He took a swing with his left hand, in which he had been concealing a blunt object, and hit Tony smack on the mouth.

* * *

'ADMITTEDLY, IT DID SEEM LIKE A BRILLIANT MOVE,' the black man said. He and Tony were facing each other, both in comfortable armchairs, between them the coffee table upon which the urn had stood. There was a pistol on it now, next to the plate with the duck breast. The man had hit Tony on the mouth with its butt.

'Excellent way of throwing us off the scent,' the black man continued brusquely, yet with an undertone of admiration. 'You saw off your partner's leg, hit him on the head with your axe, and leave him behind, next to his Krugerpark *bakkie*. A whitey didn't cross my mind for an instant. Let alone a *fokken* white-collar criminal from *fokken* Belgium.' He chuckled. A high-pitched, self-satisfied, nervous giggle. He pushed his owlish glasses back up with the top of his middle finger.

'The body had already been gnawed by animals. Did you know that? We couldn't even find the lower leg.' He looked at Tony. 'You threw it away, didn't you?' He clapped his hands. A pounding swing of a clap. 'I knew it! You threw it to the crocodiles.' He accompanied some of his words with little cries. They sounded like 'Eish!' or 'Nè?' Now and then, he clacked his tongue.

Tony pressed the handkerchief the man had given him to his swollen bottom lip. The bleeding seemed to have been stanched, but he could still taste that sweet, metallic flavour. The taste of blood, the aftertaste of fear. He hadn't the faintest idea what this man was talking about it. Was this really happening? This had to be a hallucination, an emotional aftershock. The hanky smelled of acrid sweat and barbecue-flavoured crisps.

'I don't want to sound racist,' the man said, 'but black criminals don't use new axes. They use old axes. What they certainly don't do is use axes *and* chainsaws. That's overkill. Get it? And if we do? Bantus like me? Then we don't leave them behind. We're too poor for that. That chainsaw—okay, I'd have left it behind, too. It was broken. Sand in a chainsaw? That's as bad as water in a diesel engine. But a brand new, good-quality axe? From a foreign brand? *Eish!* Even if it was in your best friend's head. Even if it was in your mother's cunt. A Bantu like me would wrench and wring it free and take it home with him. For the next job. Get it?' He looked at Tony. 'Don't you agree? That a Bantu like me would take it with him?' He got out a piece of paper that looked like a till receipt. He laid it between the duck breast and the pistol. He'd already emptied the wine glass in one swig and placed it on the carpet. 'Do you recognize this?'

'No,' Tony replied, truthfully. His lip was sore. He didn't know what to do. Co-operate or not? With the tip of his tongue, he checked that none of his porcelain crowns had come loose or cracked. He tried not to think about Rio de Janeiro and the torture he'd undergone there. The hotel room hadn't looked that different from this one. Transitory spaces, torture chambers—the same all over the world.

'Isn't the address familiar?' The man pressed on the receipt with his index finger. The colour of the skin under his nails was lighter than that around it. The nail itself was bitten down to the quick.

'No,' Tony replied. He couldn't ever remember being in a street that was called Voortrekkersweg.

'A nice neighbourhood, a decent shop,' the man said, putting the piece of paper back in his wallet and raising his buttocks to slide it into his back pocket. 'Good stuff and good staff!' Again, that giggle. Now and then, he rolled his shoulders backward and forward. A shadow-boxer doing his warm-up.

'The description from the salesman was my first clue. Maputo airport has helpful staff, with good memories, too. Almost all foreign poachers go that route. The idiots think they're safe there. Your name was simply on the passenger list. A one-way ticket, one of the few. Bought for cash.' He fetched about a dozen photos from an inside pocket and spread them out on the coffee table, one after the other. It was the way a poker player might lay down his winning hand. 'The Interpol archives provided the rest. You'd been on their wanted list for a while.'

Tony wasn't listening anymore. He was looking in panic at the postcard-sized photos. They showed another black man, dead and horribly mutilated. Close-up: the results of a crude amputation, just above the knee. The splintered bone was clearly visible, despite the clotted blood and the swollen, ragged flesh covered in insects. Close-up: a shot wound in a shoulder blade. Insects were doing their work here, too. Close-up: a mutilated face. Only the jaw was intact. An axe was sunk deep into the face. On one side, an eye dangled halfway down the cheek. Insects here, too.

'And then you should see the rhino,' the man said. 'It didn't fare much better.' His aggression was clearly increasing. What was his relationship to the victim? Had he come to take revenge? Why here, in God's name? Why him?

'Listen,' Tony said, raking the photos into a pile to protect himself from the sight of them—he laid the panorama of a beautiful landscape with an SUV on top. 'I honestly don't know what this is about.' He realized his face must be as white as a sheet. His swollen bottom lip made it difficult to articulate properly. He'd placed the dirty handkerchief next to the plate with the duck breast. 'I'm completely in the dark. I'm genuinely sorry about this. Tell me what I can do to help you. I'll do everything in my power.'

'Don't insult my intelligence,' the man said. 'Most of my colleagues gave up on the investigation immediately. The two poor suckers left are still busy combing South Africa.'

'South Africa?' Tony asked. He'd moored there just a couple of times with the *Liberty Oasis*, always in Durban. He had messed around with the son of a local Indian carpet seller, and apart from that, nothing else. What a disappointment he'd been, too, that Indian. Big eyes, small penis, touchy. Bambi in a turban.

'I'm here of my own initiative, paying my own way,' the man said. 'Nobody knows I'm here. And apart from me, no one knows you're here.' He felt in his other inside pocket and took out a notebook.

He doesn't leave a single pocket unturned, Tony shuddered. People with a gift for methodology were either geniuses, or as mad as hatters. A genius would have long spotted his mistake. Tony was stuck with the other possibility. A fantasist. A lunatic. Was he really alone? At any moment his gang might come storming in, like that time in Rio.

The man used his little finger to go through the points in his book, one by one. 'You're not very loyal. You ripped off millions from the bank that employed you for years.'

'I ripped off a bank?' Tony had resolved not to say anything else, but his astonishment had got the better of him.

'An international business bank,' the man specified. 'Your dirty tricks caused their insolvency. They're calling you a rogue trader.'

'A bank that could be bankrupted by a person like me should never have been founded in the first place.' Tony knew that it would be sensible to hold his tongue, but he just couldn't stop himself. He'd been put upon too much, he'd been bullied too often, and he'd taken the blows afterward. It was better to go down fighting.

'And how did I manage to cause the bankruptcy, if I may ask?' There was just one way out—to break down these fabrications with their own contradictions, their own lack of internal logic. 'How could one man, on his own, bring down a business bank?'

The man, with his little finger on the page: 'You rigged the accounts by setting up a pyramid scheme.'

Tony, amazed: 'What's a pyramid scheme?'

The man: 'A Ponzi scheme.'

Tony, irritated: 'What's a Ponzi scheme?'

The man: 'Long-term, large-scale fraud.'

Tony, at his wit's end: 'I'm the one being cheated! Me, and me alone. The whole time. I'm the victim!'

The man: 'The facts tell a different story. You went into hiding just before your arrest.'

Tony, rolling his eyes: 'I got off the boat and never got back on. Does that count as going into hiding?'

The man: 'You illegally downloaded company information onto data carriers, giving the bank reason to fear that you intended to pass it on to malicious journalists, or threaten authorities for large sums of money, or even a new identity.'

Tony, confused: 'What are data carriers?'

The man: 'CD-ROMs, USB sticks, external hard drives.'

Tony: 'Search me! Turn over the room! Please! You won't find them, because they aren't here.'

The man: 'Of course they aren't here. They're in a safe somewhere. Along with your two other treasures. Or have you sold them already?'

Tony: 'What? What have I sold already?'

The man: 'The horns.'

Tony: 'Horns? Which horns?'

The man: 'The rhino horns.'

Tony buried his head in his hands. What kind of a hell had he ended up in? Now that everything had finally seemed to be on the right track. His lip was sore, his head spun.

'Listen,' he began, freeing his face from his hands. He adopted what he hoped was his most honest facial expression. 'I'm genuinely sorry for you. I would love to help you, but I really don't know what you are talking about. There's been a terrible mistake. I don't have anything to do with all this stuff you are accusing me of.'

The man looked at him. He grabbed Tony's chin between his thumb and index finger, tilted his head, and squinted. The moment lasted a while. At long last, he burst out laughing. 'You're a piece of work!' He wagged his index finger. 'Hell! You almost had me fooled.' He clapped his hands, shook his head, and laughed deeply, rolling his shoulders. 'Eish!'

'I implore you,' Tony groaned. 'You are mistaken.'

The black man raised both hands, beige palms towards Tony. 'All right, all right! I give up. You win. I'll drop all the charges.' He looked around as he laughed. 'Where's the minibar?'

Tony pointed hesitantly at the commode containing the minibar. The man went over to it, shaking his head and still chuckling. 'There's just one small matter I still have to clear up with you,

Mister Hanssen. And if you deny this, too, I'll let you go.'

'Go ahead,' Tony said, relieved at the prospect and yet caught in that perennial wolf trap again. Breathing was difficult. He saw spots before his eyes. 'Ask away. Haul me through the rigging. There's nothing I'd rather.' He noticed he'd folded his hands together in a praying position. He shoved them between his thighs and had to stop himself from rocking his upper body back and forth. His fear was turning him into a spastic. 'Fire away. Go on.'

The man took two miniature vodka bottles from the bar. Still standing, he calmly downed them, one after the other, as he continued to study Tony through his owlish glasses. His paunch hung liberally over the belt of his trousers.

'Swear to me,' he began, wiping his mouth with the back of his hand, 'that you don't know who Mister Bo Xiang is. Swear to me you haven't been paid to do anything for him. Swear to me that you don't know he's the owner of this building, the architectural showpiece of his hotel chain. And swear to me that you, and not he, are paying for this room.

Tony broke. The man knew about everything. That crazy story about axes and rhinoceroses? Complete with horrific photographs? Diversionary tactics. Perfidious nonsense used to unsettle his prey.

'What do you want from me?' Tony groaned. 'What are you planning to do to me?' He really was rocking his upper body now. He kept his eyes tightly shut. The tip of his tongue feverishly counted his crowns. His lip was sore. He waited for a fresh blow.

The man, returning to his armchair with all kinds of little bottles, bent towards Tony in a paternal manner. 'You don't have to worry,' he said, patting him on the shoulder. 'We'll figure something out. Do you still fancy that duck breast? It's lying there, getting cold.'

Tony, his eyes open again, gestured for the man to help himself.

He didn't hesitate and sank his teeth deep into the meat. 'Before I forget,' he said, his mouth full, 'my name's Khumalo.' He offered his wrist instead of the greasy hand in which he was holding the duck breast. His other hand clutched a small bottle of red wine, already half empty. 'Inspector Vusi Khumalo.'

Tony shook the inspector's wrist. They looked at each other. The inspector slumped and chewing, Tony with his back as straight as a rod, suffering. From time to time, Inspector Khumalo pushed his owlish glasses back up into place.

'You do realize,' Khumalo said, when he'd finished the meat—he'd tasted just a small piece of chicory and grimaced in disgust—'you're in a difficult predicament? Even without my investigation.' He cleaned his hands on the dirty hanky and casually put it back in his pocket. 'Your boss is under serious fire—from his party, from his consortium, from his shareholders, from the international press. His imperium is toppling, his rule is over. And his wife chose this very moment to snuff it. There are crazy rumours going around. Do you have any information about her death?'

Tony looked at Inspector Khumalo. What kind of game was he playing? He watched as the inspector, one hand in front of his mouth, begin to pick his teeth with the index finger of his other hand. The finger found something. The inspector had a good look at it and then calmly put it back in his chewing mouth. Only then did he look at Tony again.

This isn't a game, he realized with a jolt. This fellow doesn't know everything. He really has mistaken me for someone else. He doesn't know a thing about me.

'I've heard those rumours, too,' Tony nodded, as neutrally as possible. He couldn't let them show—his lifeline. His grain, his morsel of hope. 'Nobody believes that that poor woman just clocked it. Something particularly unsavoury must have happened to her, for sure.' He had to stall. There was no way Inspector Khumalo had a gang. He was here on his lonely ownsome. Tony, on the other hand, had allies: the interpreter and his body-guards. They were bound to return at some point.

'Shall I tell you what happened to that woman?' Inspector Khumalo asked with a self-satisfied smile.

'Go ahead,' Tony said, repressing a smile. 'I'm ever so curious.'

'She's still alive,' Khumalo beamed.

'She's still alive in many people's memories,' Tony smirked.

'She ran off with the money,' Khumalo said, 'along with her toy boy.'

'Her toy boy?' Tony no longer needed to repress a smile. There was no smile.

'They're actually money runners, without those poor suckers realizing it,' Khumalo sniffed. 'Every now and then, Mrs. Bo Xiang has a new favourite. She and her willing horse travel arm in arm like so-called lovers, to all the fiscal meccas and offshore para-dises the world has to offer. Between the fuck sessions, she settles her husband's stinking business affairs. Business and pleasure, the perfect cover. Don't tell me you've never heard people gossiping about that?'

'No, of course,' Tony replied, harried. 'Everyone thought it scandalous.'

'You should be happy you only fell into Mister Bo Xiang's clutches,' Khumalo chuckled, 'and not into his bitch's.' He stood up and stretched. 'The Chinese and sex? They didn't just invent fireworks. For thousands of years, they've been experts at torture and warfare. Same goes for their love life.' He had gone to stand at one of the full-length windows and was looking out over the city.

Tony studied the view from his chair. A helicopter hovered above a large crossroads, like a dragonfly above a pond. An air-plane made its descent in the distance, reflecting the sun in a flash. Tony turned his gaze to the coffee table. The pistol lay next to the empty plate. Its barrel was pointing toward the window.

'Check that traffic,' Inspector Khumalo groaned, massaging his neck with his right hand. 'New York's nothing compared to this. And this is just one of the city centres. A fraction of the whole picture. There are dozens like this, hundreds. And them? How many hundreds of millions of them are there, by now?' Again, that giggle. 'I know the black man has quite a reputation with his libido, but *eish!* Those Chinese! They hit the jackpot every time they shoot.'

Tony looked at the gun. Paralyzed, unable to move, disgusted with himself. Why didn't he ever take control?

'Of course, they've got a head start of a few thousand years,' Khumalo said, 'that makes it easy. That makes everything easy.' He laid both of his hands flat on the windowpane, a little higher than his head. His legs slightly spread, as though he were standing up against a wall to be searched. 'Do you like history, Tony? I love it.' His mouth was close to the glass. A patch of steam appeared.

'They laugh at me, the young guys in our police force. They can be coloured or Xhosa, they can be called Frikkie, Shabir or Taliep. Their historical awareness doesn't extend any further than the last time they bought sneakers. We've got one Jew. Even David prefers watching rugby to the History Channel. A *blerrie jood!*' He wiped off the steamed-up patch with the sleeve of his jacket. 'I long for just one thing—to retire in one piece. And the only thing I'll do, then? Instead of hunting down drug addicts and poachers? I'll read history books about mankind, on my own.' His expression as he surveyed the heart of the metropolis became ever dreamier. 'The more you read, the more admiration you feel for those *fokken* slitty eyes. Of course you think Europeans discovered America and Australia and the Cape of Good Hope. Forget it.' He pointed at the city. 'They were the first. My favourite book is about that.' He changed his posture again. One forearm fully resting on the glass, forehead on it again, free hand in his back pocket: a little brat counting down in a game of hide-and-seek. Only he was spying under his forearm.

He made an unmissable target. Nevertheless, Tony was still frozen to the spot. He could picture the whole thing—grabbing the pistol and aiming it, an extra in an action film now. Knees half bent, arms outstretched, holding a gun in both hands that didn't go off because the safety catch was still on. Or maybe it would explode, tearing off a couple of his fingers. He'd never fired a shot in his life.

'Do you know what those motherfuckers did to avoid getting scurvy at sea?' Khumalo asked. The lenses of his glasses reflected the busy traffic. 'We're talking about a thousand years ago. They grew bean sprouts and coriander on board. They hadn't quite got as far as spring rolls. Every day, they caught fresh fish for the entire fleet. Do you know what they used to hunt and drive those schools of fish?'

'Otters,' Tony said hoarsely. He stopped looking at the table. 'Tame sea otters.' His hands were sweating. It wasn't a good day to learn how to shoot.

Khumalo gave him an admiring look. 'Otters,' he affirmed. 'On a leash that was hundreds of metres long. How did you know that?'

'I've read that book, too,' Tony said, struggling to breathe. 'It was pure nonsense. I know a little about ships and sea currents. Those junks of theirs? Those cumbersome washtubs with their unwieldy sails? They weren't built to sail across oceans, with their square prows and their ridiculously large rudders. Sometimes they had two rudders. One for port, one for starboard. You give it a go.'

Khumalo stood there, perplexed. He pushed his glasses up. 'They had watertight compartments,' he said.

'So did the *Titanic*,' Tony said. 'We all know how that ended.'

Khumalo burst out laughing—shoulders rolling, hands clapping. 'You son of a bitch,' he cried. 'They don't come any cooler than you.' Amused, he leaned one shoulder against the glass, his face toward Tony, arms folded, his supporting leg outstretched, the other at a coquettish angle.

What's wrong with the fellow, Tony wondered—ants in his pants? Every ten seconds he changed his pose. What does he think this is? A photo shoot? An audition? 'You're just jealous,' Khumalo said, 'that the Chinese got everywhere before you people did.' His amusement already seemed to have vanished.

'It's not about who's first,' Tony said, swallowing. 'It's about who stays the longest.'

'*Fok!*' Khumalo cried. 'We were able to experience that firsthand. Not just in Cape Town. All over Africa, in Congo—*your* Congo—most of all. But even there? Believe me, mister. Your show is over. It's history.' He looked deeply offended, once more.

He's not the most stable man, Tony thought. But no, of course Khumalo wasn't really that unstable. He was cunning. He was playing the oldest double role in history, alongside that of virgin and whore, Faust and Mephisto. Good cop, bad cop. Dr Jekyll & Mr. Hyde, dressed in the same uniform. Don't let him get to you, Tony. Hang on in there. They'll be here soon. The interpreter and his bodyguards. Play for time.

'Do you honestly think you can still hold this back?' Khumalo pointed at the cityscape with his thumb. 'These numbers? This energy? This violence?' His eyes spat fire. 'They've already bought up or bought off everything movable and immovable in our country. We're empty. Do you get it? We're done. We're finished. A few more years, and it'll be your turn. Don't be fooled. You must know the story of the French journalist during the ping-pong diplomacy?'

'I don't know anything about sport,' Tony said, 'and a French journalist doesn't know anything about diplomacy.'

Inspector Khumalo looked at him without moving. 'Are you trying to rattle me?'

'I wouldn't dare,' Tony said, folding his arms.

'Richard Nixon and Henry Kissinger? Early seventies?'

'I wouldn't know what you're talking about,' Tony lied.

Khumalo clacked his tongue scornfully, but carried on with his story all the same. 'After Kissinger's visit to China, a Parisian journalist was allowed to interview Mao. Party chairman Mao!' Khumalo adopted an effeminate accent, as well as a French accent. 'Chairman Mao! What do you believe the effect of our French Revolution to be on social history after 1789?' The inspector went back to his own voice and thick accent. 'And what answer do you think that Mao Zedong, heir to the oldest civilization in the world, gave the Parisian dandy?' He grinned, anticipating the punchline.

'I've no idea,' Tony said, genuinely curious now.

'He said to that Parisian asshole,' Khumalo chuckled, 'that it was much too soon to notice any after-effects of their piddling French revolution.' Again, that clap of his hands. A high five with himself. 'That Comrade Mao? He was one of a kind.'

'The results of his own revolution were noticeable soon enough, though,' Tony said. 'Famine, purges, cultural civil war, corruption, environmental pollution.'

'You're focussing on the negative,' Khumalo grumbled, with a dismissive gesture. 'Sometimes a firm hand is just what's needed. Look where they are today. We could use a couple of good Maos in Africa.'

'I think you've already gone through several dozen,' Tony said, 'and there are a dozen more in the making.'

'Bring them on!' Khumalo cried. 'With the real Chinese at the top. We tried you out for a few hundred years, and we weren't satisfied. High time for a change of approach.' He walked over to the minibar again. 'What'll it be, lemonade or beer?'

'I'll have a white wine,' Tony said. If he were going to be held hostage here twice—once by a Chinese widower and once by an African inspector—he might as well get drunk. It'd make his helplessness slightly more bearable. Why else did people resort to opium and alcohol, to God and cough mixture?

'You can give me two,' he called to the kneeling Khumalo. 'If necessary, we can order a crate of big bottles from room service. On Mister Bo Xiang's account. He's a comrade, too.'

The sarcasm escaped Inspector Khumalo. He was kneeling before the minibar, finishing off a bottle of Mandarine Napoléon. Not long afterward, he approached Tony with two small bottles of wine, as requested. The other bottle, red, was for himself. His gait was less steady than when he'd first come into the room.

They clinked bottles and sat down facing each other again. 'Of course,' Khumalo began, after a pause, 'there are things about the Chinese that I don't understand.'

'You're telling me,' Tony said. 'And not just about the Chinese.'

'They own everything these days,' Khumalo said, ignoring Tony's irony or perhaps not grasping it. 'Everything trendy and happening. The highest buildings? The biggest fleet? The most expensive wines? More and more international masterpieces? They've got them. Fifty years ago, censure and deprivation were rife. Now, it's censure and plenty. You can't think of a product that isn't for sale here in two versions—the real thing and a passable forgery. Those guys make fakes of everything.'

'Who's to blame them,' Tony said, just to say something. He started on his second bottle.

'See that pistol, there?' Khumalo asked, gesturing at the gun on the coffee table with his chin.

Tony, counting his teeth with his tongue, didn't reply.

'Bought here,' Khumalo said. 'At a market around the corner. Two dollars. It looks alarmingly real, even though you couldn't fire a bullet with it. A brilliant fake. You can find thousands like it, along with so-called Rolex watches and so-called iPhones, you name it. Most of that crap doesn't even have to work. The exterior, the shell, the idea of possession is enough for the Chinese. They may have more millionaires than tea houses by now, and all over the planet they're hoovering up the petrol, natural resources, and diamonds from right from under our noses, but still they're addicted to representations more than anything. Get it? The contemporary prints of their glorious future. Meanwhile, they can't break free from their history. They clamp onto the breakwater of their grand history like mussels.' He looked at his empty bottle. 'Shall we order those big bottles? And something else to eat?'

Before Tony could say anything, Khumalo had stood up. He tottered over to the telephone on the commode and ordered two club sandwiches and four bottles of white wine. 'The most expensive on the menu,' Tony heard him say, 'and make sure they're not French. We support those peacocks enough already. They messed up Algeria and massacred Madagascar.'

He returned with a grin. 'Where did I get to?'

'The mussels of the past,' Tony said.

'*Eish!*' Khumalo chortled. 'The past! History! I love them both, but sometimes I worry that they're nothing but dead weights. Too much knowledge about ourselves and our ancestors isn't good, either. It stops us from rising up with open minds. Do you get it, Tony? Choose your own path. Be free. That's what it all comes down to. Free as an eagle, free as a pelican.' He whirled his arms around slowly, as though he wanted to rise up from his chair. 'No millstones, no rings around our legs. Without the dead weight of all those bastards who call themselves our ancestors.' He roared. 'Our own free flight!'

Tony put his two empty bottles on the coffee table. Something horrible was about to happen. He knew it.

'Tell me honestly, Tony,' Khumalo said, still flapping in slow motion. 'If you were allowed to start your life again. Without millstones. Would you dare to fly? High in the sky? Would you dare reach for the stars? Or would you just keep on swinging obediently in your birdcage?' He stared at Tony as he flapped. 'Which would it be, man? Come on! Would you learn from your mistakes, or not?' He was making cooing noises now, too.

'Me?' Tony asked, trying to buy time.

'Who else?' Khumalo cried, before cooing again.

'I'd go about my life in a completely different way,' Tony said softly. 'And I'd make different mistakes, at least.'

Khumalo stopped flapping. 'Wrong!' he thundered. 'Wrong! Wrong! Wrong!' He hit the coffee table with his fist, causing the plate to bounce and tumble off without breaking, thanks to the carpet. Khumalo didn't even look at it. 'We can go about our lives any way we want,' he cried, his index finger stabbing at Tony's face, 'we keep making the same mistakes. All of us! Exactly the same mistakes! But,' he said, again spreading his arms like an albatross would spread its wings, 'at least we'd be able to make them without anyone's help.' Again he slowly milled his arms without leaving his chair. His voice was calm. 'At least we couldn't keep shifting the blame to total strangers.' He drifted above some kind of plane. 'Get it?'

'No,' Tony said, with difficulty. 'To be honest, I don't get any of it, Mister Khumalo.' His chest seemed to be closing up like a flesh-eating flower. He had to wait for the room-service waiters. Maybe they could do something.

'My point is,' Khumalo said, breaking off his nosedive to get a packet of cigarettes and a lighter from yet another inside pocket, 'that those Chinese motherfuckers are pillaging my country's and my continent's resources. And in return, they spew out a tsunami of cheap products that bury and suffocate us. Not that we mind.' He lit up. 'That's what we're like. We're Africans. We're not afraid of suffocating. We're used to getting by on very little. No air or hot air, what's the difference?' He inhaled deeply. 'The free T-shirts our biggest liberation party hands out at its congresses? Congresses at which our ministers argue every time that our brothers and sisters in the textile industry deserve better pay? Those T-shirts come from China, and they've been made for next to nothing. Everything's Made in China. With the support of a local strongman to appease our marionettes back home.' He plucked a thread of tobacco from his bottom lip.

'What if my continent needs a motorway? Maybe from a gold mine to the coast, or from a diamond mine to the coast, or from an oil well to the coast? Does it need to build a whole new harbour, which, right from the start, is just some kind of outpost of Shanghai? The Chinese come and build everything themselves. The Chinese bring their own engineers. The Chinese bring their own trucks. They bring their own road signs and traffic lights, they bring their own road workers, they bring their own whores. But *fokken* hell! I've made peace with all that, Tony. That's progress. You can't stop it. That's not my point.'

'What is your point?' Tony asked, as neutrally as possible. There is no point, he thought. There's only terror, someone suffering from it, and someone enjoying it. There isn't anything else. And not just in this room.

'My point is,' Khumalo began, exhaling smoke, that these slitty eyes with all their export and their high-rises, their expertise and their high-tech espionage, still believe in palm readers and old women who can predict their future from tea leaves. Exactly like our *sangomas* forecasting the weather from sheep innards and chicken bones.' He took another intense drag.

'You know what they had at that market around the corner? Where I bought that fake pistol? They were still selling traditional medicine. Man!' Again, that giggle. 'No fakes there. The real thing, Tony! You can't believe your eyes. Chinese voodoo! Rat foetuses, marinated in spirits. Snake penises in vinegar, to cure miscarriages or measles. Dried jellyfish and seahorses for warts and piles. And there were dozens of stalls selling only aphrodisiacs. What a word, *nè*?' He sampled the sounds. 'Afro! Dizzy! Yak!' He slapped his thigh, then calmed down immediately. 'They let salamanders copulate, and at the moment the creatures reach their climax, during that fraction of a second of cosmic infatuation and euphoria we all know so well, they're squashed between two planks and their innards are squeezed out. That goo of bones, blood, and sperm is steeped in rice wine. Until another 100-year-old wants to have a baby with his 16-year-old girlfriend.' He took another enormous drag. He was using one of the empty minibar bottles as an ashtray.

If he keeps smoking like that, the fire alarm will go off, Tony hoped. There were enough smoke detectors. The smoke stung his eyes and his throat. His lip was still sore.

'But what do you think, dear Tony,' Khumalo asked, 'was their most potent remedy against prostate trouble?' He opened his eyes wide behind his glasses. 'It's only sold under the counter. I'll give you three guesses.'

There was a polite knock at the door.

'That'll be room service,' Tony said. He stood up.

Khumalo pushed him roughly back into his chair. 'It's an expensive product,' he said, 'even though it's just plucked from nature. A bottle of fake perfume costs less than a spring roll. Two grams of this wonder stuff costs more than a sports car.' Another knock. Khumalo called to the waiters to leave the food and drink on the floor outside the door. There was a brief clattering, then nothing more.

'They grate it while you watch,' Khumalo said, leaning back again, 'using beautiful silver graters that are hundreds of years old. They grate it and stir it into their green tea. The richest sprinkle it on their noodles, like you'd sprinkle ground nutmeg on your *boerewors* at a *braai*.' He let his stub slide down the bottle's neck and stood up. Shakily. 'Do you get my point now?'

'More or less,' Tony lied. 'But what do you want to do about it?'

'Nothing,' Khumalo said, walking to the door. 'I just want my slice of the cake.' He banged his knee on a side table, but swayed on. 'You don't have to be a genius to figure out how much one of your horns is worth, Tony. Let alone two.' He opened the door a chink, looked each way, bent over and straightened up again, moaning and groaning, with a tray in his hands, on which he'd already placed one of the bottles of wine. 'You are my cut, my futures portfolio,' he said, walking with exaggerated caution and missing the side table this time. The bottle wobbled. 'You're my long shot.'

'Your long shot at what?' Tony asked, looking at Khumalo as if he were an assailant coming at him with a flamethrower instead of a tray.

'My last chance to start over,' Khumalo said, deadly serious. 'The pension I deserve.' He carefully put the tray down on the coffee table. The sandwiches were proper triple-deckers, with turkey and ham, tomato and cos lettuce, a handful of crudités and a generous pile of French fries. Khumalo picked up the cork-screw from the tray and studied the bottle's label over the top of his glasses. 'Did those bastards bring us French crap anyway?' he muttered. 'Puligny Montrachet.' He shrugged and screwed in the opener without removing the cap. The cork popped; Khumalo poured each of them a considerable glass and sat down again. 'Bon appétit.'

Tony neither ate nor drank. He watched Khumalo squeeze out two plastic sachets of ketchup onto his portion of fries.

'You're my redeemer, in a way of speaking, Tony,' Khumalo said, licking his fingertips, one by one. 'Do you realize what that implies?' He took a bite of his triple-decker sandwich, his mouth wide open. 'A saviour,' he said as he chewed, pushing his glasses back up again with his wrist, 'runs the risk of having to suffer. Don't look so sheepish. You worked at a bank. I invested in this journey, so I have the right to a return.' He took a second bite.

'I beg of you,' Tony said quietly. 'I don't have anything to do with this. You're mistaking me for somebody else.'

'We both know that that's a lie,' Khumalo said.

'Don't do something you'll later regret.'

'What did you say?' Khumalo asked. 'I can't understand you.'

Tony said it again. A little louder.

'My regret will depend on you,' Khumalo said, with a shrug. 'You decide what's going to happen here. But I'll tell you one thing.' He rubbed his mouth with the serviette he'd pulled out from between the charger and the plate with the sandwich. 'You can't handle pain. You might think you can; I don't know. I do know what pain is, you see. I've had to experience it myself. I thought I'd be strong enough, too. Could take a few hours. Since then I've suffered every day. Pain is my guide dog. Pain is my best friend. I get up with him, we go to the café together, we come to blows, and still I wake up next to him again in the morning.' Again, that giggle. It was sounding more and more desperate. Sometimes it was more like a sob.

'My friend brings his own friends with him, too. Mr. Painkillers, Mr. Alcohol. The first gives you ulcers, the second gets you divorced. The two together give you a persecution complex.' He took another bite. 'Why should I saddle a fellow human being with a group of friends like that?' He chewed. 'Get it, Tony?' He stopped talking.

'I get it,' Tony muttered, after a long silence. 'I get your point.' He stood up. He was unsteady on his feet, too, though not from the alcohol.

Khumalo didn't stop him this time. He poured himself more wine and munched his way through the rest of his sandwich.

Tony sat down again with Mrs. Bo Xiang's Louis Vuitton on his lap.

Khumalo looked at the bag. 'Nice piece of kit,' he sniffed. 'From the market around the corner, too?'

Without answering, Tony opened the bag and placed the fourteen bankrolls on the coffee table.

Khumalo stopped chewing. He wiped his hands, took the elastic band off one of the rolls, fanned out the notes, and whistled between his teeth. 'You've got this lying around for all the world to see?' he asked. His face betrayed neither happiness nor surprise. He held up one of the notes to the light.

'It's all for you,' Tony muttered.

'Great,' Khumalo nodded. 'This looks like more than enough.'

'Really?' Tony asked. Again, that glimmer of hope, the most deceptive of all remedies.

'Sure,' Khumalo said, twisting the elastic band back around the roll. 'His daughter will be able to survive for years on this.'

'Daughter? Whose daughter?' Tony asked. The ground was sinking away beneath his feet.

Khumalo pointed at the inside pocket containing the photos of the dead man. 'His crippled daughter. The girl he'd been trying to take care of since she was born. The father was an asshole, of course, he never should have helped you, he deserved to be punished. But whether he deserved to die? In such an inhumane manner?' He picked up his glass again. 'That child shouldn't have to suffer for it. That wouldn't be fair.'

'All right,' Tony said, after a long silence. 'It's for his daughter. So be it. Everything's sorted.'

'I don't think so,' Khumalo said. He squeezed out the remaining sachets of ketchup, this time onto Tony's fries. He'd finished his own. 'What about me?'

Tony couldn't think of an answer.

'You're not the first person Mister Bo Xiang has sent over to kill a rhinoceros,' Khumalo said. 'Mister Bo Xiang seems to be a history fan, too. Ancient history. The Greeks, the Romans, the Huns. Always the same tune. It's even in the Bible.' He began to eat Tony's fries. 'A powerful person saddles a hero with an impossible task. Either he comes to grief, or he outdoes himself. Jason and Hercules, to name just two. Didn't they teach you that at school?'

'Of course they did,' Tony said, 'it goes without saying.' He didn't want to touch his fries anymore. He drank more to compensate.

'Not me,' Khumalo mused. 'I had to teach it all to myself when I was long past being a kid anymore.' His thoughts seemed to drift for a moment, but then he pulled himself together again. 'A classical mission like that always came with a major reward: cattle, a golden fleece, a golden girdle, a passionate wedding night. But the real benefits came afterwards.' He took the bottle and emptied the last drabs into Tony's glass.

'Mister Bo Xiang puts his close employees to the test before he tells them the secrets of his imperium. The higher the position, the tougher the challenge. The crueller the challenge, the closer their relationship.' He stood up and staggered back to the door. 'You're at the start of a spectacular collaboration. Am I mistaken?'

'I hope not,' Tony muttered. 'I fervently hope that Mister Bo Xiang hasn't forgotten about me.'

Khumalo returned, holding the rest of the bottles in his arms like young pups. 'You mustn't see me as a beggar holding out my hands to you, Tony. That time has gone. The Kaffir is dead. You need to see me as the first stockholder in your career. The stake isn't those horns, but what they represent for your future. You're going to throw me some large crumbs of that cake.' Again, he popped the cork without removing the cap. It looked like it had exploded from the inside. 'Call it redistribution, Tony. Call it warrants, call it Black Economic Empowerment, call it what you like. But I have a right to it.' He filled two glasses up to the rim.

'How am I supposed to cough up those crumbs?' Tony asked. The alcohol wasn't helping to shake off his fears. He saw spots. 'I just gave you all the money I have. You're giving it to the crippled daughter of a man neither of us know from Adam. Is that justice, too?'

'That's Ubuntu,' Khumalo chuckled. 'Black humanism. You don't understand a thing about that. And it doesn't change anything. You still owe me.'

'But why?' Tony asked, barely audible.

'I've been your bitch for the past few days,' Khumalo explained. 'I've cleaned up all traces of your ass. The axe seller's written statement. The written statement from the airline staff in Maputo. The passenger list for your flight. I've put everything into a file. You can make that file disappear.'

'How?' Tony asked. He knew what was coming next. He didn't want to hear it.

'Don't tell me,' Khumalo began, 'that you don't have a secret stash on some tropical island. I've read your file, the amounts were staggering. I know your tricks. One phone call and a few code words, and the case is closed. Do it. I'm not the bad guy. Believe me, Tony. Violence isn't my thing. Here! I'll even get rid of this toy gun.' Khumalo tossed the fake weapon into a corner of the room. 'Make that phone call. I don't need to have *everything*.

We'll figure out a fair deal.' He smiled. 'Come on! Where is it, man? The Cook Islands? Cyprus? Tell me. Jersey? The Bahamas?' He leaned towards Tony as if he were a friend. 'Just say yes. Just say yes to the bitch who has gone through fire and water for you.'

And Tony said yes, no longer clear-headed, his spirit broken by fear. The man who had sworn that he'd never give up his secret even under torture, now gave it up before he was even touched. He broke because he knew he would break.

He made a couple of calls with his smartphone, obeying Khumalo's orders. Numbers, codes, passwords: Tony had everything memorized, he reeled it all off like a good boy. What should have been the nest egg for his old age became ransom money for a murder he hadn't committed.

But because there was a half-day's time difference between China and the Bahamas, Tony's trial would last longer than he'd hoped. Much longer than when he'd stood waiting in Mrs. Mercedes's *casa de turistas* with the late Mrs. Bo Xiang until the fiat from the Virgin Islands arrived.

And during those long hours, wiled away in the heart of a Chinese megalopolis, neither tiredness nor alcohol could stop Khumalo from talking at length. During which time, the inspector—partly to kill time, partly in an attempt to justify himself—told the story of his childhood and the twists and turns of his adult life in their full, technicolour glory.

And although the inspector had begun his encounter with Tony in a threatening and sullen manner, as the light faded and it became a balmy evening, his tone became ever milder. Finally—no less drunk than his hostage—Khumalo even began to excuse himself for what he was doing to Tony.

By the time the redeeming phone call came from the Bahamas at dawn, the inspector had even started feeling that the seed of that wonderful, powerful medicine called friendship had been planted between him and Tony. Because somebody had finally wanted to sit down and listen to his unpleasant life story for hours on end, in silence and with apparent approval.

He, Vusi Khumalo. Freedom fighter, a man betrayed by his comrades.

2. Southern Africa (1980s and later)

'IN THE BIBLE, TONY, IT WAS PAUL God struck by lightning from his horse. I was struck by a BMW. Not by the car as such—blinding-white with pimped-up wheels and tinted windows. It was an inscription that baffled me and made me see things differently. It ran along both sides of the two doors, in the battle colours of the party I've been a member of since my youth.

I still support our fight. But the party's no longer my own.

'I already knew how to play chess when I ended up in prison the first time. Reading is what I learned there. Strategy and geography, too. And English, even some Shakespeare—*Julius Caesar*? The play was popular with our government. "Cowards die many time before their deaths / The valiant never taste of death but once." I knew those kinds of verses off by heart.

In jail, I learned to calculate, in both senses of the word. But to argue or debate? Never. I got angry, even when it was just a practice exercise. Sparring as a boxer? No problem. Role play in a debate? After ten minutes, I'd be boxing again; it would just come over me. No one wanted to debate with me after a while. It made me fall behind even more. I realized that, but I couldn't do anything to change it. I could have gone much further in life, perhaps even got as far as parliament or the government, like so many others who'd learned everything they knew in the can.

If only I'd learned to control myself.

'The guy who sold me my first party card told me that. He didn't actually sell it—I didn't have any money—he gave it to me. Not out of compassion. He recognized talent when he saw it. But he also said, 'Vusi, restrain yourself. If you can't curb your temper, you won't be able to be a leader. And what's a movement without leaders? A tragedy.'

He was right. About our movement and about me. I was arrested unnecessarily, that was the start. The thing is, back then, I was already too stupid and conceited to keep my mouth shut. I was even too arrogant to run away.

They'd liked what I said, since it was smart, and quick. Our cops weren't used to that. Certainly back then. Can you picture them, Tony? Oom Koos? Oom Piet? Uncle Koos and Uncle Piet. Clumsy, uniformed Boers. They had the flat noses and broad shoulders of retired rugby players. They'd dry off their fat, red necks with white handkerchiefs about half the size of a tea towel. They'd scratch behind their cauliflower ears, straighten their caps, and curse at each other in that guttural equine language of theirs. They were disgruntled. Their whole unit was disgruntled. We're talking the early eighties. In front of them, a Bantu school up in flames. The smoke's rising, the traffic's at a standstill, and a group of troublemakers is standing there, celebrating provocatively.

One of them, a black kid, doesn't try to run. Not even when protesters start throwing sticks and stones. Not even after the Boers have responded with tear gas and rubber bullets. The little brat even stays standing there on his own when Oom Koos and Oom Piet decide they may as well charge with their truncheons and *sjamboks*. Do you know what that is, Tony? A *sjambok*? It's a whip made of hippo skin. Indestructible. Those creatures spend their entire lives swimming around in dirty water and their own shit. Their hides are made for that.

The first men didn't even hit me. They stormed past, chasing the runaways. Amazingly quick, as though they wanted to score a touchdown, despite their weight. The fifth was on target. I didn't even duck, thank God, otherwise he'd have hit my face, and then

I might have lost an eye, or my nose. The only thing that broke was my collarbone.

I'd told myself I wouldn't feel any pain because I didn't want to feel any. It wasn't until they'd finished with me, a couple of hours later, in the can, that I stopped feeling anything anymore. I'd passed out. I hadn't been able to keep my mouth shut there, either, broken collarbone or not. It was my first encounter with Oom Torture and Oom Pain. My new best buddies. My chess club from hell.

'I've got my father to thank for my big mouth. Not directly from him, but because he wasn't around. That's what my mom said. She often said it. She never told who he was, my dad, whether he was still alive, or whether he knew I existed.

I fantasized that he worked in the gold mines on the Witwatersrand, as a foreman, and that we never got to see him because the Boers didn't want to give me and my mom passes to go visit him, not even for a weekend. And he couldn't travel, either; he wasn't allowed to leave the mining compound because he was too dangerous. A rebel—that's the character I thought up for him. A hero in the making. Until I heard a local woman in our township mouthing off that he was an imbecile drunkard who'd raped my mom and fled. And that my mom had enjoyed it. The bitch of a neighbour said that, too. I beat up her two children for it, without the poor sods knowing why. I was big and strong for my age. They didn't have a dad, either, by the way. Theirs had died of poisoning. Too much meths; beer was expensive for him.

I'd rather have a father who wasn't there.

'I tried to make up for the loss with my big mouth. "You didn't cry," my mom always said. "You rolled out of my body swearing, and you've never stopped." I reminded her of him. She said that, too. On the rare occasion. I couldn't tell from her face whether the confession made her happy or not.

In any case, I began to berate her. I was furious with her. I was the only thing left of my dad, and she was the only person who could recognize it. I hurled the cruellest insults at her. I shouted that I'd have walked away from her, too, after a single crappy screw. That I'd start drinking, too, if I'd had to go to bed with her—a flabby cow who stank of sweat and beer and pap. In the beginning, she still hit me. Later she gave up. Definitely when I began to hit back.

God, if I think back to that, Tony. To my early teenaged years and my plump mother. It makes me feel terrible. Then I need another pill, not just for the scars on my back and the soles of my feet. Why did I berate that poor woman so much? Why didn't I support her? Why didn't anybody support her? The biggest scandal of our continent is the fate of our women.

Not that I did things any better myself, later on. I've been married three times, and I treated all three of my wives scandalously. I cheated on them, I threw a ton of shit at them, I hit one of them regularly, and I left each of them before she could leave me. I'm not proud of it. Yet I'd been planning to do it all so much better. Better than the other guys, better than my father. But, by then, I'd already got to know my bosom buddies, my chess club. Oom Torture. Oom Insomnia. They lay between me and every woman.

I didn't marry a fourth time. I could have done. Pamela. She was pretty and clever enough. She understood me, she consoled me, she was going to give me a new life. I called it quits as her fiancé before I could let her down as her husband.

'When I came out of prison the first time, still reeling from all the beatings, my collarbone barely healed—I was 13 at the most, maybe 14—I couldn't find our shack in the township. There was another one in its place. I recognized one of the corrugated sheets they'd used as a wall. My name was scratched into it. "That's our sheet," I shouted, my fists already balled. "Where's the rest? Where's my mom?"

She was dead, the few who dared to talk told me. They couldn't show me a grave. She'd died in her sleep, and after that, she'd been taken off and buried like a dog by the authorities, others said. After that, our shack had been plundered and set on fire. Everybody said that.

My first suspects were the two children of the gossiping neighbour. I beat them up again. They still swore they didn't know anything. I kept on kicking. It wasn't until later that I heard that my mother had moved of her own accord. That she'd had an accident on her way to her home village in the Eastern Cape. In a ten-seater taxi bus with sixteen passengers and four bald tyres. Missed the bend. It can happen. Still does. They buried her along the roadside, not even in her village. There was something wrong with her ID, or there wasn't enough money for the rest of the journey—who's to say? And what does it matter? She was dead; I was on my own.

That's why I picked a new family. There were tens of thousands of us. My party. She gave me more than anyone else. And not only me. To this very day. Whatever our opponents' lies or rumours suggest.

'The early years were the best. For me, that is. Despite everything. Our Struggle was simple and justified. We had to break free from our chains; after that, everything would get better.

The fight against myself was more complicated. Confusion— that was what I remember best. Not fear, not pride, not hope. They were present, too, in abundance. My insecurity was greater. I hid it behind my toughness, behind my bravado. Nobody sang and danced and chanted as loudly, and with as much conviction, as I did. And always in the front row. It landed me in prison more than once. No problem. I got my education there; my teachers were comrades. I'll be grateful to them to the day I die.

But what they had me do outside? Outside in a reality without bars? That was sometimes the opposite of the ideals they'd stamped into me. I didn't protest. I was proud of their trust in me, and I was the dream recruit. I was alone in the world, I was a big fella; it didn't take much to keep me happy, and when I was angry, I wasn't afraid of anything or anybody. Aside from that, I was happy with every pat on the shoulder, every friendly word, every shared cigarette. The perfect soldier.

I felt omnipotent. My duty was purposeful; the dead and wounded were unavoidable. *We* hadn't chosen violence. It had been forced upon us—all other measures were exhausted. But the terrible thing about violence, Tony, is that it's a cockroach. There's no other creature or plant that continues to reproduce so obsessively, in every chink, in every hole. You see one of them and you know there'll be a hundred more. I began as a guard and a courier. Four months later, I was already fighting in the frontline states. Again, in the front row. A dirty war, like every war. As old as the hills, as old as the sun. We already talked about Jason and Hercules; in Namibia and Rhodesia, I thought about Troy more than once. One of the Boers, there? His name was Eugene de Kock. Does that mean anything to you Tony? No! That's quite curious, don't you think? We have to know so much about you, and you so little about us. Perhaps that's the essence of all supremacy. The people on the bottom need to spend their whole lives playing catch-up. The people on the top can remain indifferent to everything. They don't even realize they are indulging their right to indifference. That's power.

Eugene de Kock, a quiet boy in his youth, was refused entry

into the South African Defence Force. It was because he stuttered at his army interview, psychologists said afterward. It's possible. The Boers have a really close relationship with their language. Eugene wanted to fight, anyway. He could already see himself as an officer. His father, a member of the Afrikaner Broederbond, had drummed that into him. You're going to be an officer! And now his son couldn't even be a first-class soldier because of a speech defect? They put him in charge of a secret death squad. One of the many. His would become legendary.

I saw one of his Herculean jobs with my own eyes. He had captured four of our comrades. He broke a few of their bones, then he bound them to the hood of his Casspir. Casspirs were the armoured vehicles his foot soldiers marched along behind into the bush, armed to the teeth. They were hunting us: the Communists, the heretics, the dignified blacks. Kaffirs. Their word for us comes from the Koran. Kaffir, faithless, infidel. Brought over by Malaysian slaves, adopted by descendants of the Dutch. They couldn't even be bothered to come up with a name for us, preferring to steal one from those half-Arabs.

If you see one of those armoured cars coming at you, Tony, with its human shell? And one of your pals, screaming and bleeding, pulling at his ropes? Screaming in pain with each tug because his arms and legs are broken? We shot them dead ourselves, from a distance. Even the ones who weren't begging for it. To spare them even more misery.

Each one of us knew—if you ever had to lie on the hood of a Casspir yourself, like a lamb to the slaughter? You'd be shot by your best buddy. I pulled the trigger myself. *Ja*, I still had mates back then. Or what could pass for them. When you're fighting, anyone standing next to you is a buddy. When the battle's over, you never want to see them again. Not all memories do you good.

'I won't say that the barbarity on our side was any less. No one who has fought on that kind of front can say that. More guerrilla warfare than field battle.

The Boers knew all about it. It was the way they'd had to fight the Brits themselves, once upon a time. Commandos, still riding horses, back then. Sometimes I got the impression that they blamed us. That they were offended, the Boers, because we dared use the same tactics against them that they'd used against their oppressors. Those English bastards hadn't shown us their best side, by the way. Concentration camps? We invented them. The Brits against the Boers, white against white. Try reading a few books about that, sometime. Tens of thousands of women and children corralled behind barbed-wire fences, their farms burning in the distance, plumes of smoke on the horizon. And the people—those women, children, newborns, too—starving, dehydrated, struck down by sicknesses. I won't defend the Boers, but if you realize what happened to them? Oppression is a wheel. Anyone flattened by it rolls over others the next day with even more determination. The most dangerous perpetrator is a victim.

That's probably the reason things didn't always end cleanly on our side. I can be honest about it. I'm even a victim of it myself. At a certain point, I was accused of being a traitor. Life can't get much worse than that. Umkhonto we Sizwe, that's the name of the armed wing of my party. The Spear of the Nation. I felt it, the spear of our nation. And not just in my back.

We had a rat among our ranks, or perhaps the Boers had better espionage techniques—they had America's support, and then the Brits again, and Israel. Who did we have? The Russians and the Cubans. It was already *blerrie* fantastic if their torches lasted longer than a year. Except their machine guns—they were genius. The AK-47? That's a pure Communist weapon, Tony. It shoots every kind of munition, without prejudice. After a while, you got the feeling you could put cherry pits in your AK-47 and it would still spit out death and destruction.

I digress. Probably because I don't like to talk about the darkest hours in my life. We were under fire every day that week. We walked from ambush to ambush; we were shelled with great precision. Our communications were intercepted, everyone was convinced of that.

And, all of a sudden, I was the rat.

'I don't know who had decided that, or what evidence they thought they had. They said that one of the sacrificial lambs on the hood of one of those Casspirs had begun to shout out that he'd been betrayed, and I'd killed him before he could finish his story. In those days, it was all fate needed: suspicion, and a tall story as evidence.

I can no longer remember how long it lasted, or what they actually did to me. My skin can tell part of the story, if I show you the scars on my back, the soles of my feet, my chest, my groin. My nightmares tell the rest. The blackest part. There's no pill that can deal with that, no herbal tea, no flattened salamanders.

I was half-dead when they discovered the real rat. Since then, that dumb sucker's been featuring in my nightmares, too. Every night his arms are tied behind his back again, he kneels down, there's a tyre full of gasoline around his neck. He begs and prays, and yet every time someone throws a lit match.

Being allowed to watch his execution was supposed to be some kind of consolation. They said. I've always thought it was a final warning. That's the worst thing about betrayal, it always sticks to you. Napalm is nothing, in comparison. The suspicion of guilt surrounds you like body odour; everyone turns up their nose. I don't even think it's about long-term mistrust. It's more shame about what people inflicted on you. Deep inside, they hoped you were the rat people took you for. It would lessen the remorse. Actually, there were enough people who did become rats after being tortured wrongly. If you tell someone often enough that he's no good, he can end up behaving that way.

I didn't. Never. I thought what they did to me horrible and unjust, but I accepted it. Tragedies occur in times of war; that's what I told myself every day. The Struggle was so much greater and more important than my personal doom and gloom. I was still alive, many weren't—why complain? No one put it into my head. I convinced myself. I could even understand, however painful it was, why after my interrogation, I was never fully trusted again. When I entered a room, there was whispering, or people stopped talking, or laughed too loudly at silly things. I didn't get to hear any real information. I was glad. If you don't know anything, they can't take you for a rat. And I had time to read a lot.

But without much knowledge, I kept being passed over for promotions or transfers. People asked for my opinion less and less often. Until they ended up assuming that I didn't have an opinion.

I made peace with that, too. I was an insignificant part of the organization. As long as we won, at some point.

'And we did win, Tony. Right until the end, helped on by my nightmares, I thought it would go wrong. I thought we were being tricked; I thought they'd lie in wait for us with new death squads, with heavier weapons. That they'd draw us out of our safe havens, supposedly to negotiate peace, while planning to exterminate us for once and for all. During those years of transition, there was a suspicious amount of robberies. Raids on trains and taxi buses, attacks and the settling of accounts, violence for violence's sake. Much of that was orchestrated by a state within the state, I'm sure of that. An old crocodile pretends to be dead but launches its deadly attack as soon as you've got close enough.

That was why I was against those negotiations. I had shored up much too much anger and pain to believe in a future without civil war. I wasn't even sure I'd want a future like that.

Then that day came, Tony, and I had to believe it. And I can only say one thing. I wish everyone a day like that in their lives. Just one day like that. To know and to feel that you can be free. That your life hasn't been for nothing.

I was in Cape Town on the Parade, the central square near the station. The station crowds had been emerging for hours, singing, chanting, wishing one another luck. Tens of thousands of them. The singing and the sound of stamping feet rolled through the mother city, across the entire city bowl, between Lion's Head and Devil's Peak, along the flanks of Table Mountain, and then back down again, back to the Parade. An endless wave of triumph. It was shortly after our first democratic elections.

On the balcony of our former colonial town hall—later the library I knew so well; it was where I would borrow Count Tolstoy and Chinua Achebe's masterpieces—on that balcony, a celebrated poet appeared. He had bare feet and was wearing ridiculous traditional animal skins. But he also recited wonderful verses in an impressive, gravelly voice from times gone by, times when poets didn't need books to be poets. Shakespeare couldn't have done any better. After that, there was our archbishop. Our divine dwarf clown in his own kind of traditional smock, a purple tent with sleeves—he even had that wacky purple yarmulke on his head. I don't know any other word for it: a yarmulke, even though he was an Anglican. He began his own celebratory poem, his own 'Song of Songs,' with his crooked nose and Popeye eyes, his infectious laugh, his squeaky voice, his windmilling arms, "We're free! We're free at last!"

Then he came out: Madiba, our leader, our father, our Nelson. Wearing a modest suit, his old. grey, mobile face, and his voice, dry as cork, dead-boring, if you like. But when he began to give his speech? For the first time as our elected president?

All of the choruses fell silent. Tens of thousands of mouths zippered; the wave that had rolled through the city bowl calmed. And in that superhuman silence, you didn't only hear his voice, you could hear the earth turning. I swear it, Tony. I don't believe in God, not since my trials in Rhodesia, and I've long given up on mankind. But I swear to you that I could hear the earth turning that day when Mandela spoke. The mountains around the city bowl held their breath; the two oceans embracing the Cape Peninsula in their arms rocked us gently back and forth to the beating of our communal heart. Is there any wine left? Have some yourself, too. Here's to Madiba! To *his* trials. To his strength. *Amandla! Viva!*

Though he's just a human being, really. Even he has faults. He sold us too short. That's what I think. He was so tolerant that, amongst the Boers and far further afield, he has become the most popular black man in history. That's how a whitey likes his Bantus: moderate and civilized, and without too many thoughts of revenge. For anyone other than Mandela, I would never have come to terms with a reconciliation. He made it possible. I don't regret it, either. It's worth it. There's no man who ever walked the earth I admire more. Although I've never understood how such a great man could deliver such boring and yet such awe-inspiring speeches.

Eish! You should have been there, Tony! On the Parade. What a crowd, what an atmosphere, what a day!

'At the same time you realized, then and there, that there would never be a day like that again. On the contrary. There comes another day, years later, when lightning strikes you off your horse. Because you realize that your own life is too short, as is that of your imaginary children or your children's children, to ever experience things being completely settled. Liberators aren't necessarily managers. That's putting it mildly. And a government without managers? That's not even a tragedy, it's a catastrophe.

I don't like to say it. There are so many—certainly among the cowards who emigrated, and among the bastards who supported the Boers to the end—who say that nothing has changed for the better in our country. That, on the contrary, everything is falling apart, as it did in Sierra Leone and Zimbabwe. I'd like to grab those losers by the throat. I'd drag them to the township where my mother's shack stood, to the village where she was born and where she should have been buried. I'd rub their noses in it—those hundreds of thousands of houses that have been built, and which do have plumbing, however basic. I'd like to kick them along the roads that have been built. I'd like to whip them into the court buildings, into the neighbourhoods where there was once only impunity. I'd like to show them the playgrounds—even an outdoor swimming pool—in places where children used to play football on a rubbish dump. In the library of our brand-new Constitutional Court in Jo'burg, I'd like to compare the growth figures of our economy to the crisis tables of the countries they have fled to, their tails between their legs. Countries where they, the deserters, still sit complaining, longing for the swimming pools of yesteryear, for their status as chosen ones, their dirt-cheap cleaning women, their daily G&Ts, their fat, lazy *braais* at reasonable prices. Oh, let them rot in London's pouring rain, our bitter expats. Let them be crushed by boredom in that *fokken* Australia of theirs!

The unfortunate thing, Tony, is that they could grab me by the scruff of my neck. They could drag me to many townships where crime has the upper hand. Where the hopelessness never gets stamped out. Forgive me for not sketching a more detailed picture. It's cowardly, but it's too painful for me. How could we have failed so badly?

I can forgive people who make mistakes due to incompetence. What's a person supposed to do, after liberation, with all his liberators? They all demand jobs. Rewards for the past are considered more important than competence in the present. It's all very human and very understandable. But you don't make post-war peace with it. As a result, there are hundreds of thousands of houses that didn't get built. While the bricks and the mortar and the toilet bowls lie waiting. Unfortunately, each of them at a different location. Sometimes I wonder how our Struggle ever came to a successful conclusion with so many bunglers in the ranks. I'm not even allowed to bang the drum. At the end of the day, they pitchforked me into being the successor to Oom Koos and Oom Piet. I had no experience. But I wasn't fit for anything else.

I do realize what I'm not fit for. And I've never lined my pockets, which is not something we can say about our new rats. The real debacle? Our upwardly mobile comrades who gladly feather their nests as though they were the new colonizers. A handful of rodents like that is enough to make a new building sag. And there are more than a handful.

The rat who tortured me in Rhodesia? He was one of the founders of the Spear of our Nation. A consummate villain, but the Struggle washed clean all names, reputations, criminal records. All of a sudden, he was praised for the heavy hand he'd been so feared for when he was a truck driver and a smuggler. There are people who say that, without him, our country would never have been freed. There are people who say that, due to him, our country has never really been freed. He never made his excuses to me personally. I doubt he remembers me.

He became Minister of Defence. There have been court cases running against him for years. He has been accused of large-scale corruption in arms supplies. The gangster turned into a gangster again, the war just a means to an end, a temporary whitewashing operation. Not all of the cases against him ran their full course. There were too many other big names involved. That doesn't help deliver fast justice.

And that, too, is a story as old as the sun.

'For a long time I didn't want it to concern me. I remained blind. I defended the party leadership through thick and thin. You can find rotten apples everywhere! I said that kind of thing, against my better judgement. I downplayed their pompous country houses, their car parks full of the most expensive Toyotas and SUVs, their escapades paid for by the state, diverting resources from the needy. I dismissed revealing reportages as slander, as the frustrations of whiteys, liberals, and political opponents. One of our youth leaders threw a party with bunny girls and hard liquor, using government money. He and his friends snorted coke from the belly buttons of one another's girlfriends. They ate sushi without using their hands, off the stomach and buttocks of a well-paid striptease artist.

I laughed off the revelations. We were all young, once. Wild oats, great leaders! I swallowed it all.

Until I found myself standing face to face with that blinding-white BMW.

Our party was celebrating its anniversary in a stadium in Jo'burg. Part of the security detail ended up falling on my shoulders: parking. A chair between the vehicles—that was my place during our great knees-up.

The men I'd been in prison with—my teachers? The women I'd tried to seduce at the congresses in my early years? The buddies who'd stood by my side in Namibia and Zim? They were all sitting on the tribunes, and I was watching their cars. I was on my own, and they were sitting next to people remaining silent and people laughing loudly and people who were ashamed and could no longer look me in the eye after my torture.

Some of them were even standing on the field in the witches' coven of power, the golden circle around the centre spot, the celebration's midpoint. I could watch the party's progress in that packed, churning stadium above me, on a black-and-white monitor. A giant cake was wheeled out, straight to the centre spot in the golden circle. A couple of hundred bottles of bubbly were produced and uncorked. In the middle of this badly organized farce, our former interim president—not even such a bad fella—grabbed the microphone to address the masses. The masses that were also standing outside the stadium, marvelling at the opulence on video screens. The masses, most of whom had received a free T-shirt, one of those rags produced somewhere around this Chinese city for next to nothing. And do you know what he said, Tony? The man who might even be our future president? With a cake server and a glass of champagne in his mitts? He apologized to the crowd for there not being enough cake and champagne for everyone. But we'll eat and drink on your behalf! He wasn't even booed. It was swallowed up by the sounds of the party. *We'll eat and drink on your behalf!*

I turned my face away in disgust. Then I saw it, there. As white as a new refrigerator. On both of its flanks, in yellow, green, and black, the name and logo of my party. Under that, a double slogan. One hundred years of emancipation! Free at last!

I went home without saying anything. They even sanctioned me later. An act of vandalism had been committed. On just one car. Its rear-view mirrors kicked off, headlights smashed, windscreen wipers bent, tyres stabbed. The culprit was never found. The security camera was broken, or had been sabotaged—they never found out which. It was the Limpopo county statesman's car. He didn't find it funny. He'd only had the BMW for a month. I was transferred to the lousiest departments. First, narcotics. After that, big-game poaching. Elephants and rhinoceroses. You can guess the next bit, Tony. The next bit brought me here to you.

'There is one thing I'd like to stress. I'm not like them. Those overfed rats of the present. All right, partly I am, of course. I'm not mad; I'm not blind. It's not completely legal, what I'm doing here.

But I don't harm anybody. Get it? I don't take anything from my countrymen. On the contrary, I'm helping somebody. That little girl. Her father is dead: that fact can't be changed, that crook got what he deserved. But a child shouldn't pay for the sins of its parents. I'll underwrite her future. Right away. You can't trust any donations to a foreign charity.

That's the long and short of it. That child justifies everything. That rhino? No one can bring it back to life. The two horns? If I take them back, they'll be destroyed. So we're better off selling them to the Chinese. Peanuts to them, a lifeboat to others. Thanks to my actions, some of that blood money will flow back to my home country. Is that so wrong?

I understand you're not jumping for joy. But your kind can easily survive this sort of temporary drain on your resources. That's the essence of your privileges. A setback is never fatal to you. The higher up you are, the bigger the safety nets. Life doesn't ever change for people like you.

'This is the only thing that will be different. Your sinister tracks will be erased. It will be as if you never set foot in that game reserve. As though you never bought an axe, as though you never hacked a person down, never even took an airplane from Maputo. Yet another setback neutralized! If you look at it that way, you can count your blessings.

In exchange for all of that, I'm asking for just a trifle in return. A well-deserved retirement, without having to take a rand from my country. I won't apply for my official pension. I don't want another cent from those rats at the top. Why should I? I've got you. What you're giving me is more like a bonus than anything negative. You're saving a country with hundreds of thousands of destitute people at least one pension. Look at it that way, and then tell me—what's so wrong with that?

I still have fifteen, maybe twenty years to go. I'll manage that easily, despite my many pills and the bills for the drink. I live alone, I've already got a car, I don't need slogans anymore. I just want to be able to buy books. About human nature. I want to be able to read them on my own. Chewing over my disappointment.

Without ever having to hunt down a poacher again.'

* * *

'THERE'S JUST ONE THING I have to warn you about,' Khumalo said. He was already standing at the door. His voice sounded shaky, and he was rather unsteady on his legs, too. Drink and tiredness were taking their toll. He wanted to use the tip of his index finger to push his glasses back up. It took two attempts. He looked at Tony with something like melancholy. The morning traffic jam was just building up outside, beneath a cautious sun. The Pearl River gleamed, shattered glass in motion.

Tony said nothing. Furious, exhausted. He didn't care what presented itself at that moment: an earthquake, bodyguards, room service, Mr. Bo Xiang himself. They were all too late. He'd lost his nest egg. His secret, his lifeline, his plan B. It was as though he were standing there stripped naked.

'Watch out for that wife of yours,' Khumalo slurred, wagging a finger.

'Thanks for the warning,' Tony said. He was barely listening. He reached for the lock—the sooner this man was through the door, the better.

'I read your whole file,' Khumalo said, holding the door shut with one hand. He didn't look like he was going anywhere soon. 'That Martine of yours confirmed everything under oath. You abused her trust, she said. She wants a divorce. Is that bitch crazy or something? She's been getting it on with one of your bosses. For years. There are rats everywhere.'

Tony said nothing, closing his eyes in despair. What did he have to do to get the fellow to bugger off? He'd met all of his demands; he'd listened to his blathering for hours on end; he'd drunk all the available bottles with him. What more could he want?

'Is that little girl even your daughter?' Khumalo asked. His bottom lip quivered. 'Never let that child down.'

Tony opened his eyes. He saw the situation with a disconcerting clarity. 'Inspector Khumalo?' he began, with a decisiveness he'd been lacking up to now. 'You've got what you came for. I wish you a safe journey back. And I hope I never, ever see you again.' He shoved the inspector aside and opened the door wide.

'You're right,' Khumalo sighed. He checked his packet of cigarettes. It was empty. 'I should go home.' Standing in the doorway, he turned around and grabbed Tony's hand. 'I wasn't planning on telling you this,' he whispered, 'but I find you a likeable son of a bitch.' He looked touched again.

'Thank you,' Tony said. He'd rather die than return the compliment. He couldn't wrench his hand free.

Khumalo pulled Tony closer. 'Get out of here as soon as you've sold the horns,' he said. 'There was a trial project running in Krokodilspruit. It went horribly wrong.'

'Why am I not surprised?' Tony asked, freeing his hand.

'To deter poachers, a fast-working poison was injected into the horns of six animals,' Khumalo whispered. 'Four of them died. The poison seeped out of the horns and into their bloodstream.' He stepped warily into the lift and said just one more thing as he took leave, his back to Tony. Slurred but intelligible.

'You took out one of the survivors.'

3. Guangzhou (eighty-first floor)

WE FIND TONY HANSSEN on the eighty-first floor of a skyscraper in the centre of Guangzhou, in the unvaryingly cool air-conditioned climate of an international hotel chain. He'd closed the outer curtains yesterday evening; the light seeping in around the edges reveals the dawning of a new day. The traffic is moving again, now, just audible at this height despite the double glazing.

Tony is sitting in an armchair with his trousers and pants around his ankles. The porn film he ordered with the remote control is drawing to an end, judging by the group orgy featuring actors from the previous scenes.

He is finding it hard to come.

Is jet lag the problem, or the Japanese actors? Trimming your pubic hair was not popular in the Land of the Rising Sun. Not even for the women. They were pale-skinned and delicately built, eternal schoolgirls with correspondingly modest bosoms. They showed off their mops like a bricklayer his tattoos. It was a question of taste.

It wasn't Tony's taste. It had been the same thing with the porn film he'd ordered earlier. He'd muted the sound then, too. From the cries, it seemed the Japanese were more into pain than pleasure in sex. The cacophony an approach like that must lend to an orgy was something Tony was happy to forego. He loathed group stuff, anyway. He focussed on the best-looking couple, pleased that the silence was disturbed only by his own familiar panting. But he didn't come.

Perhaps the problem was the reflection of himself that he saw in the widescreen, superimposed above all the activity. No longer the hardened, proud hunter he had driven along in front of himself on a motorway in the African night just a few days earlier, a hunter with a steering wheel in his hands. Here sat a piteous misery-guts, an asshole Tony didn't want to be, one he'd resist until his last breath. Only in the most intimate moments did he give the putz in himself free rein. So that's what the jerk looked like. Slumped limply, bared knees grotesquely spread, his fist pumping away without much enthusiasm, his face gradually illuminated with each close-up of naked buttocks on the screen. Sometimes you could make out the outlines of a luxury suite behind the bore.

Between Tony and the TV was a coffee table, on the carpet under it a plate with a used knife and fork, a dirty napkin, and gnawed spare ribs, a double portion. On top of the table were four beer cans, empty and squeezed in the middle. Next to them his pride and joy: the big horn and the smaller one.

They, too, were regularly lit up by the close-ups of copulating bodies.

Tony—the hunter, not the bore—had given the horns a first rudimentary clean just before crossing over the border into Mozambique. He'd used his last bottles of mineral water, his penknife, and his already soiled T-shirt for the purpose. When he'd finished, he'd torn the T-shirt and the rest of his safari outfit to pieces and left them behind in a rusty dustbin at the roadside. Petrol over it, lit match. He'd thrown the penknife out of the window a few kilometres further along, counting on an acquisitive finder. It was a completely unnecessary gesture, but he liked the pathos it inferred. In the rear-view mirror, he watched the red penknife bounce across the tarmac onto the verge, away from him.

There was a risk of one last, tense moment at the border, but his phone call to the Chinese embassy in Maputo had born fruit. A customs officer was waiting for him, just at the roadside, a couple of hundred metres before the barrier. Tony paid him for his tourist visa, the road tax, the compulsory temporary insurance—all of it at ten times the normal price. Nevertheless, it was peanuts compared to the value of his cargo.

He washed the horns for a second time in Maputo, in a hotel not far from the airport. He scraped the remaining bits of meat, blood, and dirt away with a broken glass from the minibar—patiently, carefully, ensuring not to damage the horns any further, particularly at the base. It had kept him busy for a while. In the meantime, Mr Bo Xiang's embassy man was arranging his flight. Tony's suitcase would pass over the border in Lourenço Marques Airport as diplomatic baggage, not checked by anyone. Tony had left the four-by-four on the Avenida Patrice Lumumba that morning, not far from the popular Museu de História Natural. Doors unlocked, key in the ignition, tank full of petrol. The gun and ammunition would be a gift for the sharp-eyed thief. It was guaranteed that the car and the gun would begin a new smuggling adventure the next day across the entire continent, as far as Dakar or Mogadishu. It would take a genius to ever put the pieces of that puzzle together. Let alone connect the start of both trails to a certain Tony Hanssen.

He'd washed the horns for a third time in Guangzhou—the first thing he'd done after the long flight, before even taking a shower himself. He used lukewarm water, no soap, no shampoo. By now he had grown fond of the texture of his horns, infatuated by their earthy smell, their surprising weight, their mere presence. Look at them! He had actually managed this on his own.

After the double wash—first the horns, then himself—he'd treated himself to both bottles of Veuve Clicquot from the minibar in the commode. He was relieved, glad he could catch his breath in this cocoon of crystal and wall-to-wall carpeting, before the hard work began. The world stage was calling. Soon, Tony Hanssen would be making a comeback.

Like it or lump it.

That had been days ago. Since then, his suspicions had been kindled and had flared up. He hadn't slept a wink the previous night. How long did Mr. Bo Xiang and his entourage mean to keep him hanging on? He hadn't heard anything more from them. It seemed like they regretted the fact he'd returned successful. Had it all been empty promises, cruel deception? He'd experienced enough of that himself over the past year: orientals liked to make a fool of occidentals. There was something retaliatory about it.

A kind of practical joke—had he been the victim of one? The thought was too awful to entertain. He'd murdered a man, mutilated a corpse, committed forgery, tricked and bribed civil servants. His lip hadn't healed yet, his neck hurt every time he moved, he could have broken it, or his jaw. He could have been shot by poachers, and if the police had caught him, he wouldn't have got off with just a year behind bars. In most countries you'd get life, in someone of them, a death sentence.

Barbaric joke or not, the game had gone on long enough. Tony was proud of his horns, but he had to get rid of them, the sooner the better. Not at any price, though. He wouldn't sell himself too short. He'd negotiate with Mr. Bo Xiang and his small army of assistants, daggers drawn, even though he was all alone. That last bit hurt, suddenly. Since he'd stamped his BlackBerry to death in Brussels Central Station, he hadn'd minded being a loner, an ant in a city of millions. Now he did, with negotiations up ahead. You were weaker on your own. One like-minded person was enough to reinforce your position, and to keep you on your toes if you were being conned.

But where could you find a committed ally on demand? An

associate with whom you could discuss fiscal strategies, put together escape routes—someone good at reading the small print in contracts? An old-time bore—someone like that would be useful. The real bore, the one on the trading floor who had compared Tony to a pigeon fancier, the loser who'd been fired shortly after that, and, like so many, had instantly disappeared off all the radars in the trade. He would have made an ideal sparring partner. Plenty of experience, few hobbies, no illusions anymore. What was his name again? Could he be dug up via Google or Facebook? On the other hand, how long would it take for someone to get here? Supposing he did say yes. Oh, forget it. Tony didn't need to have any illusions, either. He was alone. That was his power; that was his doom.

But where had they got to? Mr. Bo Xiang's lackeys with their demands?

Shortly after landing at Guangzhou Baiyun airport, Tony had been informed of possible complications. The creepy interpreter had called him while Tony was being escorted to the hotel by four bodyguards.

None of the colossuses had spoken English; all four were wearing sunglasses and monkey suits. Tony felt like a parcel-post package, so indifferently was he treated. They took his baggage out of his hands, though, surrounded him, and swiftly piloted him out of the noisy arrivals hall. But they looked around them with just as ridiculously surly expressions as, in a practically empty car park, they walked over to a sand-yellow Porsche Cayenne, Tony still in the middle. A film star on the Croisette in Cannes. But then, without any fans or journalists. Without anyone, in fact.

The four-person escort had given Tony a feeling of importance at the time, a confirmation of the grandeur of the test he'd brought to a happy conclusion. Now, a few days later, he saw in it a bad omen. Why hadn't the interpreter himself come to meet him? Why those colossuses? Was he a guest or a prisoner?

He'd been sitting on the back seat between two bodyguards when his iPhone had rung. A Porsche Cayenne might be known for its spacious interior, but Tony felt squashed, beset on either side by a wide ass and a gorilla's back. The colossuses looked outside, each through their own window, their torsos twisting— at other luxury cars, at motorcyclists screeching past, at walls and banners covered in Chinese characters, at businessmen in bespoke suits who unabashedly spat on the ground, at toothless beggars, at motorized rickshaws, at lethargic cyclists whose two-wheelers were hidden by constructions made of polystyrene transport crates, all of them empty, tied together with string, piled three metres high, leaning over, prey to gusts of wind. The Cayenne also passed numerous cranes, drills, and bulldozers. The racket outside must be furious.

Inside, music by Michael Jackson was playing. To please the important visitor, Tony guessed. He couldn't imagine the bodyguards being crazy about songs like 'The Girl Is Mine' or 'We Are the World'. He was happy when his iPhone rang. He got it out, gesturing with his free hand to the driver to turn off the music.

The man reduced the volume with apparent reluctance. For a Chinese who must have grown up under Mao Zedong's government, the interpreter's English was surprisingly good. He spoke French, too, he'd told Tony, but not very often. It reminded his boss of Cambodia and Vietnam, and investments that had been lost there, causing disastrous deficits. The interpreter had winked that his boss preferred to join forces with the Japanese these days. The remark must have contained a funny joke; the interpreter had almost choked on his laughter.

The interpreter confided in Tony quite often. Sometimes he declared, uninvited, that he liked Tony. Much more than others of your kind! He mentioned friendship. His smile was to be seen as proof. Bared nicotine teeth, some of them more black than brown.

Tony got the hint. He began to lionize the man even more than he had done previously. He regularly took the trouble to go on a night out with him, slinging back great quantities of brandy until early in the morning, usually ending up in a building with sixteen karaoke rooms, each for a maximum of ten songbirds. Most of the cubbyholes were occupied by couples.

In one of these rooms, Tony and the interpreter fraternally massacred an international repertoire of light music, slurred and blurted out in the light of a tatty television set. Tony threw half of the brandy under the table without the interpreter noticing. When the first whores showed up, he discreetly left the room, walking backward, blaming his religion with a show of regret. The interpreter never asked which religion it was. He nodded understandingly, allowed Tony to give him an intense handshake so he could accept the necessary banknotes without losing face. He immediately ordered a new bottle of brandy over the intercom, for himself and two of the harlots. As he exited, Tony saw, through the chink of the closing door, the three of them toasting and launching into a Whitney Houston number. He had to keep on the right side of this man. His direct line of access to Mr. Bo Xiang. The tyrant's right hand.

But even without such perks, the interpreter was strangely fond of Tony. 'You're one of us!' He said that more than once, even without any brandy going past his nicotine teeth. 'You're my brother. You're a Chinaman.'

The interpreter had sounded remote and dejected through the iPhone in the Cayenne. Not a trace of fraternity or friendship. Tony should have realized, there and then, that there was a hitch.

The creep had first passed on sincere congratulations, both from his boss and himself, but had gone on to beg Tony to understand that Mr. Bo Xiang wouldn't be able to meet him in person. A regrettable delay had occurred, something dramatic in the personal sphere—he would give Tony the details later in person. For the time being, Tony would be a guest in the pearl of Mr. Bo Xiang's consortium, the most expensive hotel in Guangzhou, which had a Cantonese top chef and a sommelier from Geneva. He could make his wishes and desires known to the reception, and they would be fulfilled immediately. The interpreter bid him a good day and asked him to be at the ready. As soon as the painful hold-up had been smoothed out, he would get in touch with Tony for a meeting with Mr. Bo Xiang, during which they'd get down to business immediately. Decisions with major consequences. He hung up before Tony could ask for more information.

A stony-faced Tony put away his iPhone; the driver turned up the volume immediately. 'Beat It'. Even louder than before.

The porno film had finished, the credits were playing, and Tony still hadn't come. It irritated him. He was used to getting what he wanted, come hell or high water. Were his nerves playing tricks on him? His negative forebodings?

Stop being so gloomy, he told himself as he switched off the television with the remote control. You weren't a navel-gazer before; don't start now. What kind of a threat could topple you now? After all you've managed to pull together, in darkest Africa, of all places! Maybe—he thought, reassuring himself—he was simply suffering from decompression after his overwhelming adventure. The erection that had so unexpectedly come upon him in Mpumalanga, well, it was surely taking its toll. He'd discovered the hunter in himself. The hunter longed for action. Real action. Life-and-death tension in a dangerous, grubby half-light. Not clumsy masturbation in an insufficiently darkened golden cage. He grinned. After Krokodilspruit, a man needed more stimulation than there was to be had from Japanese porn and canned beer.

He began to worry again immediately. How would that ever work when he returned home again shortly? How would his new yearning for extreme stimulation reconcile itself with his rather domestic, if not to say bourgeois, homesickness? His banal longing for a daughter and her mother? That homesickness and that longing weren't in any way lessened.

Certainly not now that their reunion was so close. All thanks to those two boys, there! His horns. His certificate, his access card, his trophies. He bent toward the table without pulling up his trousers or his underpants.

His horns! His valuable, fabulous horns. He held them like a nursing mother would hold twins, one in each arm. Their jagged bases rested in his crotch. His still half-inflated prick hung bashfully between them, shrinking pathetically.

These two, here—that was what it was about. They guaranteed his participation in the brand-new international consortium that he was going to help set up. Mr. Bo Xiang was putting up the initial capital and the staff; Tony was putting up his guts and his algorithmic talents. Thanks to these two boys, he'd definitely proved to the magnate that he was totally reliable, trustworthy to the core, afraid of nothing, prepared for anything. Thanks to his memory sticks, he also possessed enough knowledge of the loopholes to make a breakthrough on any competitor's playing field. If they were well employed, the sticks also offered opportunities to assert light pressure, without having to resort to downright blackmail.

Knowledge was something he'd always possessed, but his horns also gave him power. He'd dismiss the allegations with them; he'd hire the most expensive lawyer to clear his name for good; he'd reclaim his place amongst equals. He caressed them with his cheek, his two boys. Despite the washes, they still had their earthy, primitive smell and power. Might it be true? The thing he'd read on a lot of websites? That, contrary to scientific evidence, they did work as an aphrodisiac?

He grinned. Why not give it a go? If he still struggled to come after that …! You didn't find Viagra in your minibar—not even in this city. Why not chew on a bit of rhino horn? It didn't hurt to try.

And who would miss that one splinter out of more than—what was it? Ten kilos? Twelve? They were selling for three hundred thousand dollars a pair on the black market.

He investigated the smaller horn from close up. There were enough slight indentations and marks where you could easily scrape off a splinter with a knife without it being noticeable.

At the same time, he was growing hesitant again. The marks he came across didn't fuel his passion for experiment, but reminded him of the unfortunate animal's life. How, from a young age, it would have had to defend itself against God knows what animals and dangers in the bush. And how it was brought down all the same—ruthlessly, from a cowardly distance, it hadn't stood a chance. And the rhino calf that had got away—where was that now? Had anyone found it? Had other rhino cows been willing to look after it? There was more chance, Tony realized, that it was no longer alive. Such a sweet little baby.

His thoughts turned immediately to Klara. Not only because, to put it bluntly, she was his own offspring—an infant that he'd been forced to abandon. But mainly because he didn't know how he was ever going to admit to Klara what he'd done in that game reserve. Yet he'd done it to win her back. To be able to go home to her with his head held high, and give her the future a daughter of his had a right to. Aside from a computer-clever-clogs, Papa had also turned out to be a genuine hunter. A murderer. He didn't know how he'd ever be able to confess the truth to her mother.

Martine—oh, his Martine! After that hastily broken-off session in the Internet café in Istanbul, he hadn't dared use Skype again. He was wary of being tracked down, now that he was finally at the point of being able to put everything right. Martine! How anxious she'd looked just before he'd had to break the connection. Desperate, without her usual sangfroid. But still just as pretty. He missed her so much, it hurt. A sweet pain. He cherished it. The further you were from home, the clearer you could see yourself: his feelings for Martine were a beacon of authenticity in the cesspit of deceit and hypocrisy where he'd earned his wage for so long. He'd been able to put up with it for so long because of her. He could only see that clearly now. She had been his antidote.

She always would be. He couldn't do without her. He'd rarely felt that so strongly. Only love that hurts is true love. He may have recently become a hunter, and perhaps inside he had always remained a rock rebel—above all, he was an eternal adolescent. A 40-year-old juvenile begging for attention. Hopeless, doubting, suffering. Love didn't only hurt because of the beauty of your beloved. It hurt because it was too big for a well-disguised fool like you. It flattened you, it belittled you, it spat at you because at the core of your being, you were too cowardly and too lowly, too insignificant in its glare. And yet you longed constantly for its sweet reprimand, for your gentle defeat when it appeared, for the exquisite pain of love. Oh my God! To be able to lie in Martine's arms again, soon! To be able to kiss her again! When would he be able to? After all this bloody wasted time?

He closed his eyes so as not to pollute his imagination with the reality of this depressingly extravagant hotel room.

They'd start kissing as soon as they were reunited in Wolvertem. Still dressed, still in the narrow hall of their home, his suitcases still in the car. Kissing. Kissing. Until he tells her to go and have a long shower with a lot of hot water, 'nice and relaxing', while he prepares everything in the bedroom.

She would obey him with sham reluctance—her favourite seduction technique. As she took a shower, he'd arrange the incense sticks and put on ambient music. He'd half close the venetian blinds, drape their softest beach towels over the entire bed. He'd put the bottle of massage oil on the radiator to warm up. This time, he and Martine would take the time. Their time. All the time in the world. Their mobile phones? Both of them on flight mode.

When everything was finally ready—he'd even made jasmine tea, with Jules Destrooper almond biscuits on the side—she would make him wait, divine bitch she was, that she still was, thank God. Even without him as anchor and shining light. Despite the pressure of being Klara's sole carer weighing down on her delicate shoulders for over a year.

All of a sudden she padded into the bedroom, not saying anything, barefoot, garbed only in a bathrobe that fell open to show a white G-string, and a whiff of Chanel. She let the dressing gown fall to the floor, twirled around slowly twice, like a model, to prove that in his absence she, too, had been slaving away in the gym, and only then did she lie down. On her stomach. Legs slightly spread, the string barely visible: sly, inviting, challenging.

He began with her back, sly, too. It was a quarter of an hour before he moved on to her legs. She spread them just a little, and then just a little more. Giving his fingers room to manoeuvre, and a while later, finally, anew, his tongue. Apart from his saliva, he also used a little oil to prepare her. He would take her twice. She knew it, and groaned in anticipation.

Tony opened his eyes and saw, to his contentment, that his imagination had done the job that two Japanese films hadn't. His member had risen again longingly, pulsating hard in time with his heartbeat. He laid his two horns aside and began to jerk off, snorting with lust and anticipation, his eyes closed fanatically so that his imagination would not be bombarded by his reflection in the widescreen TV again.

He felt the climax approaching, sooner than expected, more intense than ever, thanks to the hours of unintended foreplay. And yet he slowed his rhythm for a while, just to tease himself, to draw out the pleasure, to increase the explosion. Then he sped up again. The finish was approaching. Just a little while longer! He tensed the muscles in his legs. Now!

There was a knock at the door.

His sperm seeped out awkwardly, without much pleasure, as he wondered aggressively who in their right mind would disturb him now. A cleaner? Impossible, so early in the morning. As he bent over to pick up the dirty napkin from the plate with the remains of the spare ribs, he saw on the television display that it was almost nine o'clock. It could actually be room service with a breakfast he hadn't ordered. That had happened yesterday, too, and his name had indeed been on the bill. Mistakes could happen, even in top hotels, even two days in a row. This time they could bloody well get stuffed, with their coffee and croissants. He would take breakfast in the restaurant in a while, or in a coffee bar elsewhere—the city was big enough. He made no move to get up.

The knocking continued. More persistent, louder, more nervous.

This couldn't be room service. A waiter would take the tray away again, or leave it at the door. Was it the interpreter, perhaps? The bodyguards! The meeting was about to happen!

'Hold on!' Tony cried, flustered. 'Give me a minute!' He'd already cleaned his hands and his dick with the napkin, which he'd thrown back on the plate. Now he stood up, pulled his trousers and underpants back up in a single movement, closed his zip, buckled his belt, ran his hand through his hair, and started toward the door. His eye fell on the horns.

'I'm coming!' he cried, as he hid away his trophies in the commode. They just fit.

'Here I am,' he said a moment later, as he opened the door.

He stood face to face with a European with a wild gaze and a swollen bottom lip, just like him. The man looked a little older, though, and was almost as tall but slightly heavier. His bottom lip was thinner, his face puffier, his hair straighter and lighter in colour. Given the bags under his eyes, he hadn't slept much, either.

'*Spreekt u Nederlands?*' the man asked. He didn't offer a hand.

'Indeed,' Tony replied, in amazement. He kept his own clammy right hand in his trouser pocket.

'And you're Tony Hanssen?' It didn't sound like a question.

'I'm Tony Hanssen,' Tony confirmed, with growing suspicion.

Then the man said something weird and wonderful. He said, 'Me, too.'

For a minute, Tony didn't know how to reply. Then he asked, 'And what happened to *your* lip?'

* * *

'NOW I UNDERSTAND WHY MISTER BO XIANG couldn't see me yet,' Tony said, both relieved and yet worried. 'But why were you al-

211

lowed to know that his wife had died, and I wasn't?'

'I was there when the poor man got the message,' Tony lied. 'It broke him. He doesn't want to see anyone, for the time being. His wife was his muse.'

'Why, if I may ask, were you with Mister Bo Xiang at that moment?' Tony asked. He tried to hide his circumspection. He also felt a peculiar stab of jealousy. 'What kind of work do you do for him?'

'More or less the same as you,' Tony bluffed. 'Let's call a spade a spade. You don't work for a man like Mister Bo Xiang because of his pretty eyes.'

They looked at each other. Not unfriendly on the surface, yet still sizing each other up. They both experienced the atmosphere as slightly tense and a little surreal.

That could also be due to their mutual lack of sleep.

Quite some time had passed since Tony had been invited by the other into the room to tell his story. They'd even decided to have breakfast together. As they waited for room service, they'd tentatively exchanged small talk.

Two years older? You wouldn't think it. Come on, don't flatter me. And where were you born? Really! I've driven past it quite a few times. Where did study? Leuven *is* better if you want to study law. Cairo *and* Bangkok? I've always lived in my hometown. I envy you. And me, you. How many people can say they're happily married these days? I just haven't met the right person yet. It may still happen! And so on.

Neither of them spoke their mind, and both of them concluded—relieved without letting it show—that they weren't related to each other. Not even distantly. Then the breakfast arrived. Continental for two. With an extra pot of coffee.

Tony poured himself a big cup right away. His own breakfast, he thought silently, must have been brought to this room yesterday. He had assumed that his order had got lost in the chaos—hundreds of rooms in one high-rise hotel. Now he knew better. The other, that bastard, had even stolen his breakfast. Thankfully, the coffee was bitter and strong. Tony poured himself a second cup immediately. He wanted to be alert. This trickster, this murderer bearing his name, would be made to pay for what had happened to him that night.

'Another cup for you, too?' He asked. With a smile.

'Please,' the other replied. Also with a smile.

Immediately after Inspector Khumalo had disappeared behind the closing doors of the lift, Tony had dragged himself to the bathroom, spent and exhausted. Naked under a cold shower, he had pulled himself together. Yes, he was all washed-up, and yes, aside from some vague promises made by a Chinese real-estate crook, he no longer had a brass farthing to his name. But there had to be a way out. Whatever the cost.

His teeth chattering and eyes closed, he'd run through all the elements of the past night. All of Khumalo's stories, all the details. Tony puzzled and pondered until the conclusion simply presented itself. He turned off the cold-water tap. Another Tony Hanssen must be staying in this hotel. They'd given Khumalo the wrong room number at reception. A single phone call would be enough to find out that other number.

Tony had seldom been so sure of his case. He stepped out of the shower cubicle. Winning at roulette? With your first bet? On a single number? That might happen. A chance in a few million—but why not? That's how he'd met Mr. Bo Xiang in Macau. But for the same lucky winner to have a namesake from the same country, and for an inspector from yet another country and continent to travel thousands of kilometres to look for a Tony Hanssen in this very place? And for the inspector—of all the possibilities in the largest country on the planet—to pick this city and this hotel? The probability fell short by several zeros to the right of the decimal point. The man really did exist, and he, too, had connections with Mr. Bo Xiang, that's why he was in this building at this very moment. *He* should have been threatened and cleaned out, not me.

Another possibility came to Tony, drying himself, his teeth no longer chattering but clenched. Khumalo's account had been true from start to finish. The murder, the horns, the test set by Mr. Bo Xiang. Why would an inspector like Khumalo get it wrong? He'd been right about all the rest. He had at last opened Tony's eyes to the role he'd played: toy boy, money courier, stupid motherfucker. And him thinking, all that time, that the old witch had wanted to go to Monaco and Liechtenstein for shopping and a bit of hanky-panky.

He became furious when he thought back on it. He no longer felt an ounce of pity for that bitch. She'd deserved to die. His only regret was that she'd been able to cross over to the other side in such bliss. The happy corpse? To hell with it. And her husband? He could fuck off with his grief. Sending your elderly wife around the world like an ageing whore? Bravo. Even Mamaatje and Papaatje hadn't gone that far to arrange a safe haven for their undeclared earnings. Amateurs! They could learn a trick or two from the Chinese.

He thought of another possibility, completely dressed by now, tying his shoelaces and almost snapping them in his anger. The trickster he had to thank for last night's horrors was about to close an enormous deal, according to Khumalo. With Mr. Bo Xiang. There was a—what did they call it in business and politics?—an opportunity, there. Tony would insist on a seat at that table. It was his turn, now. He had a right to a slice of the cake, too. A big slice, after all that he'd been through.

How? That would become clear. The trial he'd been through overnight had given him one advantage. He knew the whole story; his namesake didn't. Knowledge was power. And forewarned is forearmed.

'Did you really mean,' Tony asked in surprise, 'that you have experience in the financial sector, too?' His interest in this loser had finally been piqued. He had hesitated to ask him in. The guy looked a mess; there was something unnatural about him. But it wouldn't do any harm to listen to his story, just to kill time. How often do you meet someone with the same name? And at the other end of the earth, at that.

Now the loser was turning out to be interesting and—who knows?—maybe even useful. He was treated like one of the family at the Bo Xiangs' and he also had some experience. Not a bad start. Maybe they should order another pot of coffee. The loser was drinking it like it was water. He must have had a rough night. Ecstasy? Coke? Then it hadn't worn off yet, apparently. What a greedy bastard! The pastries and the spreads were finished. Only the fruit was left.

'Oh, experience can mean so many things,' Tony said—drinking, gorging himself, chewing. He was hoping to allay his mounting migraine with food. The first cup of coffee had been very bitter on an empty stomach. He shouldn't have let Khumalo have that duck breast last night. 'And what is "the financial sector"? It's a damned broad concept. If not an umbrella term.'

Tony gave the loser an amused look. 'I'd never looked at it like that,' he smiled. 'The financial sector as an umbrella term. You've got a good sense of humour.'

'That's not the first time I've been told that,' Tony said, with a smile of his own.

'Joking apart,' Tony said, quickly plucking a grape from the bowl before the cokehead ate all the fruit, 'where did you pick up enough experience to earn Mister Bo Xiang's trust? I had to go to great lengths, myself.'

I know, Tony almost blurted out. What he did say: 'I don't have what you might call a specialism. My starting point is the bigger picture. The philosophy of common sense.'

'Let me guess,' Tony chuckled, after a pause. 'You work in PR. Fair-weather boys. Lots of words, not much work.'

'That's me,' Tony admitted, smiling, too. 'Getting on with clients, coming up with slogans, communications strategies. That's my department.'

'No one can come up with slogans and strategies,' Tony replied, salvaging another grape, 'without a solid knowledge of the business.'

Tony: 'Of course they can't.'

Tony: 'Where were you trained, then?'

Tony, after a silence: 'All over the place, really. I'm a traveller. Just as long as I'm with like-minded people.'

Tony: 'Which branch most caught your fancy?'

Tony, after a silence: 'It depends what you mean by branch.'

Tony: 'Accountancy, law, credit rating, data provision, equity sales.'

Tony, after a silence: 'Providing data has always been close to my heart.'

Tony: 'What a coincidence. That's my specialism, too.'

Tony, after a silence: 'I wouldn't really call it a specialism. I can find my way around.'

Tony: 'Who were your biggest accounts? Goldman Sachs? Bank of Scotland? Salomon Brothers?'

Tony: 'We did business with all of those, from time to time.'

Tony, amazed: 'With all three?'

Tony: 'Not at the same time, of course.'
Tony: 'Business?'
Tony: 'Deals. Projects. Synergies.'
Tony: 'Shall I tell you something?'
Tony: 'Be my guest.'
Tony: 'You know sod-all about banks. You're bullshitting.'

If you were caught out, Tony knew—thanks to his experience with cruise-ship passengers, who could start up endless conversations and expect you to agree with them—there was only one way to rescue the situation. Tell the truth. Or a retouched version of it.

He opted for a heavily touched-up version. If you were lying, it was better to carry on lying, and do it well. And you had to put yourself down. Everyone fell for that. He started by humbly conceding that the other Tony, that bastard, was right. He meekly begged him for forgiveness, pleaded with all his heart for the other Tony to hear him out, and then confessed that, he was right, he didn't understand a thing about any of that financial business. That's how he'd got tangled up in it.

He had allowed himself—'through my own total idiocy'—to rack up gambling debts with Mr. Bo Xiang. To pay them off, he had become his international cash courier. He'd become, he had to admit, a crack hand at it. He had paid back almost all of his debts, but Mr. Bo Xiang was very keen to keep him on. Mr. Bo Xiang was about to embark on a new venture that would put all his previous ventures in the shade. Tony happened to know his namesake would play a key role in this. Was he wrong? Well, then. How did Tony know? Sorry. He had his sources.

It wasn't the only thing the sources knew. Was he mistaken to suggest that the other Tony had just carried out a difficult mission in Africa? Calm down, calm down! Tony didn't need to be afraid.

He was congratulating him. And he knew how to keep his mouth shut. What's more, he was involved, too. He was up to his ears in it. He wanted to be part of the new deal. He was proposing a partnership. Why not? The tycoon trusted him, and Tony was used to intercontinental wheeling and dealing, even if it was only with cash. So the other Tony had nothing to fear. He and Tony were natural allies, they were namesakes, compatriots, and partners in adversity. Weren't they? To strengthen their bond, Tony would reveal something about himself. Something delicate, something no less thorny than the other Tony's African mission.

He, Tony, had been travelling in Mrs. Bo Xiang's company when she died. In Buenos Aires. Argentina, if you please. He'd been at the bank office, assisting her with a major transaction. The poor woman had simply collapsed right in the middle of the negotiations. Massive heart attack. Tony had tried to save her with mouth-to-mouth resuscitation. To no avail. After that, he'd helped to repatriate her. Secretly. Hush money here, a bribe there. The outside world must never, ever catch wind of it. Well! Now Tony and he were on equal footing where the truth was concerned.

And all the time, as he pleaded and argued and wheedled and lied, Tony never lost sight of the fact that the man in front of him was a crook, a thug, and a charlatan. That cold fish hadn't even blinked when Tony had brought up Africa. How could anyone be so barbaric and yet so phlegmatic, almost to the point of being charming? It remained confusing, even disturbing, that the other not only was called Tony but also looked a little like him. Like a younger and—admittedly—rather more handsome version.

But Tony refused to let that vague resemblance get to him. It was his turn, now, to let someone else do the dirty work. Finally he'd turn his losses—financial and otherwise—into solid profits. He still didn't know how, but he had it coming to him. Inspector

Khumalo had been more than right. Retaliation is a wheel; the most dangerous perpetrator is a victim. And who had more right than Tony, a multiple victim, to exact ruthless revenge? I'll take my pound of flesh, he thought—laughing, lying, placating—if necessary, from someone who shares my name. Correction. Especially from someone with the same name. This stupid name has cost me enough.

It was payback time.

What a loser, Tony thought—nodding, listening, evaluating, still keeping his cards close to his chest. The poor guy was shaking with nerves. He couldn't even carry off a simple pitch without his body language betraying each of his lies. His story had more holes than a chunk of Swiss cheese, in any case. Him? A cash courier! What a loser! Everyone knew about Mrs. Bo Xiang's reputation. It was alluded to, or laughed about frequently enough, even in her husband's entourage. This crybaby had been one of her gigolos. You didn't need three guesses to figure out what had been deposited in Buenos Aires, aside from dosh in a secret account. You had to want to go there, with an old carcass like that.

Still, he might as well stay on good terms with this fool. He had his ear to the ground, there was no denying that. He enjoyed Mr. Bo Xiang's confidence; he'd been present when his wife had died. Secret weapons weren't to be scoffed at. But thank God he didn't know anything about the dead gamekeeper. No one knew about that tragedy, thank goodness. Blackmail was the last thing Tony needed.

Some questions gnawed away at him. Why had no one ever told him that this fool even existed? Was it some kind of plot, or just a harmless oversight? Maybe Chinese people thought that Hanssen didn't stand for a family, but for a clan. They had so many Chings and Changs, it got you in a muddle. And the two Tonys, then? Most Muslim fellows were called Mohammed. Not everything was a conspiracy. Maybe it was down to Tony himself. Maybe he'd simply failed to pick up on the message. The interpreter had scornfully talked about "others of your kind" often enough. The creep had probably just been referring to this particular clumsy oaf.

A loser like that should be forbidden from bearing my name, Tony thought. From a distance, he even looked like a scruffier version of himself. We'll see how much use I can put him to.

After that, I'll dump him. I'm not the Salvation Army.

* * *

'THEY'RE MUCH BIGGER THAN I EXPECTED,' Tony said. He was actually holding the smaller of the horns. He studied it from every angle and was genuinely impressed.

This could have to do with the fact that he, and he alone, knew that they were deadly weapons. Not because they could impale you. For that, they would have still had to have been stuck on top of the forehead of the living animal as it charged at you, ready to pierce your innards with its protuberances before trampling you. No, this trophy—and certainly the bigger one, there, which the other man was holding—no longer needed a bearer to be fatal. It contained enough poison to bring down another rhinoceros, in silence, without bloodshed.

Despite that, the horn was beautiful. It felt solid. Totally different from ivory but just as noble, just as mysterious. So this is it, Tony thought, still studying the horn from every side, this is all that's left of a life. An existence that, considered retrospectively, served only to produce this, here. A suggestive object, a symbol. Something to powder and stir into your drink. And yet, oh so very lovely. Should he tell the other about it? About the poison?

Nah, he thought. All in good time. It would only spoil the mood. And maybe it wasn't even true, what Khumalo had blurted out just before he left.

'They're truly superb,' he exclaimed. 'Magnificent!'

'You should have seen the creature they were attached to,' the other Tony boasted. 'I had to shoot three times before it went down. Tough customers. More stubborn than an elephant and more dangerous than a buffalo.'

They were standing together at the window, looking out at the metropolis at their feet, each of them holding a horn. Waiting for a sign from the interpreter. From time to time, they furtively checked their mobiles. When would it come? Both of them were exhausted.

A war of attrition, without either of them knowing it.

Tony was the one who had asked, quite out of the blue, and for lack of other topics of conversation, whether he could see the horns. Waiting together, and the listless boredom that accompanied it, had worn the sharp edges off their mutual scorn.

As Tony had hoped, the other complied with his request immediately. Vanity and flattery, the bedrock of all human interaction. 'It wasn't something I enjoyed doing,' the other lied, after he'd brought the horns out of the commode. 'Nobody likes putting down such a wonderful example of such a splendid species.' He sniffed, feigning modesty. 'But you do it because you have to. Because there's nothing else you can do. Do you understand, Tony?' He looked out over the city as though surveying his kingdom.

'Absolutely,' Tony lied. 'Cheers!' After breakfast, they'd had a bottle of wine brought up. Not Puligny Montrachet. Tony had long hated that stuff; he'd warned the other. The other had agreed completely. Nothing wrong with a good Italian red. He loved Montepulciano himself. What—Tony too? Well, what do you know? Soon they'd be finding out they had more in common than they thought.

They both smirked.

'Isn't it unbelievable,' the other began, the big horn in one hand, a glass of wine in the other, 'that two chunks of a corpse can open the door to everything that lies before us?' He gestured at the city with his glass. The wine waltzed with it. 'I'm growing to love it more and more, Tony, that infinite mystery called China. The oldest cradle of mankind.'

So now he was a poet, too, Tony thought, not just a charlatan and a killing machine. 'I'm entirely of the same mind,' was the only reply he could come up with. 'China, *mon amour. Santé!*'

They chinked glasses. For the second time.

'Do you know what you still haven't told me?' the other Tony asked, after a pause. He glanced at him for a moment, then turned to the Pearl River again, there in the depths, between the bridges and the viaducts with their thousands of vehicles.

'I have no idea,' Tony said, on his guard. The small horn was a pleasant weight in the crook of his elbow.

'How did you hurt your lip?' the other asked, slyly.

'Oh, that?' Tony shrugged. He stroked his horn. He'd put his glass aside; it was already empty. The migraine seemed to have been suppressed; his head was pleasantly empty, slightly rosy. It was nice wine.

'Come on,' the other Tony said. 'Tell me, my man.'

'You first,' he grinned.

There was a silence. They both grinned.

'I hurt my lip in Africa,' the other said finally, telling the truth. Then he lied: 'My chainsaw got jammed. Then I went to fetch my axe from my four-by-four. You won't believe it, but I stupidly managed to bang my mouth against the open door of the boot.'

He smiled, shaking his head. 'There he stood, our great hunter. Bleeding like a pig from his mouth.'

Even the way he brandished his so-called stupidity was boastful, Tony felt. He laughed along while mentally picturing Khumalo's photographs. The close-ups of the victim. That axe. This yuppie was capable of horrifying atrocities. Tony mustn't ever forget that, however dangerously chummy and suspiciously cosy things got in this room—this aquarium, this horizontal snare. He had to stay on his toes.

'I was much more clumsy,' he lied, echoing the other man's laughter. Imitation had its charms.

'Impossible,' the other chuckled. 'What could be dumber than hitting your mouth on your own car boot?'

'Well,' Tony laughed, 'I walked into the toilet door.'

'Pull the other one,' Tony roared. 'The toilet door?' He slapped his thigh with his free hand. 'The toilet door?' His laugh threatened to derail.

'I swear it,' Tony lied. His laugh threatened to derail, too. The stress, the fear, the tiredness were turning into hysteria, into reciprocal nervous shrieks. 'I banged into the door like in a cartoon. A leg and an arm on either side. My face in the middle. Smack into the edge.'

They each knew the other was lying, but neither of them cared. They roared with laughter. The fit of giggles of one Tony kept setting off a fit of giggles in the other. Minutes passed.

'I fell flat on my ass,' Tony said at last, in fits and starts and a squeaky voice. 'I saw stars! I was happy about one thing, though!'

'That you could still *see* stars?' the other Tony asked. He was bent double, out of breath, his face bright red.

'No!' Tony shrieked. His eyes watered, his face was turning purple. 'That I still had teeth!' He clapped his hands and bent double, too.

The other had to lay the big horn aside so as not to drop it in his fit of hysterics. He bent over, his hands on his now-aching abdominal muscles. He screeched in a strange falsetto: 'I can just picture you! On your arse! Next to that door! Your hands full of teeth! And your mouth completely empty!' He had to sit down before he fell over laughing. 'I can just picture it!' he hiccupped, several times.

'It was a very close call. I wasn't far off,' Tony said, finally getting his laughter under control. He wiped his tears from his eyes with the thumb and forefinger of his free hand.

There was a silence. Not an uncomfortable one.

'Can I ask you a favour?' the other asked, out of the blue. He had his hysterical laughter under control now, too. 'It's something personal.' He wiped the tears from his eyes.

Another silence. A pause that was something like a settlement, a potential covenant. An armistice in a room with too much crystal.

'Don't worry,' the other reassured him, 'it doesn't have anything to do with Mister Bo Xiang. It's purely personal.'

'Ask away,' Tony said, after another silence. The atmosphere in the snare had become almost pleasant. Why not? The other Tony was a human being, too. Who could say what kinds of things he'd been through, what kinds of misfortunes and disappointments had turned him into the kind of man he was. At the end of the day, you could call Tony a killer, too. He'd driven Mrs. Bo Xiang to her death. You had to see everything in context. 'What can I do for you?' He looked the other in the eye. Sincerer than sincere. Retribution would just have to wait. It was so nice to hang around with someone you had a few things in common with, for a change. And who spoke the same language, to boot.

'Do you have a Skype account?' the other asked.

'EASY NOW, EASY NOW!' THE OTHER TONY SOOTHED, still in the suite on the eighty-first floor, but quite some time later. He clutched Tony tight in the way you'd try to calm down an epilepsy sufferer during a fit, contrary to good sense. 'Keep on fighting, pal! Keep breathing!'

He picked up the struggling Tony and carried him with great difficulty over to one of the showpieces of the suite, an antique chaise longue. Anyone who didn't know better would have sworn they were fighting.

Shortly beforehand, Tony had slid out of his chair, unable to breathe, his eyes rolling, delirious, striking out around him, his back arched in a spasm, just short of foaming at the mouth. It was his own fault—he'd just had time to think as he'd slid downward. A flash of lucidity during a fit of rage.

He had unexpectedly got a new shock. Shame and rage had taken hold of him, rather than just heartbreak. He hadn't Skyped with Martine, as the other had asked him to.

He had, supposedly to practice, Skyped with someone else first.

Before it had come to that, Tony had spent an hour trying to get out of having to Skype with Martine. He wanted to spare the other the news that his wife was going to leave him in the lurch, and undoubtedly want custody of their little angel, and lay claim to all their joint property. Their house? He could forget about that. There wouldn't be much left in Wolvertem to go back to.

Tony didn't want to be the bearer of all that bad news. It wasn't even altruism that drove him. He would need the other at the negotiating table shortly, calm and collected.

But none of his obstructiveness was equal to the other man's determination.

When Tony had countered that neither of them had a computer, the other had called reception and asked for one to be brought up immediately. 'I always do it this way,' he explained. 'I don't have my own, anymore. Much too dangerous.' Room service arrived with a state-of-the-art model. 'Ah, a Samsung—great as long as you keep them away from the Delilahs.' He seemed disappointed that Tony was unable to laugh at his joke.

When Tony lied and said he didn't have a Skype account, the other just made one for him. Location Buenos Aires, Tony saw to his dissatisfaction, reading over the other's shoulder. He said nothing. He didn't want to offend him because of a misplaced joke. A much bigger blow was on the horizon, once he got that wife of his on the line. Talk about Delilahs, Tony thought darkly.

The other had already become wildly euphoric. He couldn't stop saying how beautiful his wife was and singing the praises of true love, even after years of marriage, even after months of unwanted separation. He couldn't stop talking about Klara, either. Tony had started to hate the little bitch already. The way her father kept raving and boasting about his cute little princess? To him, Tony—still a total stranger, after all, despite their shared name. Tony didn't get it. What kind of drug was it, what virus, that turned people into blathering idiots as soon as they got onto the subject of their progeny?

He was full of admiration for the way the other could stay focussed as he raved on, the way he managed to keep typing away on that little keyboard. His fingers seemed to have fused with it. He'd just start by reformatting the whole computer, he'd boasted at the outset, as though it were the most normal thing in the world. Only after that would he install the software and an extra firewall.

Cookies, bugs—he'd double-check everything first. 'You never know who might want to track us down. Better safe than sorry.'

Tony hadn't even known what that all entailed—cookies, firewalls, reformatting. Much of the Internet had remained mumbo jumbo to him. He had enough problems with everyday on–off switches and operating instructions. If nobody took the trouble to explain to him how the microwave worked, frozen meals either remained frozen or were burnt to a crisp.

'You're the ideal person to call Martine,' the other had insisted, typing away with a vengeance. 'You pose as a digital tourist looking for people with the same name. It happens all the time, these days. The world's a village; everyone walks in and out of other people's houses uninvited, whether it's via Twitter or Facebook. We're Wi-Fi neighbours, all of us.' He smiled, tinkling and typing away. 'No one is safe, anymore. Unless you know the right pathways and techniques.'

The other Tony was no stranger to paranoia, he sensed. Perhaps he should use that to play for time. 'Your wife isn't stupid,' he said, starting with a compliment. 'She'll see through me and cut off the line straightaway. We'll be worrying her unnecessarily.'

'Bullshit,' the other Tony said. 'I know her. She's dying to hear from me, no matter what. I'll stay out of sight, myself, until I'm sure she's alone.'

'And what if she isn't alone?'

'At least I'll get to see her while she talks to you. That would mean a lot to me. You'll understand when you see her. My adorable Martine. *O la la!*'

'What if Martine's laptop isn't switched on?'

'We'll Skype with her mobile first. I've topped it up. Her smartphone is on twenty-four hours a day.'

Why am I not surprised? Tony thought, gnashing his teeth. He could already picture the kind of woman she was. Who would marry a computer jerk from the banking sector and stay with such a vulture for so many years? You couldn't be quite right, yourself. You'd have to be a monumental cunt, just out for the dough. Tony would rather die than make a phone call to a dyed-in-the-wool bitch like that. She'd see right through their silly set-up; she'd order the other to show his face and give him the goods. She'd tell him she was going to clean him out and dump him. She'd tear into him, demoralize him, destabilize him. Tony needed that like he needed a hole in the head. Everything seemed to be finally under control, at last, almost manageable, even. He couldn't deal with any more fuss, let alone a screaming harpy. Tony had had enough—he'd been broken on the wheel, he was done. He shouldn't have started drinking again after breakfast. What had he been thinking? The Montepulciano was eating away at his very last scrap of resistance.

'Are you ready?' the other asked. He seemed reborn. Barely an hour at work and he was already clad in the many automatisms of his profession: coercion, condescension, excitement, mouthiness, cockiness, and radiant, ineradicable optimism. He briskly turned the laptop to face Tony.

The built-in camera hadn't lit up yet. If necessary, Tony realized, the entire living human race could look him in the face through that one tiny lens. The eye of the square Cyclops. Tony returned its gaze in horror. Confronted with that oppressive sum, the suffocating cumbrousness of millions, billions of lives, all of them as vulnerable and meaningless as his own. They could have been bacilli, teeming under a microscope.

Tony had made another two desperate attempts to win time, hoping for a last-minute rescue by the interpreter and the bodyguards, as he'd hoped for that night with Khumalo. They'd have to arrive at some point, surely.

Again, his resourcefulness didn't pay off. First he lied that he'd never Skyped before, and that he was so clumsy he was bound to mess everything up, starting with the conversation itself, maybe even the programme, and the laptop, too. It wouldn't be the first time he'd made a computer crash, he said, entirely truthfully.

The other had given him a withering look. 'No one's that much of a loser,' he said, with a tinge of irritation. He sensed that Tony was dragging his feet. It wouldn't take much for things to get nasty. 'You just keep your paws off the keys when you talk. I'll do the rest.'

Finally Tony lied that since he had never Skyped before, he was scared of having his very first video conversation with—he was sorry—a stranger. He knew what he was like—he'd freeze up. Martine would get suspicious and cut him off before they'd even got going.

'All right,' the other sighed, his mouth contorted, eyes rolling. He had neither pedagogical skills nor patience. 'First we'll practice with someone you know. Out with it! Who do you want to call?'

'Excuse me?' Tony replied.

'You don't mean to tell me that there's nobody you'd like to call?' the other snorted. He began to sound downright hostile. 'Do you want to work with me, or not? This bodes well! Come on, man! Who are you going to call?'

It had turned into a threat.

And Tony gave way, as he always did. He said his father's name: 'Alexander Hanssen.' It rolled off his tongue before he'd realized, with a speed and a certainty that shocked him.

It was a sorry state of affairs, after all those years, all that travelling the world, that the only person he could think to name was one of his progenitors. Not even Mamaatje, but *him*, of all people.

This betrayal, plus the anger that he didn't have any connections left, aside from those two creatures, sapped Tony's strength even more than the treacherous Italian wine. His ribcage began pinching once again; the flesh-eating flower was making its comeback.

He saw the other happily tapping away at the keyboard, digitally searching for the lucky winner, as though it were a phone-in contest, a late-night quiz for sleepless squires. 'And your prize is … Ta-daah! A tête-a-tête with your long-lost son!' With a bit of luck, Mamaatje and Papaatje weren't home, Tony hoped. They weren't exactly computer types, was his guess. Like father, like scion. They probably didn't even have an account, he fervently hoped.

'We've got him!' the other shouted triumphantly, in English. 'Hanssen, Alexander. There's just one in the whole of Belgium.' He turned the laptop back toward Tony.

The square Cyclops made a ringing sound, though its built-in eye wasn't yet glowing green.

Tony looked at the screen, taken aback—it displayed a portrait photo of an old man who could be none other than his father, albeit fed through the Wringer of Time. Covered in wrinkles. Emaciated. Grey, well-coiffed hair that looked like it might be a wig. Unnaturally white teeth. Tanned skin verging on the orange. Tormented eyes, despite the repulsively cheesy smile. The electronic ringing sound stopped. A green icon reminiscent of an antique telephone blinked on and off above the portrait photo.

Why was that elderly mutant grinning at him? What was he up to, that ghost from Tony's past? He felt like he was being assailed and stared at from all sides—by the other Tony next to him, by the little photo in front of him, by the currently dead eye of the Cyclops above him. The ringing sound continued.

Please let them not be home, Tony prayed, please let Mamaatje and Papaatje have gone to the Waregem Races again, dressed in their Sunday best, or a VIP tent at the Tour of Flanders, or the Dead Pigeon's Ball, the Antwerp bird market, the Antiques Fair, the seafront at Ostend, the hell that was Bokrijk Open Air Museum, or simply to hell itself.

The ringing stopped.

The screen opened up like a flower in a time-lapse nature film, though rather less sharply focussed. The face staring out at him was made up of rough, jerky blocks in pastel colours. 'Hello?' This wasn't Mamaatje or Papaatje. This was a young woman's voice. From time to time, the jerky blocks merged into a plausible image. The girl who appeared was not unattractive, and about 25 at the most. From the look of her, one of her progenitors was black. Mother Nature had endowed her with a pronounced bosom, and her mouth wouldn't have been out of place in a lipstick commercial. The cleaners in Belgium were getting better-looking, Tony thought.

'Who am I speaking to?' the girl asked. She had a sweet accent, but she was frowning. 'Who are you?' Her dark eyes peered at Tony in confusion through the screen, thousands of kilometres away. The built-in green eye above her image was staring at Tony, too. That green eye used to be much bigger, he thought, and there was a triangle around it. *Mind Your Language. God Sees All!* That had been the slogan on those framed Catholic prints that had hung behind the counter in all the pubs in Belgium. To no avail. They swore themselves rotten. Tony sat there, frozen, staring at the girl. He'd lost his tongue. It was stuck to the roof of his mouth.

'Who are you, then?' the girl asked again. 'Can you hear me? Hello?'

'I'm sorry,' Tony said at last, with a great deal of difficulty. 'This must be a mistake.' He felt the other, who was politely staying out of shot, give him a kick on the shin. 'Talk,' the other hissed at him, not without malicious glee.

'Tony? Is that you?' the cleaner asked, all of a sudden delighted, if not to say over the moon. 'Unbelievable! It's really you!' Her face changed temporarily into a Cubist masterpiece before turning back into a realistic portrait of a handsome young woman of mixed race. Her voice changed, too, from time to time—from melodiously attractive to electronic croaking, and back.

'It's so cool you've got back in touch at last! I'm so happy!' She continued to sound excited, although the frown had returned to her forehead. 'You should come around sometime, Tony, you don't have to call ahead. And don't you worry, everyone would be happy to see you, we've all been waiting for you all this time. I knew you'd come back one day, I can sense these things. I've heard so much about you, honey! Where are you? Are you in the neighbourhood?'

'Not really,' Tony said. He looked in astonishment at the interior behind the girl who had just called him honey. Aside from a couple of paintings, he didn't recognize anything. It all looked suspiciously modern. 'Who are you?' he asked. 'And where are you, in God's name?'

'I'm sorry,' the girl grinned, 'I'm Lindiwe, but everyone just calls me Linda. And this, what you can see here—'she turned coquettishly and made a curling, upwards movement with her hand, as if she'd just pulled off a magic trick, 'this is the living room. Shall I give you a tour of the whole loft?' She turned her laptop ninety degrees as a starter.

Linda *was* in a suspiciously modern living room. Immense and bare and stylish, with high ceilings and smooth concrete walls and large sliding windows that seemed to look out on—unless Tony's eyes were deceiving him—some kind of river. Yes, look at that—a barge came into view.

A barge? 'Where's our house gone?' Tony asked. Was his voice turning into electronic squawking from time to time, too? If so, was there any difference? He stuttered, and his voice sounded bad enough as it was. Modernist concrete weighed down on his chest.

Linda laughed. A beautiful, spirited, candid laugh. Tony gave the other a sideways glance. He wasn't looking at Tony anymore, but at the screen. His mouth gaping at so much beauty, at sex on legs.

'We moved out of that ugly house about three years ago,' Linda cooed. 'Who still lives in Hicksville, in this day and age? It's so much nicer in the big city. Your father has really perked up since we moved here. Just the view of the Scheldt river, to start with! And boats going past the whole time?' She smiled in satisfaction. 'It gives you such a lovely sense of longing for all those far-off countries. At the same time, you can get everywhere on the bike. We'd never want to live anywhere else.'

'On the bike?' Tony asked, amazed. 'My parents live in Antwerp and they ride bikes?'

Tony's smile faded from her face. Beauty and tragedy, reinforcing each other—an Old Master portrait. 'Tony,' she stammered, 'I'm sorry. I thought you knew about your mother.'

'What's there to know?' Tony asked. He knew already, but wanted to hear it from the mouth of this gravedigger, this whore. She was younger than he was, for fuck's sake. Quite a lot younger.

'I don't think I should be the one to tell you,' Linda said. She'd laid her right hand on her breastbone, above her décolleté, as though she wanted to spare Tony's feelings by covering her own heart. Her nails were long and painted Bordeaux red. She looked around, searching for help in her aesthetically-pleasing bunker with its stunning light.

'Stay on the line, please,' she said, her face right up to the camera all of a sudden. Her face bulged horribly—from Vermeer to

233

Hieronymus Bosch in a second. 'Please don't go! I implore you! Not again!' Her lips were monstrous, the dismay in her gaze repulsive. 'It would kill your father!' Were those tears welling up? Ridiculous. 'I'll go see if he's in his office! Wait for us!' Her face disappeared abruptly from view, leaving behind a gaping vacuum. Even the barge had disappeared.

'Alexander?' you could hear her shout, off-screen. 'Alexander?' Increasingly shrill and distant. 'Alexander!' She sounded hysterical, as though she were in pain. As though the smooth concrete were on fire. And she with it.

Tony didn't even slam the laptop shut. He swiped it from the table, against the window. The screen burst with a satisfying crack. The Cyclops' eye dulled. A few loose keys clattered away. At the same time, Tony felt his back arching and himself gliding from his chair, fighting for breath like a spastic with asthma. What issued from his mouth sounded like crying, in the way that wounded wolves cry when they make noises in the night.

The other Tony misunderstood the situation. He rushed to help, thinking his future partner needed consoling. He caught the thrashing Tony and carried him in his arms to the chaise longue. 'You have to be strong, buddy.' That was the kind of thing the other Tony said to him. 'Let it all out. Just cry; you'll feel better.' He laid Tony down and stayed seated at his side so that the jerking body wouldn't slide off the chaise longue. 'I'm sorry, buddy. I didn't mean for this to happen.' He even said that. An apology because he thought Tony was mourning.

What the other Tony could neither know nor guess was that Tony wasn't fulminating simply about the loss of a progenitor, but about everything she'd embodied all these years. Most people made love their foundation; Tony had lived off hate. The object of his hatred, however, had come to seem eternal, immutable, in

234

his mind. He'd never counted on the cycle of life, on evolution. The thing he'd hated suddenly turned out not to exist anymore.

That made his hate ridiculous, and him, too. Like a rebellious animal that had pulled and tugged at a familiar chain for years, only the chain wasn't attached to anything anymore. The stake in the ground might have never even been stuck into the ground. Tony had lost two things in one and the same second. His actual childhood, and the image of it that he had cherished as a justification for his actions. Both had vanished, dissolving like flesh in hydrochloric acid.

What really made Tony feel so bitter, and drove him mad, was that this loss could still turn him inside out. He, who had so often boasted that he'd left 'that whole bloody mess' behind long ago, had to admit, to his fury, that he hadn't been able to discharge it until today. And not even permanently. This was the most shameful, the most abhorrent thing of all. Although Tony had sunk away into a bottomless delirium, this fact was still clearly branded into his mind. What he had lost, twice, would always be inside of him, albeit in a cancerous form, an allergy. Like if you had an arm amputated, and the scar wasn't the only permanent reminder. No, there was the pus, too, and the itch, and the maddening pain that predicted the arrival of rain. They all lodged themselves in the place where that missing arm had been.

Even though you'd lost it, you never got rid of it.

There was something else that Tony would remember later, fragments looming up out of the shadows of his delirium. The other bringing him a blanket and cold water, and saying, 'Don't you worry. Just lie down here for as long as you want.' Tony even remembered waking up for a moment, and the other sitting by him, looking at him, looking into his eyes searchingly, just like a doctor would do. The other even laid a hand on Tony's cheek and said, 'You need to sleep. I still need you, pal.'

'Martine?' Tony asked with difficulty, thick-tongued.

The other Tony: 'Don't you worry about her. We'll call her after it's done.'

Tony: 'Done?'

The other Tony: 'The interpreter called. The meeting's tonight. You can come, he said. No problem.'

'Where to?' Tony asked, just to say something. He didn't give a damn about the meeting. But he wasn't sorry to feel the other's hand on his cheek. It wasn't the embrace he'd expected from Pedro the golden boy, that phony undertaker in Buenos Aires—how long ago was it now? A week, a year, a century? But a caress of the cheek was already worth quite a lot. It was more than he thought he deserved.

'In a restaurant, of course,' the other Tony chuckled. His hand stayed where it was. 'Where else? You know them, don't you, our Chinese friends? In that regard they might as well be Belgians or Italians.'

'What do we need to take?' Tony was referring to the horns. It was the last question he could think of before falling back into a restless sleep.

The other Tony's words, intended to reassure, barely registered. 'The same as ever. A reinforced-concrete gut for the food and a stainless-steel liver for the drink.'

* * *

TONY TOOK HIS HAND AWAY from the clammy but cold cheek. The loser had fallen asleep again. Would this idiot, this woeful mess, be in any state to offer assistance during complicated negotiations? Would he even be able to come along to the restaurant?

It was unbelievable, Tony thought, shaking his head in exhaustion, that two people with the same name and more physiognomic similarities than differences could be so unlike each other. Thank God!

He left the loser on the chaise longue. It was high time that he crawl under the sheets for a serious power nap himself. A couple of hours would suffice. He had always been like that.

As he got undressed, ready to dive into bed, he heard a scream. He hurried back into the sitting room. False alarm. The poor idiot had screamed in his sleep. Tony sighed. It was better not to leave him lying there on his own.

He took the loser in his arms again, picked him up, and carried him to the bedroom. Amazed at himself. Because he felt something he hadn't felt for a long time, except for Klara and Martine.

Care. Concern.

4. Guangzhou (in a restaurant)

WE FIND TWO TONY HANSSENS on the other side of the metropolis, in a fish restaurant very close to the harbour. The restaurant could seat more than two hundred guests, yet there was still a lengthy queue of locals, running along the outside of the building. They smoked and chattered on the wide pavement beside a six-lane boulevard on which, even at this late hour, there were still tailbacks. Half of the front of the restaurant consisted of an artificial rock face, three floors high, waterfall included. The water poured down into an elongated aquarium with tropical fish and turtles, right on the street, picturesquely lit.

The table the Tonys had sat down at was generously sized, though laid for only five. It was screened off from the rest of the establishment with a heavy curtain hanging from ceiling to floor in stately folds and decorated with traditional motifs. The walls and the ceiling were decorated, too, as were the fitted carpet and the high-backed chairs. Everything was decorated, with the exception of the crisp white tablecloths and napkins. The woodwork was lacquered in black or dark red, with decorative golden edging. The lighting was provided not only by gently swaying pagoda-shaped lanterns—bare tube lights and colourful neon swirls also set the scene. An antique Chinese theatre crossed with a contemporary amusement arcade.

One of the Tonys sat staring into space, as though he were simultaneously a few continents away, thanks to a special meditation technique. It could also have been that he was waiting—a standard business-meeting technique for duos—for the ideal moment to launch an unexpected, incisive intervention, in which he would make a final proposal that the opposing party wouldn't be able to refuse without undermining the whole deal.

The other Tony wasn't keeping quiet. He was running through all the other meeting techniques with verve and a raised voice: playing the charmer, sulking, sucking up, thumping the table with his fist, feigning indignation, drawing an optimistic growth chart on his napkin with a ballpoint pen.

Wasted efforts. His adversary, the interpreter—despite being his secret drinking and karaoke companion—proved implacable during this sparring match between equals, two prizefighters fighting as though this were their last battle, for life or death. Their concealed friendship deepened the malice with which they had verbally clashed for more than an hour, now. The tone became ever fiercer, the discussion evermore complex. The silent Tony had lost the thread of the combatants' conversation after just a quarter of an hour, so labyrinthine was the construction, so specialized the subject matter, so international the arena.

Mr. Bo Xiang was sitting to the left of the interpreter. Silent and motionless and just as mentally absent, though that could have been a tactic, too. In his case, it could even be part of his raison d'être as tycoon. A person like Mr. Bo Xiang didn't need to argue or flatter. He had henchmen for that. He had henchmen for everything. He wore, indoors, and even at this time of day, vintage Carrera sunglasses, and, instead of his crumpled suit, a dinner jacket. A wilted carnation was stuck through the buttonhole. Where had he come from? The silent Tony couldn't help wondering. From a funeral or a society ball? All Mr. Bo Xiang had done so far was eat and drink and smoke and listen.

From time to time, the tycoon laid his parchment claw on the porcelain hand of his other escort aside from the interpreter. A Chinese beauty of no more than 20, in a skirt suit with a Parisian cut and a stylish neckline. Her long earrings seemed to be made of platinum and emeralds, but her sad eyes sparkled like polished anthracite. Cleverly worked gold shone around both of her wrists, but she didn't need a necklace—the hollow of her breastbone and the shadow of her décolleté were decorative enough. Although she seldom smiled, her mouth may have been her most impressive jewel. Delicate, sculpted lips with a matte finish, always slightly parted, obscene and innocent alike. She was called Chloé, the interpreter had informed them as he greeted them coolly.

Chloé had been keeping silent all evening, too, eating and drinking like a bird with anorexia but smoking like a Turk. The only thing she did, apart from that, was to cast the occasional languorous or concerned glance at the man next to her, the man in sunglasses, her lord and master. Once she even wiped his sweaty forehead with her napkin.

Mr. Bo Xiang didn't even blink, as though he considered the attentions of such a stunning girl the most normal thing in the world. He had everything. On one side, Chloé's perfect beauty. On the other, the interpreter's perfect menace, with his nicotine teeth and his pockmarked skin. Between them, the man himself, Mr Bo Xiang. Cool, unfathomable, terrifying.

Where was his grief now, the silent Tony wondered. Or was this the way Chinese men of his standing grieved? This icy scorn? Maybe he's on something, Tony thought, just like me. He dismissed the thought at once. A man like that wouldn't take pills, he thought; a man like that would take it out on something or someone, an entire sector if necessary. A man like that knew no better remedy than punishment, domination, and oppression. He'd been reminding Tony all evening of his father, Alexander the Not-so-Great. Despite his age, he'd also got himself a young filly as a comfort woman. Must make a nice change from a bypass op.

Linda and Chloé, Chloé and Linda—the names echoed around Tony's mind. What drove pretty young women into the arms of powerful wrecks? Were they all really looking for surrogate fathers? Is that why they spread their legs the minute a senior citizen started showing a little interest? Chloé and Linda, Linda and Chloé. If Tony had known that this chain-smoking babe, this designer slut, would be present—with all the memories and connotations the girl evoked—he would have never let the other Tony convince him to come to this lair. You could see where it was leading, all this misplaced solidarity. What am I doing here, he wondered, for the umpteenth time since sitting down. What do I have to do with any one of these people? And where was it, his reward, the thing he'd been so solidly promised. It hadn't been mentioned at all. No one even seemed surprised that he'd turned up along with the other Tony. What did they think he and the computer prick were? Bosom buddies? Brothers? Partners in crime?

He should have stayed away.

No, he should have escaped when he had the chance. Before Inspector Khumalo had knocked on his door, before that corrupt black schmuck had infected him with the hope that he, Tony, could take a slice of the cake, just as long as he did his very best. What an illusion. A role like that wasn't reserved for him. There wasn't anything for him to skim off. There was nothing he could pocket, nothing he could rectify, nothing he could even destroy properly. He could do nothing, and he was a nothing. He should count himself happy if his gambling debts were halved. If that happened. It probably wouldn't. Cheated again, fucked over again. At a roulette table, that was all right—but he didn't belong at this restaurant table. It reminded him of the fatal put-down he'd received from another old fogey, the professor of civil law who had failed him and even laughed in his face during his final year of university, his final year of Flanders, his final year of Europe: 'On est au *banquet de la vie, infortuné convive!'* The bully had shouted out a translation afterwards: 'We are unfortunate guests at the banquet of life, Mister Hanssen! But you and I will never see each other at this table again. Now sod off!' Never thought I'd think back to that moment, Tony thought, smirking momentarily. If only he knew, that narrow-minded bastard. He was probably dead by now and buried and rotten and decomposed.

Tony gave the other a sideways glance. His namesake, his companion, to his right. Look at us sitting here! The odd couple, sitting nicely together, shoulder to shoulder, the two of us facing a unified Chinese triumvirate.

Poor Tony, Tony thought, no longer smirking. Look at him sweating, the toady. Our self-declared genius clearly can't believe that he's having to beg for what he wants. His dream, his world consortium, his return ticket to normality. He demands them all as if they were a human right.

A right? Look at them, his credentials, his proof of payment— his pathetic horns. The other Tony had carted them here in his chic suitcase. The proof of the murder and the fraud he'd had to commit to earn his place here. They lay there stupidly, they'd lost their shine, they'd become two absurdities, useless relics of a brute that had decomposed by now, or been eaten. Folkloric junk, nothing more. Insignificant, dirty, primitive. They lay neglected on this overloaded table, between the overflowing ashtrays, enamelled earthenware teapots with dregs of green tea, half-empty wine and cognac glasses, dishes with slurped-out, eyeless fish heads, picked-out crab legs, snail shells, oyster shells, all manner of carcasses.

And even then, Tony had managed to avoid the most repulsive dishes.

* * *

THE EVENING HAD BEGUN BADLY for them, a couple of hours ago. They hadn't been picked up by the bodyguards in their Cayenne. They'd even had to charter a cab, clutching a foolish piece of paper on which the receptionist had written the address of the restaurant in Chinese characters.

The other Tony had spent the entire ride grumbling that this had no class, and that he wasn't used to this from Mr. Bo Xiang, nor from anyone in those echelons, anywhere in the world. He'd imagined his victory march toward reparation rather differently. His baggage, his cargo—the horns in the boot—was worth a fortune, he whined. He'd managed to convince the driver to allow the suitcase on the back seat, between the passengers. The boot wasn't an option. Next thing you know, we'll be robbed, too, he sighed a couple of times. His voice had something plaintive about it, a timbre Tony hadn't heard from him before.

To make matters worse, the taxi had got caught up in a monstrous traffic jam. They stopped at the highest point of a viaduct, part of a motorway that ran through an area full of tumbledown, but still-inhabited, concrete blocks. The engine idled away, while three floors up, twenty metres away, behind dusty windows, a family sat eating soup and watching TV without paying heed to the uninvited spectators stuck in traffic. At first you looked away from the family in embarrassment. Then, out of sheer boredom, you ended up watching TV in their living room from your taxi. A Premier League match.

Two goals were scored before the traffic got moving again.

They'd reached the restaurant with a half-hour delay. Under the insulted gazes of the queuing people, they were led inside by a matron with overly made-up eyes and a scornful mouth. First past the open kitchen, then past dozens of tables with either large families or businessmen in their shirtsleeves. The combination of the hubbub and the clatter in the kitchen sounded like a good-natured revolt. Only the smallest children, surprised and giggly, watched the foreigners, one of them pulling a wheelie suitcase behind him. One toddler started pointing and crying, was barked at by his mother, and began to cry even louder, without anyone paying any more attention.

The matron held open a curtain and pointed out the table at which the Chinese triumvirate sat, waiting for them. The interpreter, sullen; Mr. Bo Xiang and his Chloé, coolly indifferent. There was also another person present at that stage: standing, surly, unamused. One of the four bodyguards, the colossus. He accepted a red envelope from the interpreter, who seemed to launch into a verbal attack. The colossus shrugged, stowed the envelope in his inside pocket, and strode out of the curtained-off room. He didn't bother to look at the two Westerners whom he'd had under his care until recently. He very nearly tripped over the suitcase.

The colossus wasn't the only person who came by in the course of the evening for a red envelope. Some envelopes looked thicker than others. It was like payday in a nineteenth-century copperware factory. To all appearances, most were being laid off. The bulk of them were silent as they accepted their envelopes, albeit with disgruntled expressions. A few swore back when the interpreter snapped at them. One or two cried and tried to kiss Mr. Bo Xiang's hand. Impassive, he didn't allow it once. Chloé, on the other hand, wiped away a tear from time to time, the silent Tony noticed. There was some emotion in that bitch, then.

While the procession of suppliants and rejects continued, the two Tonys were summoned by the matron to 'go and pick out a dish in the kitchen', as the interpreter told them gruffly. What the Chinese triumvirate would eat had apparently already been decided. They stayed seated. Hear, see, and don't speak. Three monkeys in a row.

Tony had expected to find a buffet of hot dishes, like in a Greek restaurant. Moussaka, oily pasta, white beans, Greek salad—everything spooned onto your plate by the cook beside his hot oven. But the two Tonys were taken to a separate room with pale-blue tiles on the walls, next to the kitchen. It turned out to be a small fish market.

All kinds of basins and aquariums were set up in a horseshoe shape, most of them made of thick green glass and filled with products from the seven seas, without any regard for species or attractiveness. Peeling glossy photos of skyscrapers, racing cars, and pastoral scenes featuring pagodas were stuck onto the steamed-up tiles above the fish tanks. The lighting consisted entirely of fluorescent tubing.

The cooks extolled the virtue of their goods with gestures. They thrust lobsters at the two Tonys, monsters with eyes on stalks and pincers that snapped in the air. Next—like elderly Down's syndrome sufferers at a Flemish country fair—they used little fishing nets to catch tropical fish with despondent eyes and dumped them on a pair of hanging scales. The fish gasped and floundered. Even the smallest weighed more than a kilo.

After that, they showed the two Tonys ten kinds of toad, ten kinds of tortoise, sea snakes, squids, sea roaches—stopping short only of baked maggots. The body of the largest crab was the size of a child's head, its legs were longer than iron pokers, its claws wider than the shuttle on an antique loom. A young crocodile more than a metre long lay waiting for some adventurous customer, its jaws tied.

The molluscs formed the real pièce de resistance. Nothing illustrated evolution's unfortunate detours better, thought Tony in disgust, than the world of invertebrates, from abalone to zebra mussels. They were available in every size and shape, and came with all imaginable spin-offs and offshoots. Tony couldn't believe his eyes. What kind of country was this? People here ate anything that had ears, eyes, feet, or tentacles, everything that could crawl, swim, fly, or dig, everything that could breathe, suck, bite, or glow. As long as it was fresh, they'd stick it in their mouths.

His namesake clearly didn't share Tony's disgust. He looked around like a famished child in a sweets shop, all contentment. He'd already digested the humiliating taxi ride and the embarrassing delay. He was feeling the flush of victory, a priori. 'Holy Christ, just look at this menagerie. How on earth do they manage it?' He must have seen it as proof of resourcefulness and resilience, if not to say supremacy. He couldn't wait to participate. To the chefs' merriment, he pointed out one freakish creature after the next.

Tony didn't. Even the thought of a *moule parquée*, a raw mussel with white wine sprinkled on it, turned his stomach. He couldn't manage more than two oysters. The most striking mussel here looked like a white piece of elephant trunk, thirty centimetres long, bordered by two crescent-shaped shells, like a hot dog bun with a sausage that was much too large, not to mention mouldy. There was an obscene cavity at either end of the trunk. A creature with two anuses? Tony went for the least of the evils. A modest lobster and a medium-sized grey fish.

The vendors looked offended, but that was probably their role. First they pointed appreciatively at the compliant Westerner, their thumbs raised. Then they pointed disapprovingly at Tony with dismissive gestures and expressions as though they could smell shit. Tony pretended not to understand them and kept on shaking his head at each saltwater monstrosity and snake they held up to his face. He'd done what other people wanted enough, recently. It was high time he thought about himself for a change.

The cooks unexpectedly backed down, roaring with laughter,

even. It had just been a game, a practical joke. One of them gave Tony a pat on the shoulder with his wet, briny hand. His colleague scooped a lobster and a trout-like fish from their basins, showed them to Tony one last time, and gestured that he and his companion could return to the table behind the curtain.

Once there, their choices were served incredibly quickly, accompanied by a little bit of sauce and a lot of noodles, a few spices and a lot of vegetables, lightly fermented tofu and heavily fermented black beans.

The business discussion didn't break out until the dessert and cognac. 'They even have that in common with the Italians and Belgians,' his namesake hissed at Tony behind his hand and in Dutch.

Back then, at the beginning of the discussion, he'd still beamed broadly. Still that spoiled child in the sweets shop, ready to demand his due.

* * *

IT WASN'T THE SILENT TONY WHO FINALLY broke the impasse in the curtained-off room. It was the tycoon, Mr. Bo Xiang himself, long after the discussions had degenerated into trench warfare between the two negotiators. The interpreter looked ashen, the other deathly pale; both of them had shouted themselves hoarse and, judging by the expressions in their eyes, were ready to drink each other's blood.

Mr. Bo Xiang unexpectedly thumped the table with both fists, roared something in Chinese, reached across the table without warning, knocking over a balloon of cognac on the way, grabbed the silent Tony's hand, and began blubbering like a fishwife. Tears rolled out from under the lenses of his sunglasses, snot ran from his nose, dribble from his mouth. As he snivelled, he launched into a litany in Chinese that didn't seem aimed at Tony, but at the interpreter.

Looking like he'd been struck down by the hand of God, the latter sat, staring up at the ceiling, pallid, beaten, exhausted. Chloé looked at her plate of food, less than half of which had been eaten. A newly lit cigarette balanced between two of her delicate fingers. Her eyes teared up, too, enough to make her mascara run, but she didn't do anything about it, allowing her black sorrow free rein. Her face was stuck in a grimace somewhere between despair and embarrassment; her chest with the pretty hollow and the elegant décolleté went up and down as though she were suffocating. She kept on looking at her plate as though she couldn't believe she'd been served such rubbish.

Mr. Bo Xiang was nowhere near done with crying and talking, and he still clutched Tony's hand. He took off his sunglasses with his free hand so that he could look Tony in the eyes.

It was an unsettling sight. Mr. Bo Xiang squinted and seemed drunk. His rather small eyes were swimming around forlornly between his swollen, watery eyelids. One of his nostrils was blowing a snot bubble, sweat was dripping from his forehead, his mouth hung open with misery. Now he was actually addressing Tony. He said all kinds of things that were apparently difficult to put into words. He also lowered his voice. A nun praying on her deathbed was loud in comparison. The good-natured revolt of hubbub and kitchen clatter simply carried on in the background.

My God, Tony thought, this fellow really has taken pills. More than I have. Look at him. He's lost to the world. Was this the most powerful man between Macau and Guangzhou? This, one of the secret drivers of the world economy? This was a needy old man with a sorry-looking carnation in his buttonhole and dribble on his chin. Had he had a stroke or fallen from the stairs? In a fraction of a second, Tony had seen enough; the desperate strength with which his hand was shaken pronounced the verdict. Mr. Bo Xiang was still there, he was still clinging to his former decorum, his past authority. But his empire was finished, his existence over. Shattered glass, no longer in motion.

'What's your boss saying?' the hyperactive Tony asked the interpreter. 'What's his final proposal to us?' He didn't seem to realize what had just happened at the table. Probably a matter of self-protection, the silent Tony thought. If the other had understood, he never would have asked his question. He'd have packed up ready to make a quick getaway. Instead, his voice sounded hopeful, almost triumphant. He imagined himself the victor. He wasn't asking the interpreter for information, he was asking him for capitulation.

And the interpreter obliged. 'Mr Bo Xiang,' he began, reluctantly and yet in a solemn tone that was appropriate for this irrevocable turning point, 'has the honour and the satisfaction of notifying you that he will agree to all your proposals and all your plans with pleasure. He finds them downright masterful, even ingenious.' The grin with which the interpreter said these last few words suggested that he wasn't translating, but coming up with them himself. The oblivious Tony picked up on none of the irony. 'Mister Bo Xiang imposes just one condition,' the interpreter continued. Again, a mocking curl around the mouth with its nicotine teeth.

'And what would that condition be?' the other Tony asked warily. He was sitting, holding his iPhone, ready to rend the condition into percentages and profit forecasts. He gave Tony a sideways glance, looking to him for support. A confirmation of their alliance, now that the grand finale of the fierce negotiations neared.

Tony didn't look back. He was still trying to locate the bottom of Mr. Bo Xiang's gaze. The Mariana Trench. That was the name,

Tony remembered, of the deepest point on earth in the middle of the Pacific. They'd sailed over it a few times in the *Liberty Oasis*.

Mr. Bo Xiang didn't let himself be distracted, either. He whispered all kinds of things to Tony—Tony, whose language he didn't understand, and who couldn't understand him without the involvement of a third party. Look at us sitting here, Tony thought, trembling, suddenly almost touched. Mr. Bo Xiang and me, the tycoon and the willing horse, connected by a handshake and little more than that. Two communicating vessels exchanging emptiness, nothing more. Not only were Mr. Bo Xiang's eyes swimming in their own moisture, his head was rocking unsteadily, he was sweating, his breath stank. At his side, Chloé repressed a sob. She extinguished her cigarette in the mother-of-pearl of an oyster shell. Even the interpreter seemed more moved than cynical by now.

'Could we hear the condition now, please?' the triumphant Tony asked sternly. He obviously enjoyed adopting a vengeful tone with the interpreter. He was the only person at the table who wasn't affected, the only one who didn't understand that, by now, something quite different was at play than the deal he had come for.

The interpreter, too, exchanged a glance that angled for confirmation. He caught Chloé's eye when she looked up briefly from her plate. She nodded and looked away in embarrassment. 'Mister Bo Xiang,' the interpreter began, 'insists that the new consortium be named after his late wife.'

The triumphant Tony did his best to conceal both his relief and his happiness. He didn't succeed. 'You mean Mrs. Bo Xiang, sir?' he asked, nodding modestly, full of mock sympathy. He still had his iPhone at the ready.

The interpreter nodded, genuinely moved. 'Mister Bo Xiang prefers her maiden name,' he said. 'Li Na Yunho.' There was an almost devotional silence.

'I can't see a single problem with that,' the victorious Tony said, as humbly as possible. 'You won't regret this.' He finally put his iPhone away. 'We're going to write history, folks. All of us. Thanks to our consortium, Li Na Yunho International.'

When he heard the name, Mr. Bo Xiang let go of Tony's hand. Whimpering softly, he let his head fall forward. His forehead landed just next to his dirty plate—he'd had crab and sea roaches with lentils. 'Li Na Yunho,' he muttered.

'All we need now is to raise a toast,' the interpreter said to the winner of the negotiations. 'We'll leave all the red tape until to-morrow.' He said this with another sarcastic twist to his lips.

After that, things moved quickly and dramatically. More quickly than Tony had wanted. More intensely that he ever could have imagined.

The victorious Tony politely offered his excuses to the triumvi-rate. He had to use the men's room. 'That's what comes of all this wine and green tea.' As he got to his feet, he gave Tony a discreet wink, and said in Dutch, 'Without you, we'd never have reached an agreement. Thanks, buddy.' He even patted Tony's shoulder. 'I knew it was the right thing to drag you here.' He turned around and disappeared behind the curtain, toward the sounds of the good-natured revolt.

Immediately, a waiter entered the room through the same cur-tain. He was wearing white cotton gloves; a round silver dish was balanced on the fingertips of his right hand. He bent over the table, respectfully took hold of the smaller of the two rhino horns, laid it on his dish, and disappeared back behind the curtain with it.

Chloé and the interpreter paid no attention to this. Tony did. What's the man going to do with it, he wondered. Prepare it? Serve it with tofu and black beans? He felt strangely guilty about not asking for an explanation via the interpreter. After all was said and done, those protuberances were worth a fortune, and still belonged to the other Tony. Didn't they? In any case, he felt the same stab of gross negligence as when he'd realized in Buenos Aires that Mrs. Bo Xiang's mortal remains had been kidnapped by a conman.

He was given no time to reflect. The interpreter came and sat down next to him in the chair the other Tony had vacated. He didn't look relieved. He had the expression of an abandoned animal that had been left chained to a tree. 'I'm fond of your compatriot,' he began at once. 'I've done everything I could to try to change his mind, but he won't listen. He can't see; he's blind. You have to warn him before he does something disastrously stupid.'

Tony nodded, but couldn't for the life of him figure out what the interpreter was talking about. 'Do you want to call the consortium something else, perhaps?' he tried.

The interpreter's expression suggested that he thought Tony was pulling his leg. 'There isn't going to be a consortium,' he said. 'There isn't going to be anything. Why do you think we're sitting in this restaurant, hidden behind a curtain? Mister Bo Xiang's houses and cars have been seized, the offices sealed, the casinos placed under state control, the accounts confiscated. Those fanatics have even taken away his dwarf rabbits. That's how big an example they want to make of him. The poor man has nowhere left to go.' He got out his packet of cigarettes. Tony saw Chloé taking care of Mr. Bo Xiang on the other side of the table. She whispered something in his ear. The wreck didn't react. He left his head where it was. On the tablecloth. His arms hung limply next to his body.

'His crime is that he carried off with panache what they only managed small-time,' the interpreter said, exhaling smoke. 'Now those rats are punishing him, in the hope that they'll get off scot-free. For years he was their idol, their shining light, their walking wallet. Now they want to put him on trial? Those people? You can't judge Mister Bo Xiang by the same standards as an ordinary mortal. That man has broadened our minds, broken open our horizons. You don't talk to the man; no one did—you listen to him. Just look at him.' He gestured towards Mr. Bo Xiang.

Chloé had actually managed, Tony saw, to get the tycoon to lift up his head. He hadn't just lifted it up, he'd laid it on her delicate shoulder. He wasn't moving. Is the guy still breathing, Tony couldn't help thinking. The sight of this complete motionlessness brought back unpleasant memories of Buenos Aires.

'He was like a brother to me,' the interpreter continued. 'My better self, the whetstone keeping all of us sharp. Even now, in his hour of tribulation, his heart goes out to his employees. He is sharing out what little money he has left. And do you think they are thanking him for it? No, they're stabbing him in the back. His best friends and his distant associates have united, and are preparing to tear him apart.' He poured himself another glass of cognac.

'I, too, had talent. I, too, had plans. I put all of them aside for him. A person should know his place when he meets his superior. And now? I'm nearing 60; imagine that I make it to 70—how am I going to spend them, Mister Tony, those ten years? I'll tell you. At his side. I'll go wherever he goes. Even if we have to rot away together in the penal colonies of this country he made great.' He downed his cognac in one.

'I won't forgive you for Mrs. Bo Xiang's death. He does. He's too good. He's also blind. Blinded by love. Before giving himself up, tomorrow, he wanted to say goodbye. To you.' The interpreter gave Tony a sour look. Again, a trace of scorn. 'You, the last person to see the great passion of his life, his reason for being, who tried heroically to save her.' He tapped the ash from his cigarette into the fish head. 'Honestly? That kiss of life of yours? I have my doubts. But they're irrelevant. I'm asking you just one thing. Don't shatter the illusion. Play along, at least for tonight. Mister Bo Xiang has suffered enough loss of face. Grant him the farewell that he wishes, before he gives himself up to his executioners tomorrow.' He put out the cigarette in the fish head and returned to his seat.

Right away, Chloé came around to Tony. She walked anticlockwise around the table, the interpreter clockwise. An almost symmetrical ballet that unavoidably reminded Tony of something he thought he'd long forgotten: his grandparents' meteorological cuckoo clock. How was it possible, he wondered in amazement, that a person's brain could dig up the most irrelevant details from forty years ago, but that he didn't understand a thing about everything around him—the biggest issues, first and foremost. His grandparents' clock had been a barometer, too. On either side of the little wooden bird that shot out of a collapsible hatch, there were two niches whose walls were covered with painted-on ivy. A farmer's wife would pop out on the left, or a farmer on the right, depending on the weather. The farmer wore a smock and a cap. He was the harbinger of rain and darkness. The farmer's wife, in an Austrian dirndl, promised bright intervals and sunshine.

Chloé was wearing Dior or Yves Saint Laurent, and it remained to be seen what kind of weather she brought with her. She sat down in the vacated chair and crossed her legs. Her lord and master, Tony saw, had laid his head on the table again. The interpreter sat next to him, his arms folded. The last bodyguard, the last samurai.

'Mr Tony?' Her voice, broken by emotion, sounded deeper than you'd expect from such a fragile, young thing. She spoke French. 'I'd like to thank you,' she said, 'for your considerate treatment of my father.'

Her father. Tony tried not to let this information sink in. It had too many barbs and implications. He was sitting here, for one thing, with the daughter of the woman he'd fucked to death. Why had she never mentioned a daughter? Perhaps she thought it clashed with her vulgar longings? Perhaps she had a jealous streak—she didn't want to tempt her toy boy with a younger version of herself. Or perhaps she was simply ashamed of Chloé. At the end of the day, Tony knew so little about Mrs. Bo Xiang! He had never known that she'd been called Li Na Yunho when she was young. He didn't want to imagine that she'd ever been young and attractive. To him, she was eternally old, and dead forever. He wanted to keep it that way.

'There's so much I want to thank you for,' Chloé sighed. She looked even more beautiful close up than at a distance of two metres. Amazingly, she spoke perfect French. 'You were at my mother's side in her most intimate moments, at the instant of her deepest suffering. But even before that, you meant a lot to her. She often spoke about you, and always with affection.' Chloé, too, took out a packet of cigarettes and avidly lit up. Unbelievable that there's anyone left in China who doesn't have cancer, Tony thought, and that they still outnumber us—us, with our smoke-free pubs and our pictures of black lungs on each pack. He tried hard to bring to mind the other off-putting pictures on cigarette packets. He wouldn't have minded counting them or listing them, as long as he didn't have to think too deeply about what Chloé had just told him.

She wasn't done yet. Blowing out smoke like a beautiful, fragile dragon, she said, 'My mother even told me that you were the son she wished she'd had.' Here, she let a sad smile register. 'If she hadn't had me, of course. As far as their offspring are concerned, my parents have always remained faithful to their ideals, more so than a lot of other people in this country. One child? Done. Isn't that ironic? I'm the only mitigating factor they'll have to concede to my parents. At any show trial.' She leaned in and kissed Tony on the cheek. 'Do justice to her memory, Monsieur Tony. I loved her; I'm mourning her.' Since Tony didn't react, she kissed him a second time for a fraction longer, and closer to his mouth. '*Merci pour tout ce que vous avez fait.*'

The other Tony came back from the toilets at that moment. He observed the kiss with a pitying look. 'I'm not interrupting, am I?' he scoffed in Dutch at Tony, as Chloé reluctantly got to her feet to make space for him. She walked back around the table, outshining the city lights with her haughtily raised head and her perfect bare back.

Tony's namesake watched her with admiration. 'Looks like our deal has been well and truly sealed,' he chuckled, still in Dutch. 'We can go. Or do you want to stay a while longer, you old dog?'

Tony didn't reply. His eyes were fixed on the waiter with the white gloves, who, in the wake of the other Tony, had come back into the curtained-off room. He was carrying the silver dish on the fingertips of his right hand again—a small, glittering launch pad. The small horn lay on the launch pad, sawn into pieces. Around the shavings, there was everything necessary for the toast in hon-our of Mrs. Bo Xiang and the worldwide consortium that would bear her name. One teapot and five cups.

And a silver grater.

5. Guangzhou (outside, on the street)

NOTHING HAD HAPPENED. Tony breathed in relief. He still couldn't believe it. That he, himself, was safe and sound, healthy in body and soul, walking along the pavement of this wide boulevard—that was only to be expected. He hadn't touched a drop of the turbid ghost tea.

But the fact that the other Tony was walking along the same pavement, singing, even, radiating vitality, delirious with euphoria and selfish ambition—that was absolute proof that the horns couldn't have contained any poison.

His namesake had even knocked back two cups of the stuff.

Inspector Khumalo must have tricked me, Tony thought. That sadist may not have tortured me physically, but mentally, he wanted to put the fear of God into me. And he'd royally succeeded. Tony had died a thousand deaths in the restaurant during the preparations for the tea ritual.

Now he knew better. If grated rhinoceros horn could be said to have any effect, it didn't come anywhere near that of hemlock—the ingredient in Socrates' poisoned cup—but was closer to magic mushrooms, which Tony had messed around with as a student. Although those shenanigans were well in the past, Tony had recognized all the symptoms in the others—elation, fits of giggles, love for all mankind. Although Tony wasn't sure the other Tony needed any grated horn or mushrooms to get high.

His drug was the flush of victory.

The other Tony danced in zigzags across the pavement, shaking the hands of perplexed Chinamen, asking a girl or two for a kiss—they all said no, most of them with a dash of outrage. He didn't care. 'I'm sure it was somewhere around here,' he called out to Tony intermittently. He was looking for his favourite karaoke bar. 'Singing! Karaoke!' he chuckled to the passers-by, along with accompanying gestures. 'Dance, drink—Whitney Houston! Freddy Mercury—We Are The Champions! Where? Where?'

Each word sounded like a mating call. He was practically galloping along the pavement, and with every stop, he screamed out his horniness like a rutting stag, the kind on the souvenir mugs you get in Bastogne. A head with imposing antlers proudly arched back, eyes wide, randy foam on the lips, and all you have to do now is bellow at the does. Except that the other Tony's silhouette wasn't drawn against the outline of a forest in the Ardennes; instead, there was a night skyline of a boundless metropolis with brightly illuminated towers and viaducts, beneath heavens full of stars and the navigation lights of Boeings and Airbuses. The high chimneys of the harbour refineries flared in the distance. Occasionally, a meteorite cut a fiery but swiftly fading scar in the firmament as it grazed the atmosphere.

When am I going to tell him that the contract isn't going to happen, Tony wondered. When should I dash his hopes and dreams? Let him babble on for a while, first, let off steam; he's got too much energy. He trailed a couple of metres behind his namesake. Close enough to keep an eye on him, far enough away not to be involved in the public nuisance of an over-exuberant foreign louse.

＊ ＊ ＊

THE INTERPRETER HAD BEEN THE PERSON to do the honours in the curtained-off room, grating a chunk of horn into his tea and stirring. No one said a word. The verbal battles had been concluded; now all they were waiting for was the closing ceremony.

Only Tony—with terrified eyes, and as white as a napkin—began to make objections. He used his sensitive stomach as an excuse. He looked like he was already exhibiting the symptoms that he said drinking the tea would give him.

'Impossible,' the interpreter said, swirling the teapot around with his hand on the lid. 'This tea is good for everything: stomach, heart, liver, blood pressure, and defecation.'

'It's not bad for your libido, either,' the other Tony chuckled to his compatriot in Dutch, nodding his head toward Chloé.

'Even if it doesn't strengthen the heart,' Chloé said in French, 'it's still worth sampling its exquisite taste. And, of course, there's the emotional value.' As she said this, she laid her delicate hand on her father's claw. He had only eyes for the teapot. His lips moved soundlessly.

'I'm afraid I'm going to pass,' Tony said. He crossed his legs and folded his arms. This time he wouldn't budge, he resolved. Enough was enough. Let the others drink themselves to death. He'd taken enough risks. It was their decision; he didn't have anything to do with it. What could he say? That they'd better find some other horns quickly because these weren't clean enough? And that he was the only one to have known all this time? Because a black detective with a drinking problem had flown all the way from South Africa especially to tell Tony this? They'd suspect him of plotting against them. Tony pictured the interpreter and the other Tony in sudden rediscovered camaraderie, insisting that he take on the role of taster. He could just imagine it. Them holding him down, assisted by a couple of those monstrous chefs. Forcing his head back and emptying the whole pot into him until it came out of his nostrils. Waterboarding with a toxic green brew. No, thanks.

'You're not going to start being difficult, are you?' the other Tony asked.

'I've already started,' he replied, also in Dutch.

'I don't want the two of you conspiring in your own language,' the interpreter said.

'What's the matter?' Chloé asked, in French.

'Our pal's eaten too much,' the other Tony said, in English.

'Just one cup of this tea,' the interpreter said, 'and he'll feel better.'

'I don't think so,' Tony said, in English.

The interpreter, surly: 'No tea, no contract.'

Chloé, upset: 'Do it for my father. And my mother.'

The other Tony, in Dutch: 'It's only a cup of tea, you know.'

Tony, likewise: 'I have ethical objections.'

The other Tony: 'To drinking tea?'

Tony: 'If we carry on like this, rhinoceroses will become extinct.'

The other Tony: 'If *you* carry on like this, you won't live much longer, either.'

Chloé: *'Mais qu'est-ce que vous dites, tous les deux?'*

The other Tony, in English: 'He'd prefer a cup of coffee.'

The interpreter, passing everyone a cup: 'No tea, no contract.'

Tony: 'I'm not doing it! I won't drink this crap!'

In the end, Chloé burst into tears, Mr. Bo Xiang sat there, mumbling and staring into space with an abandoned look in his eyes; the interpreter began to roar, and Tony did something he hadn't done for a long, long time. He held his ground. He didn't allow himself to be browbeaten. He'd had his fill of that. He'd rather knock over his cup; he'd rather pitch it through the restaurant like a hand grenade; as far as he was concerned, it could land in the market hall of aquatic monstrosities and exterminate all the gleaming, teeming, snapping, flapping life in there. Anything was preferable to taking the tiniest sip. And even though he didn't drink anything, it didn't dispel his sense of horror. He could already see himself surrounded by a dying tribunal. Four bodies vomiting blood along with their semi-digested meals of sea snakes and roast maggots, four poltergeists clawing at him and gargling accusingly that he was a coward, a sadist, a barbarian. Why had he let himself be dragged along to this inner circle of hell?

This time, it was the other Tony who ended the impasse. 'Friends, friends!' he appeased the two still-active members of the Chinese triumvirate. 'Let's not let things get out of hand on this wonderful, important evening.' With aplomb, he cast the only meeting technique he hadn't yet used that evening into the mix: the touched-up truth, broached with a smile full of bonhomie. 'With all due respect, you can't ask my friend to drink this. Calm down! Calm down! He suffers from various severe allergies; there's a chance he'd react disastrously to the horn. If you'll allow me, I'll drink in his name, in memory of the lady the consortium will be named after.' He raised two cups at once, his and Tony's, one in each hand. 'To Li Na Yunho!'

'Li Na Yunho!' Mr. Bo Xiang echoed loudly, to everybody's astonishment. He raised his own cup without a trace of animosity. As high as his doddering distress would allow.

With that, the dispute was settled. It wasn't *that* important, the ritual. As long as Mr. Bo Xiang was happy. Everyone, apart from Tony, drank.

After that, they said their goodbyes like casual acquaintances who wouldn't see one another again for a long time, and didn't seem too broken-up about it.

* * *

TONY HAD IMAGINED THAT VICTORY WOULD TASTE quite different. He walked along the pavement with the sluggish loser and roared with triumph. He shook the hands of passing Chinese men and tried to kiss their wives; he happily made a fool of himself, casting off all restraint.

But his display of delight felt bitter, too. It was, he realized, a form of flight.

Okay, he'd landed his big contract; he'd wiped the floor with the interpreter—that sneak, that hypocrite. He'd simply outdone the great Mr Bo Xiang; he'd even impressed the gazelle with the pretty décolleté with his courage and perseverance.

The loser next to him? He'd had to rescue that twerp at the very last minute from a humiliating breakdown that had jeopardized the contract. Who on earth refuses a cup of tea when he senses it's part of a crucial ceremony? The tea had been disappointing, though. What a let-down. His horns, his boys. He'd imagined their taste would be richer. To be honest, it had tasted like what it was: offal.

Honesty forced him to admit that the loser had proved his usefulness during the negotiations. Even if it was on purely sentimental grounds. The old man had a soft spot for him, and bada-bing! He'd bowed like a reed. It beggared belief, but that's the way things were, Tony shrugged. Emotion and timing were everything, not just in comedy and in tennis, but in business, too. The business world may have been invoking the collective rationality of a free-market economy for centuries, but it was still held together by chance and emotion. Not to mention feuds and bluffs. Just like life itself, at the end of the day.

That was why he loved doing business so much. He was born for it.

So, he'd expected to enjoy this moment with every fibre of his being. What was the matter? He'd achieved everything he'd ever got off on in his wildest fantasies.

Yet something was gnawing away at him. He walked further and further away from the restaurant, the site of his victory, ostensibly looking for a karaoke bar with the loser in his wake, going against the stream of the hundreds of locals out on the tiles. But he wasn't looking for anything. He was walking away from something, and not just the restaurant. The further he walked and the more he looked around, the more clearly he understood what was going on. He'd fallen for this city. Not even the city, itself. He was head over heels with the life it held out to him, like the creatures the chefs had offered him. Abundant, within arm's reach, inexhaustible and quivering with life force. His future was here. He never wanted to go back to where he'd come from. He couldn't care less about clearing his name and his reputation.

How had he managed to cope for so long back there—in that backwater, that sewage hole, that malodorous belly button of a worn-out continent? Everything was deadlocked; you were knocked down before you even began. Everything hemmed you in; everyone did their best to shoot you down, so that you conformed to the suffocating standard of mediocrity crowned with the most presumptuous of titles: 'Europe'. Germany or France might have been a different story. But no, he meant Belgium. Wolvertem. Not London or Madrid.

Tony had no business there anymore. Mpumalanga had changed him for good. He'd become a hunter, a big-game hunter. He couldn't cope with smallness anymore. It didn't suit him.

At the same time, he was fleeing the consequences of this metamorphosis. The thought made him uneasy, even sad. There would be no place for Klara or Martine in this new existence. It was cruel to say it, but they were part of that smallness. They would never flourish in this country or in the life he aspired to.

If mother and child even wanted to give it a go. He knew his

Martine. She was capable of a lot, but she knew her limits. There was nothing wrong with that, in principle. But recently, her limits were not keeping pace with his. It wasn't so surprising. She couldn't begin to imagine what he'd been through. It made their estrangement irreversible.

Tony knew of only one way to alleviate the pain of this insight, which was so confusingly mixed up with the joy of achieving his dream. For the time being, anyway, for tonight. Running, screaming. Energy. It was a way of stamping his feet that didn't look like stamping his feet to the outside world, but like wonderful madness.

He was unreservedly happy about just one thing during this veiled foot-stamping and crying, this running of his. To his amazement, he was pleased the loser was still following him.

I've grown attached to him, Tony noted, like—with all due respect, mind, I'd never say it out loud—a tramp is attached to his dog. Perhaps when he worked out the details of Li Na Yunho International, he'd create some kind of unimportant board position for the loser. The man brought him luck.

You shouldn't be in a hurry to get rid of a person like that.

* * *

'OF COURSE, WE'RE NOT OUT OF THE WOODS YET, I do realize that,' the other Tony panted with an air of humility. Nevertheless, he peered upwards deliriously at the cloudless sky, high above the penthouses on the boulevard. He and Tony were sitting on the edge of a marble planter. Their faces were lit up by streetlamps and neon advertisements.

'For the Chinese,' the other Tony explained patiently to him, who was wiping the sweat from his face, 'a contract isn't the end-point. The negotiations begin afresh each day. Our consortium will always be a work in progress. Don't let anyone tell you otherwise.' This didn't stop him from looking around in ecstasy, as though he were already picking out locations for a skyscraper with his name on it.

My God, thought Tony at his side—even though he was doing his best to seem outwardly enthusiastic—that peacock still hadn't cottoned on. His modesty about his achievement was all for show. The vainglorious man imagined himself an emperor. What did that say about his powers of judgement?

Tony tried to look at him with fresh eyes.

The sight was just as shocking as that of Mr. Bo Xiang, earlier in the evening. He had always assumed that the other Tony was a star player, a leading light in his field, high above his own status as unimportant outsider. Now he saw the truth. This was a prawn who fancied himself a swordfish.

If the other Tony was really such a genius, why was he so incredibly relieved and self-satisfied? A true professional would have thought it the most normal thing in the world that he'd landed the contract. A professional wouldn't have first let himself be packed off to Africa on such a foolish mission. His Chinese employers had sent him away, all right, but in the hope that he'd never come back. Who was the real loser, here?

I've looked up to him too much, Tony concluded, because I know nothing about his specialism. That makes it easy for me to look up to him. But even he was punching above his weight tonight. Brilliant at programming, a beginner in real trade.

That was why he was so happy.

'The thing I want to focus on most with Li Na Yunho International,' the other Tony beamed, still catching his breath, 'are elephant deals.'

'Elephants?' Tony asked. 'I thought you were into rhinos?'

'You need to look for the ivory where you can find it, pal,' the other grinned. 'It's in pension funds and charity boards. There's nowhere else you can find so many muppets in one place.'

'They were elephants just a moment ago.'

'Elephants have a disadvantage. They have good memories. Muppets don't. That's what they're called in the City and on Wall Street. They're a separate human species.'

'Hand puppets?'

'Even better!' the other Tony snorted. 'People Who Don't Know What Questions To Ask. They'll invest in anything as long as they have faith in you. That's the advantage of life, in our day and age. It's too overwhelming and too complicated for everyone. The longing for governance and paternalism has never been greater. And if you can fake that, Tony? Persuade them that you're the big leader? The guide the masses trust and follow, the enlightened guru in whose hands your money is safe? Then you're sitting pretty.' He burst into a fit of giggles again, into nervous hysterics, like the day before, when the two of them had been standing at the window.

Tony didn't join in this time. The other's laugh sounded too hollow, too forced, for that. He wanted to go back to the hotel. Up to now, the walk had done him good, after all the emotions in the restaurant. But now he'd had enough.

His namesake didn't take Tony's silence to heart. He fell backward, giggling, his arms spread. The flowers and shrubs in the planter caught him, like an audience catching a rock-and-roll idol who stage-dives into the audience, blindly trusting that his fame will save him from a broken back.

'There are even muppets,' the other screeched, 'who buy subprimes after a mega-bank has wrongly assured them that they're solid. Do you know what the bank does next?' He almost choked and began to cough. It took him a minute to be able to continue, at first with a frog in his throat, still lying back in the plants. 'They pass on the information to a hedge fund they're friendly with. The latter, of course, immediately begins to speculate on the collapse of the instruments that contain the muppets' toxic mortgages. Bingo and bingo. Do you understand, Tony?'

'Completely,' Tony lied. 'Shall we get a taxi to the hotel?'

The other Tony indignantly freed himself from the supportive audience of the plants and flowers, and stood up. 'Come on,' he roared, 'don't give up. It must be somewhere around here.' He began walking again. 'Come on, Tony! I want to drink, I want to sing!' His step was unsteadier than before, but he had stopped bothering the passers-by. Anyway, there were fewer people out on the street by this time. Tony sighed, but carried on walking behind him.

'The bubble should never have been allowed to burst,' the other Tony ranted on as they walked. 'We should have just carried on. If a person performs too many reality checks, in the long run there's no reality left. That's the paradox.' He was panting more and more. 'Plus, on top of that, money doesn't even exist. The speed of turnover is the thing that counts. But be careful! That doesn't mean that the hippies and anarchists are right. What would we be without money? Without balance sheets, without banks? Cavemen. Cro-Magnon curs.'

'Totally,' Tony said; he was having trouble keeping up.

The other Tony stopped abruptly. 'Can you hear that, too, buddy?' he asked. He was clearly unsteady on his legs now. He had his eyes closed and held his index finger in the air.

'No,' Tony said. He didn't feel like lying anymore. It was time to get real. 'I can't hear anything in particular.'

His companion chuckled. 'How can you not hear that?' He stamped his feet with joy, just like that, in the practically deserted street near Guangzhou's massive harbour. 'I can hear them, I can see them!' He spun around with his arms outstretched and almost toppled over. 'Oops, better have a little sit-down.' He sat down on his bottom, smack bang on the pavement. 'This is it, Tony. The karaoke bar I was looking for. It's here. Can't you hear the singing? Listen then! Look!'

'I can't see anything,' Tony said. 'I can only hear the gulls, and a lot of traffic in the distance.'

'Look around you, man,' the other said. He seemed to have lost all the strength in his arms; they hung feebly. Tony wondered whether he should try to help, but he didn't know how.

'People like Mister Bo Xiang,' the other Tony continued, blinking like a madman, 'can at least say: that bridge there? I made it possible. That building? I financed it. Without me, that factory wouldn't produce any shoes or concrete mixers. How many people can still say that today?' He paused, nodding and biting at the air, a nervous tic.

Then he toppled over inelegantly and hit his head hard on the pavement.

Tony had rushed to his aid too late. Fear washed over him as, kneeling, he took his compatriot in his arms. He observed him from close up. It was uncanny, having his face so close to someone with the same name, a man who, against all odds, had become so familiar in such a short time. He laid his hand on the other man's cheek, as he had done with him. Only yesterday.

The other Tony was foaming at the mouth. A thin stream of blood ran from each nostril. But he was still smiling. 'Hey, loser!' he said, giggling, 'What *can* you see, then?' He shivered, even though it was spring.

'Shall I call an ambulance?' Tony asked.

'Why?' the other Tony asked gleefully, looking up at the sky. 'This is the best thing that ever happened to me.'

PART THREE

Hope

TONY HANSSEN SHOWED HIS PASSPORT to the woman at the ticket desk. The flight he wanted to catch had already been announced at Departures, but there was still just enough time to check in and get through security and customs without hurrying. He didn't expect any problems, but there was no telling what might happen. The past weeks had offered conclusive proof of that.

The ticket lady would be a test run without her knowing it. If she considered the passport valid, Tony would soon be safe and secure in his seat belt. If she made trouble at this stage, he'd be in a jam, now and for a long time to come. An announcement jingle echoed through the high, futuristic-looking departures hall, after which a female voice announced in formal English that the flight to Beijing unfortunately had a fifteen-minute delay, and that Air China offered its excuses for the inconvenience. She carried on in Chinese, presumably with a repetition of the announcement.

The ticket lady looked at the passport photo, then at Tony, then back again. She double-checked the details he'd written down for her on the hotel notepaper. Finally, she returned the passport to Tony, along with his change, told him that his ticket was being printed, that he could take only one piece of hand luggage, and that he could proceed to check-in, desks twenty-one to forty-one. Tony waited until she'd handed over the ticket before thanking her warmly.

It had worked. It had been confirmed. It was official.

No one would ever be able to say that the other Tony had suffered much in his death throes. No one would ever know anything about it.

During the taxi ride, he had continued to happily spout non-sense, smiling drowsy-eyed, although his nosebleed returned at intervals. He dabbed the blood away himself with a napkin he'd slipped into his jacket pocket in the restaurant. He studied it up close and marvelled at the red spots. A child staring at ladybirds in fascination, before pulling off their legs and wing cases.

When they'd arrived at the hotel, no one from the reception desk had rushed to help Tony. They all thought his companion was blind drunk after a night on the tiles, and assumed Tony would want to manage things on his own. A bellboy and a recep-tionist nodded at each other, sniggering. The Western duo stag-gered into the lift. The one leaning more heavily on the other was having more fun.

When he'd finally got the other Tony laid out on his bed, he was still tittering, but he'd also began frothing at the mouth again. Tony wiped it away several times. Finally, he dragged over an armchair and kept vigil next to the bed, dozing off now and then. A few times, he was awoken by the other Tony's shrieks of laugh-ter.

A few times, Tony stared, close up and in astonishment, at the other Tony's face that was growing ever paler, and which, never-theless, still showed so many similarities to his own. A few times, the desire to apologize crept over Tony—because he wasn't do-ing anything, because he didn't want this, and because he didn't know quite what he should have done. Which was why he'd done nothing.

The story of his life, in a nutshell.

In the early morning, Tony swapped his wallet with that of the other man, looked at him one last time, and then closed his eyes. Judging by the expression on its face, he was leaving behind another happy corpse. He didn't just close the door to the suite—he left his life behind and began a new one.

The first thing he did was take the lift to the eighty-first floor. He'd swapped his key card with that of the happy corpse.

He was free.

* * *

THE FIRST THING TONY LEARNED ABOUT HIMSELF on the eighty-first floor was that he couldn't complain about either his taste or the amount of stuff he owned. Suits, ties, shoes, shirts—everything was well cut and of impeccable quality, and all of it from well-known labels. He'd just have to get used to that. Just like the fact that he was now the proud owner of three watches, half a dozen pairs of silk underpants, and a generous supply of cash.

Tony ordered breakfast over the phone—'Just make it a continental'—and took a shower. In the bathroom, again, he couldn't be anything other than delighted at his good taste. The most modern razors, the most expensive aftershave.

Out of habit, he turned the tap in the shower to cold. He'd have to get out of that habit, too, later. It no longer went with who he was.

He opened the door in a bathrobe. His first appearance as himself, face to face with other people. The waiters' response wasn't negative. They took him as he was. "Would you sign here, please, Mister Hanssen?" He improvised the signature he'd seen on the many credit cards in his wallet. The waiters bowed down deeply before his nonchalant calligraphy.

As he ate his breakfast, he watched the English-language news on CNTV. The longest item was about a real-estate magnate from Guangzhou who was said to have links to unscrupulous speculators and criminals from the betting world, and who'd come under heavy fire from the government over the past weeks, even though he was a former member of the ruling party. He'd been found dead the night before. Along with his daughter and his right-hand man. The police spokesman presumed it was an act of retribution, but couldn't rule out a suicide pact in which they'd all taken poison. Tony turned off the screen with the remote control and went into the bedroom to pack his bags. There were two left—the third was probably still in the restaurant. These had a fancy label, too. Tony would give them away empty once he arrived at his destination. He didn't want to own any suitcases anymore. It was time to put down roots.

Just before he closed another door for good, the one on the eighty-first floor, he left a tip on the commode for the cleaner that was generous enough to match his new status. He could only hope that all the tips were added together and shared out between the staff, so that cleaners who had to clean more difficult rooms could also share in his generosity.

Downstairs, the shuttle was already waiting. 'Just put it on the consortium's bill,' he'd said to the receptionist over the phone when he'd booked it. The good little girl had done as she was told. Mr. Bo Xiang's imperium had been decapitated; the commitments it had undertaken would still hold good for a while, just as an eel without a head continues to writhe.

At some point, the convulsions would stop. And if, later, an overzealous sergeant from Mr. Bo Xiang's debt-collection squad got it into his head to try to collect Tony Hanssen's betting debts for his own gain—Tony Hanssen, former favourite of the late Mrs. Bo Xiang—he'd be in for a rude awakening. You can't squeeze blood out of a stone, and you can't make a happy corpse cough up. At the most, the sergeant would think it a curious coincidence that a debtor and a creditor had died on the very same night. Usually it was just one of the two who died, taken out by the other.

It wouldn't be the only unsolved mystery surrounding the death of what was once the most powerful man between Macau and Guangzhou. The rumours were as wild and plentiful as when he'd been alive. Most suspected that certain high-ranking individuals hadn't wanted things to get as far as a trial fearing a rancorous tycoon in the dock.

* * *

IN THE DEPARTURES HALL, there was an announcement that Tony's flight, too, had a thirty-minute delay because of a technical fault. Enough time, then, to get his chic suitcases wrapped in plastic before check-in. This, too, befit the man of the world he had resolved to be.

For once, plastic was a status symbol. You were letting it be known that your luggage was valuable enough to be doubly protected.

With satisfaction, Tony watched the playful yet measured movements with which the wrapping machine's operator placed one of his two suitcases on a circular platform, pulled the plastic wrap from an upright holder, stuck it loosely to the front of the case, and then pressed a button that made the platform rotate.

Spinning around and around, the case wrapped itself with cling film until the man judged it to sufficiently resemble a cocoon. The man pressed the button again, bringing the rotating platform to an abrupt stop. He cut the stretched plastic with one swipe of his Stanley knife, put the case on its side, and immediately spun a second layer of film over it, at right angles to the first. To finish it off, he lifted the case from the platform and casually cut free the handle, the pull-out handgrip, and the wheels.

Tony watched with approval. This suited him. His last journey should be made in style. And when he settled for good, presently, he could also invest a lot of energy and money into building a nest that befit his current rank and station. He could already imagine it in detail, even now. It would be a spacious country house full of modern design. Never before had Tony had such a clear advance vision of the house where he'd spend the rest of his life. It gave him a strange and unaccustomed peace of mind. It was so much easier playing someone else than being yourself.

'Mijnheer Hanssen? Mijnheer Tony Hanssen?'

Tony turned around, amazed that anyone in Guangzhou Baiyan airport spoke Dutch.

And he was even more amazed that that person had recognized him.

Before him stood an athletic-looking young man of not yet 30, overdressed for his age, with red hair and the milky white skin that goes with it. Apart from his cheeks. They showed large red spots; it wasn't clear whether they indicated shame, excitement, anxiety—or, who knew?—anger.

His expression didn't suggest malevolence, in any case. Without being subservient, the boy radiated polite expectation, a preparedness to submit to the inevitable. He didn't have any luggage, Tony noticed, not even a briefcase.

'Can I be of service to you?' Tony asked. There was no point denying who he was.

'I'm Diederik Vanbergen,' the young man said. 'I'm one of your successors at the bank.'

'As far as I know,' Tony said, after he'd got over his astonishment, 'our firm went bankrupt.'

'We changed our name,' Diederik said, 'but, apart from that, we stayed the same. Except for one thing.'

'It must be either a minor deficiency,' Tony said, 'or a rather formidable one.' This was the kind of answer, he felt, that was consistent with the man he now was. Cool and keen-witted, with a touch of mystery.

'It's a capital deficiency,' Diederik replied. 'You, Mister Hanssen. You are what's missing for us to be able to shine like we used to.'

* * *

ON THE NIGHT OF HIS DEATH, the other Tony's delirium hadn't just made him giggly, but also indiscreet. Stretched out on the bed, he had spoken as though his Martine were in the room. He'd sworn to her by all that is holy that he'd see to it that she wanted for nothing. He certainly had the means to do so, he'd babbled to her, blissfully. Because he hadn't told her everything about the fall of the bank, he admitted with a chuckle.

Not all of the accusations were lies.

Tony had interrogated his compatriot, asking specific questions. His suspicions were soon confirmed. The other Tony had also set aside a secret nest egg. Not on the Virgin Islands or the Bahamas. On the Caymans.

A few more questions later, and the other—giggling, weakened, slowly slipping away—gave up his codes and passwords to Tony, believing he was sharing them with his beloved Martine. He pleaded with his wife to understand his decision, and said he'd miss Klara terribly.

That was the last thing he said.

Tony had bought a flight to Mexico City from the ticket lady; there must be flights from there to George Town, in the Caymans, close to Cuba and Jamaica. Good music guaranteed, exotic cocktails, too. And always good weather, aside from a few annual storms.

He wouldn't neglect Martine and her child. He owed that to the other Tony, he thought. In any case, his nest egg was large enough to make a sumptuous meal for both of them.

That would be the perfect way to avoid any further trouble. Tony would accept a divorce from Martine, including substantial alimony, even, as long as he could transfer it all in one go, without having to have any personal contact with his former spouse.

He would say it was because she'd deceived him enough already.

Was that a cruel plan? Was it taking advantage? Tony had agonized about it briefly, still in the shower on the eighty-first floor. The cold water pattered down on him as he weighed up the pros and cons. When he stepped out of the shower cubicle, he was convinced that he was blameless. Essentially, he'd be doing a good deed.

Even without him, Mr. Bo Xiang and the other Tony would have still drunk the tea. The secret treasure trove on the Cayman Islands would have been lost for good. Now, Martine and her child would at least get a substantial part of it. In the alternative scenario, all the money would have gone to Caribbean tax pirates.

Those buzzards were just waiting for deaths like this one, so that they could rake in the frictional profits, on top of the mountains of gold they were already earning from the dirty money that washed up on their buccaneers' coastlines from all over the world, in more generous quantities than the driftwood and treasure fleets in former times.

All of the loose ends would be knotted together into a beautiful tassel. No one would ever ask questions. One of the Tony Hanssens was dead. The other was a crook, living off private means, like so many other crooks on so many sunny beaches.

Tony would have the passport and the lifestyle to lay claim to that for the rest of his days. Accidentally, without even trying, he'd still managed to get his slice of the cake. Just like Inspector Khumalo before him. But leaving even less of a trace.

And now Diederik Vanbergen had turned up to ruin everything.

* * *

THE YOUNG DIEDERIK VANBERGEN could turn a phrase. In little more than ten minutes, he'd summed up the situation, cleared up a few misunderstandings, and offered a solution that would be acceptable to all parties.

Tony was hardly listening. In this immense, high-tech hall, the apogee of all transit spaces, he was flooded with waves of exhaustion and melancholy. His escape from the maze had seemed so close by. He'd thought he'd caught sight of daylight; he'd thought he'd smelled the fresh air.

Once more, he'd been wrong. For years he hadn't been able to escape the old Tony Hanssen. Now, escaping the new one seemed just as impossible.

Diederik didn't notice a thing. He was overwhelmed by enthusiasm and expectation. He wasn't the only person responsible for the fact that he was standing here, he assured him. All the whizz-kids at the bank had insisted that they try to get Tony Hanssen back on board.

'You've earned yourself something of a cult status,' he beamed.

'To some people, you're a hero. A rebel.'

It was meant as a compliment, Tony realized.

The whizz- kids' superiors had granted permission, on the condition that they stayed well under the radar while getting Hanssen back. They hadn't had much faith in a successful outcome.

'And now we've showed them,' Diederik beamed. And because he thought it would interest Tony-the-computer-nerd, Diederik gave a recap of the investigative trail.

'One of your old credit-card numbers was used a few days ago in your hotel.' It looked as though he was ashamed by this. His cheeks coloured a shade redder. 'They tried to charge a couple of films you'd ordered for your room to it. You must have used the card once before at the same hotel chain, maybe years ago—these things tend to haunt the Internet. The researchers sent me here immediately. I called your hotel as soon as I landed, and they said you'd just taken a shuttle to the airport. Then I walked around until I found you. *Voilà*. It was dumb luck.'

The explanation was so absurdly simple, it sounded plausible, Tony thought. Certainly coming from the mouth of this young man. Not a shadow of doubt, not a jot of arrogance. An honest, open chap with a positive attitude. He won't hold out long in his present job. That was something Tony thought, too.

'You shouldn't expect to get any confessions or information from me,' he replied to Diederik. He had decided to play hard to get, in accordance with his new persona.

'Your bank has nothing to gain from me, apart from time wasted and sky-high lawyers' fees.'

'But, Mister Hanssen,' Diederik chuckled. He seemed amazed. 'The bank dropped all its accusations and charges against you a long time ago. If we'd wanted to go down that route, you'd have been tracked down and extradited long ago. No one stays unfindable. Not even you. But if you ask me…' He gave Tony a roguish look.

'What?' Tony asked. He was getting irritated like his old self by now. This kid was a real smart aleck.

'The bank's reputation,' Diederik began, 'would have suffered much more in the press if you had been found and questioned, than if you hadn't. And there's always been the possibility you would return of your own accord one day. Admit it, Mister Hanssen, isn't that true?'

There was an announcement in the departures hall that Tony's flight would be leaving on time, after all. He checked the main digital board. His flight had appeared on it, the last in a long line. He looked at Diederik again.

It only made his melancholy worse. He realized in a flash who this boy reminded him of. One of his fellow students, a goody-goody swot, a superficial but doggishly faithful friend, the last person Tony had broken ties with before skipping the country. Tony couldn't even remember his name. How young they'd been! And blind, and inept. Twenty-five years ago, now.

There was one difference. This Diederik was much more handsome. His hands were broad but not boorish. A sportsman's hands. He had attractive red lips; Tony noticed them now. The reddish stubble suited him, too, his hair standing out against his white skin. He was more attractive than you might first think, Tony had to admit. That was often the case with redheads. Love at second sight.

'Your name will be cleared,' Diederik promised with his pretty lips. 'You'll be able to simply pick up your former life. You'll be your old self again, sir!'

'How old do you think I am?' Tony asked in amusement. This milksop was cockier than you might suspect from looking at his angelic appearance. Might he ever be able to see something in me,

Tony wondered. Why not? His father had got together with that Linda. Anything was possible. I've spent so long not living, Tony thought. I'm still young, really. It's high time I stopped dying and cast myself into the current.

Diederik smiled. 'You're younger than most people your age, Mister Hanssen.'

My God, Tony thought, he's got lovely teeth, too, and dimples in his cheeks. But he also thought: if I want to catch that flight to Mexico, I can't waste much more time. His plastic-wrapped cases lay at his feet like packed, suffocating pets awaiting transport.

He tried to imagine what it would be like if he didn't fly to Mexico, but back to his country of origin. Still with the same name, but with a different family background, a different personality, and a different past.

It would have its charms, he thought with a slight tingling sensation in his stomach. I'd be able to find out who I am, and how others see me, at last. Each encounter would be a voyage of discovery through a minefield. Would I be able to bullshit my way out of it each time? It was never a problem on the cruise ships. Why should it be a problem in real life?

He felt a mild curiosity growing. What would it be like, after all these years, that chunk of land where he'd first seen the light of day? His memories had surely exaggerated the bad sides and covered up the good ones. Why not prowl around in the wake of the bank's whizz-kids for a bit? He could always run away again if he didn't like it. His only duty was to Martine and her kid—Klara. He could do his duty over the phone or by secure Internet banking anywhere in the world, if necessary even from the city where the mother and child lived. As long as he didn't bump into them, there wouldn't be a problem. But even then: how would they recognize him?

Even his own father would best be avoided. Though he would have coughed up quite a large part of his new fee to have a conversation with that Linda of his. How long would it take to get her gossiping about Papaatje and his pathetic love life?

'No one else has your talent for algorithms,' Diederik continued to argue. 'That's what everyone says, even the competition.'

'Well, I'm not sure I'd still be as good today,' Tony sighed. 'To be honest, more and more of it is getting beyond me.'

'Beyond us, too,' Diederik reassured him. 'It's developing so fast, we're all getting out of our depth. But my colleagues and I would support you where we could. And even if you didn't do anything at all, your name alone would guarantee us new accounts and major contracts. You underestimate your reputation.'

'I'm happy to hear that,' Tony said. 'It's not something people say to me very often.' If he wanted to go to Mexico, he'd have to head for the check-in desk at once. Around him, travellers hurried off to all the metropolises and one-horse towns of the world.

'Do you still have those memory sticks?' Diederik asked, suddenly more cautious.

'Of course,' Tony said. He remembered packing them. They were in the wardrobe in a shoebox. Twelve pieces of unsightly trash, no larger than half a chocolate bar.

'My bosses asked me to stress,' Diederik said, 'how much they appreciate the fact that you kept the information to yourself. It wouldn't have helped anyone.'

Tony looked at the suffocating luggage at his feet and then the line at the check-in. And what about her, he wondered, dejectedly and yet instantly furious, just like old times.

If I did go—would I be going back to a fatherland or a mother's grave? Knowing her, she wouldn't have been that crazy about gardens of rest, or columbaria, either. She and Tony had always had more in common than he would have liked. What's the betting she was lying under a layer of Belgian marble? Maybe granite. Her name chiselled out in handsome letters, an enamel plaque with a portrait of her in better times next to it, for sure.

It would be waiting for him, her glorious grave, her sepulchre, forcing him to go and visit with a bunch of expensive flowers in one hand and a silk handkerchief in the other. His head bowed, at a loss for words to pay his respects to the creature who had forced him to spend his life roaming the earth, knowing full well that escape wasn't even possible, from the day that she'd squeezed him out of her. He knew he would resist but end up going. He'd cry the soul out of his body, a granite sheath at his feet, that pointless slab of marble with her name on it.

'I'm genuinely sorry,' Tony said to Diederik, 'but there's a plane waiting for me. Your words were flattering, but they didn't change my mind. Adieu and best of luck.'

He held out his hand.

Tony could see from Diederik's face that his decision had caused deep disappointment. This boy was accustomed to getting his own way. He didn't even accept the outstretched hand. He'd been one hundred percent sure he'd bring off this assignment, cocking a snook at his superiors. For the first time, a trace of anger appeared in that almost-medieval face with its beautiful, thick hair—strawberry blond, is what they called that colour? Or did it need to be a little lighter for that?

'You don't mean that,' Diederik said quietly. 'You can't do this to me.'

The worst of his anger, Tony saw, had now made way for something else. Sincerity, touching supplication. Clearly a lot depended on whether he could carry off this assignment or not. Perhaps his job; perhaps his entire future, his self-image. Would he be prepared to do anything to get his way, Tony wondered, anything at all?

'Please say yes,' Diederik urged him. 'How are we going to manage without you, Mister Hanssen?'

'Call me Tony,' Tony said, more friendly than his new self was supposed to be. He saw on the digital board that his flight to Mexico had already moved up five places.

'Make us happy, Tony,' Diederik insisted. 'Come back to the bank you made great. We'll start all over again. Together. As though nothing had ever happened.'

'And that would make you happy?' Tony looked at his cling-wrapped suitcases and back at Diederik.

'It will make you happy, sir,' the latter said. 'I'll do everything to make that possible. I promise you.'

Tony looked his successor deep in the eyes. 'Go on, then,' he succumbed, yet again. 'In that case, I'm your man.'

Author's note

My research involved too many articles, websites, and books to list here. I'm happy to mention the three most important ones. First, Joris Luyendijk's blog *Going Native In the World of Finance*, written for *The Guardian* but also published in Dutch in *De Standaard* and *NRC Handelsblad*. Second, the largely fictive non-fiction bestseller *1421: The Year China Discovered The World* by Gavin Menzies. Finally, the reference guide *50 People Who Stuffed Up South Africa*, as informative as it is entertaining, written by Alexander Parker, with cartoons by Zapiro.

Fortunate Slaves is a work of fiction. Any resemblance to living persons or events is purely coincidental.

For more information or to receive our newsletter,
please contact us at: info@worldeditions.org.